Praise for
A Terrible Love
~

"*Romantic, edgy, angsty, and thrilling.*"

—Bookish Temptations

"*Intense, sexy, and intriguing.*"

—The Autumn Review

"*I'm speechless! This book was unstoppable.*"

—Book Crush

"*Eros very much has this sort of skat, rat-a-tat, jazzy improvisational writing style. . . . It gives her whole entire work real character.*"

—Contagious Reads

"*A beautiful tale of redemption, full of suspense and mystery.*"

—A Book Vacation

"*Eros's dark and twisty prose adds a depth and dimension that is addictive.*"

—Martini Times Romance

"*This story had a cup of dark, a quart of thrilling, and a damn pound of super freaking sexy!*"

—LipSmackin GoodBooks

ALSO BY MARATA EROS

A Terrible Love
A Brutal Tenderness

The DARKEST JOY

MARATA EROS

GALLERY BOOKS

NEW YORK   LONDON   TORONTO   SYDNEY   NEW DELHI

G

Gallery Books
A Division of Simon & Schuster, Inc.
1230 Avenue of the Americas
New York, NY 10020

First Gallery Books trade paperback edition February 2014

GALLERY BOOKS and colophon are registered trademarks of Simon & Schuster, Inc.

For information about special discounts for bulk purchases, please contact Simon & Schuster Special Sales at 1-866-506-1949 or business@simonandschuster.com.

The Simon & Schuster Speakers Bureau can bring authors to your live event. For more information or to book an event contact the Simon & Schuster Speakers Bureau at 1-866-248-3049 or visit our website at www.simonspeakers.com.

Manufactured in the United States of America

10 9 8 7 6 5 4 3 2 1

Library of Congress Cataloging-in-Publication Data

Eros, Marata
  The darkest joy: a novel/Marata Eros
     pages cm
     I. Title.
  PS3602.L647D37 2014
  813'.6—dc232013032686

ISBN 978-1-4767-5221-1
ISBN 978-1-4767-5222-8 (ebook)

Beth Dean Hoover

PROLOGUE

~

"*B*rookie," Mom begins in a warning tone. I sigh but oblig-ingly pop my earbud out of one ear. I have to actually pay attention, because somehow moms can sniff out half attentive-ness like last night's rotting dinner, even across a crackling cell connection.

"Yes, Mom," I say with resignation. I lightly tap the brakes, trying to survive the treachery that is I-90 from Spokane to Seattle. And like any other college sophomore, I'm aching for home and hearth, especially Mom's cooking. I survey the slick, stupid mess of the highway. I'd hoped to beat the rush.

Not going to happen.

I downshift, keeping one hand on the wheel with one ear pressed to the cell as to assist my brakes as the blue and red strobes pulse along the banked snow at the sides of the road.

What the hell? Great, I think.

"Be careful, honey, I-90 is sloppy right now. Your father and I have been listening to the weather reports for the Snoqualmie Pass—"

I roll my eyes. "Mom," I interrupt, trying to be the Good Daughter and missing it with the irritation in my voice. "There's been an accident up ahead . . ." I squint my eyes as I take in the pileup. Medics are already swarming the vehicles.

"What?" Mom asks anxiously and I can see her put her hand to her heart. Drama R Us.

"Not me, Mom." I look ahead. "There are three cars ahead of me, but . . . I won't be home for supper. There's no way."

"It's more important to have you home safely than for you to be reckless."

Like that would ever happen, I think.

"Did you remember your sheet music?" Mom asks as I watch the police officer's hands, his orange baton guiding our slow progress around the crunched cars in my lane. My eyes sweep the wreckage and I swallow, my stare shifting to the blooming red that spreads underneath the huddle of medics, so red against all the snow.

Blood.

I shiver, setting the phone on my seat, Mom oblivious as my hand lands on my binder of sheet music on the passenger seat without looking. It's full of music I practice, music I've written . . . audition scores as well. I'm more likely to forget my purse than to leave my music binder somewhere. I hear her tinny voice and scoop up the cell again.

"Yes . . . right here," I say, distracted by the scene reflected in my rearview mirror.

"Good, because Aunt Millicent is coming to hear you play for Christmas, dear."

Christ, I think, mentally rubbing my head. My great aunt is 120 at least. She'll never die because she's from Alaska. She was one of the early pioneers of that area back in the forties with a bunch of other salty old crabs as she calls them.

Aunt Milli never lets us forget it. Y'know, the old story: *When we were kids we walked to school backward in ninety-mile-an-hour winds in ten feet of snow.*

My eyes drop to the odometer. *Shit* . . . thirty miles per hour. At this rate I'll be home by New Year's. The dark night crowds in around my Scion as Mom talks about how much Aunt Milli appreciates my piano-playing talent; she claims music runs in the family.

Uh-huh. *Blowhard.*

I scowl, thinking about the piano-playing puppet I've become to the family.

I guess it's better than being that Asian kid who could speak four languages by the age of five. But not by much.

My parents have pushed me because I'm the local piano prodigy.

I'm just a girl. I never tell anyone what I can do.

What I'm compelled to do. It's kind of embarrassing. As soon as someone knows my talent with the keys of a piano, it defines me. I wish it didn't. I just want to be Brooke Elizabeth Starr.

Mom asks me a question. Twice.

Oops.

"Yeah?" I say, my eyes trained on the road, the yellow dashes making me nauseous as huge snowflakes fall. I feel like I'm trapped inside a snow globe.

"I need to let you go, honey. You don't need the distraction of talking on your cell." That's Mom, conservative to the core.

I hear a chime in the background. Our doorbell.

"What's that?" I ask anyway.

Mom hesitates. "I don't know, we've kept our calendar open; just your brother, Dad and you tonight. Oh . . . and Aunt Milli."

I give a small groan at that.

"Bill?" I hear Mom ask in a loud voice from what I know is the kitchen. I can see her in my mind like a painted picture. Her back leans against the wall, a finger twisting the long cord of our 1980s vintage wall phone. The guts show through the clear acrylic housing. It lights when it rings.

I can tell Mom's holding the phone against her shoulder as she calls out to Dad.

There's a muffled noise . . . then a shuffle.

Those old phones are archaic as hell but they convey sound very well.

"Mom?" I ask because it's odd that she's not responding. I sit up straight in my seat as the hot air blowing out of the heater vent becomes suffocating.

Then I hear a sliding crash that sounds like a load of glass falling onto the tile floor. My memories of our home floor plan go into overdrive.

Trophies . . . my piano trophies are on that glass tabletop in the foyer.

I unconsciously clench my cell.

A car behind me honks and my eyes dip again to the odometer. Twenty miles per hour.

I don't accelerate.

Sweat breaks out on my upper lip as my hands begin to shake.

"Mom!" I scream

A gurgle that makes my stomach drop greets me as I hear the receiver bang against a hard surface.

It's so loud it almost causes me to drop my phone.

The driver behind me lays on his horn, passing on the left, taking the icy road at forty miles per hour.

He flips me off as he does.

I hear the phone *clunk* against the wall. I see it in my mind's eye like a movie, unwinding at the end of its long cord, spinning . . . hitting the wall with a hollow slap of plastic. . . .

Then nothing.

A piercing scream fills the receiver and I gasp, a sob erupting from my mouth. I know that scream.

Joey!

I put on the brakes in the middle of the highway, my ear pressed to the cell, as my hand leaves the steering wheel and covers my mouth.

Cars pile up behind me, some drivers leaning on their horns.

I hear the phone stop banging, then something dragging.

Like a body.

This isn't real, my mind numbly says.

Thunk.

Someone taps on my window as I begin to lose circulation in my ear.

Breathing. That's what I hear now. Every sense I have goes off-line except for my ear against that cell.

It's all I hear.

Someone is breathing into the receiver.

Then they slowly hang it up in its cradle.

Click.

My cell phone silences.

It drops to the floorboards of my car, sliding underneath the gas pedal.

Someone opens the door.

It's the police officer who was directing traffic.

It can't be, that was hours ago, I think.

"Miss . . . ?" He looks at me and I stare back.

I can't think. Feel . . . move.

Mom was just asking me when I was coming home.

I'm sure she's fine. Something just fell.

She's not dead. Nobody's dead.

My body begins a fine quaking that I'm helpless to quell.

Aunt Milli is there . . . being the old-relative cheek pincher she is.

Everything's fine. Everything's . . . definitely not fine.

Just breathe. Breathe.

"Miss, I'm going to have to ask you to step out of your car." A flashlight moves over my face and I don't blink, his voice sounding like it's underwater.

I don't move, I can't move. Because all I hear is breathing.

It's so loud it drowns out my thoughts.

The cop moves toward me and I pitch forward face-first.

Darkness greets me where consciousness had been.

Sometimes that is the mind's only way to protect itself.

Two weeks later

He's hunkered down in front of me. My mind is searching, searching . . . Oh yeah, *Decatur Clearwater*.

FBI. That's right. The memory sluggishly plugs into place in the slow-moving river of my mind.

The debris of my grief makes it crawl.

Marshal Clearwater gives me a sad smile of sympathy, his eyes flicking to the sheen in mine. "I know this is difficult, Miss Starr . . ." he begins slowly, spreading his hands out to his sides as he balances on his heels.

My gaze shifts to his, traveling from orbs so dark they almost blend with the pupils, to a fresh-looking scar that stands at ugly attention at his throat. It's bright pink, angry.

Somebody did that to him.

Suddenly the violence of that wound reminds me of my family and I swallow hard past the lump in my throat.

I'm not going to lose it yet again, I tell myself.

I bite my lip until I taste the metallic flavor of my own blood. Then take a deep breath.

I nod, my hands clutching the Christmas gift that Aunt Milli had brought me. I close my eyes, the vision of her frail broken body softer than the reality.

The Feds had told me just enough to fill in the visual gaps.

Clearwater stands and presses his card into my hand. "If you need anything, I'm here."

I think people just say those things. They know that people for the most part inherently do not want to impose on others. Especially families like mine: upper-class white—prestigious.

No, we white-bread snobs don't inconvenience others with our dirty laundry.

I look again at Clearwater, whose dark skin signals his mixed ethnicity. He returns my stare with level, honest eyes. He doesn't see me as a white rich girl, with that critical gaze fueled by the common assumption that I'm privileged, spoiled. Marshal Clearwater is color blind. Don't ask me how I can tell, but I just can.

He turns to his partner, a tall, tattooed Fed with cool eyes and an indifferent disposition. Tough. He wears a suit, they all do . . . but it doesn't cover his neck. Ebony ribbons of ink circle his thick throat and I swallow.

A small hand squeezes my shoulder.

Lacey. I cover her hand with my own.

"It'll be okay," she says in a whisper. The empty sentiment runs off my consciousness like water off a duck's back. Lacey is the last bit of glue from the remnants of a childhood now gone. The one thread in the fabric of my past that's been there since the beginning. I can't think of a time in my life when she wasn't a part of it. Her eyes tell me it'll be okay.

But nothing will be okay. Ever.

I try to keep my focus narrow but it widens as I sit there. The Feds pick up small plates filled with appetizers provided by our upscale neighborhood in Magnolia.

A house isn't a home without your family.

I clutch the gift tighter.

Our neighbors use the china Mom kept locked behind glass cabinet doors. I take a deep, shuddering breath as I see the slim, delicate plates being passed. Cups of real espresso are next, the creamy porcelain moving in a parade of hands.

Suddenly, the background of murmured condolences, china and glass clanking . . . my home full of strangers, is too much.

I stand. All I see is black. I can't see the colors of my family for the sea of black-clad mourners who fill every corner of my house.

I choke on my grief.

Marshal Clearwater sees me, his eyes meet mine.

No one else does.

His face grows alarmed as he sets his dish on the edge of the coffee table. Black eyes grow larger as he draws nearer, weaving through the bodies in black. My breath comes hard and fast.

"Hey," he says as he moves between the last people blocking his way to me.

I can't breathe; something heavy is on my chest.

"What's wrong with her?" I hear Lacey ask in a tight voice, her concerned hazel eyes above mine.

I'm on the ground now, a tight wheeze the only breath that comes through.

People crowd.

"Step back," Clearwater says in a voice like a bell.

"Deca—" the big Fed begins.

"Hyperventilating," Clearwater says in terse reply.

My eyes roll to that package from Aunt Milli. It tumbles from my fingers. My panic rises in my eyes, tightening my chest further.

"I'm here, Brooke," Marshal Clearwater says, those dark eyes never leaving mine. "Breathe slowly . . ."

He sees me glance at the package.

Clearwater picks it up and sets it in my hand. Tears squeeze out of my eyes, running down each side of my face, pooling in my ears.

"Jesus . . . Brooke," Lacey says, dabbing at the tears, her own mingling with mine as she gives Clearwater a dark look, like *he's* the enemy, not my grief. Always ready to champion me, defend me against all comers.

I stare into Marshal Clearwater's eyes. Thanking him without speaking.

The corners of the Fed's eyes crinkle as he looks into mine. "You're welcome."

My hand holds the small package tighter as my breath comes in a sudden whoosh.

"There you go," Clearwater says as eyes stare at me as I lay on the floor of our living room, needles from the Christmas tree making it smell like pine.

I take another breath . . . Another. They hurt.

He holds out his hands and I take one, Lacey takes the other.

They pull me up. I turn and scoop up the package again.

I steady myself, slightly dizzy. Feeling like the lamest of fools. "I need some air," I say, head down.

Clearwater nods. His partner's root-beer brown eyes follow me out to the patio that overlooks Puget Sound. I let the smell of the sea overwhelm me as I lean against the railing, Lacey at my back.

"Brooke . . ." she begins and I hold up my palm. She continues anyway. "They mean well." Lacey looks at me as she always does: determined to fix my problems, or just determined.

I nod. *I know.*

I look over the water. How everything around me appears so normal. People walking in the chilled rain. Leaves lingering in trees too stubborn to release them.

The waves churning in angry abandon.

None of it cares that time doesn't move forward for those who grieve.

My chin dips to my chest and I sit down on the patio furniture, the temperature too cold for my light outfit of a simple black wrap dress, heels, and thin nylons. It's what I can manage.

All I can manage. Oh yeah, I brushed my teeth. I give a little hiccupy laugh.

Slowly, Lacey lowers herself opposite me. I look at her, round eyes meet mine, dark blond hair frames a face I've known since infancy, through dolls, makeup, boyfriends and now—death. "You don't have to do this, y'know."

I nod. I know.

"The police have handed it over to the Feds . . . and they don't have any questions for me. I've been cleared," I say and laugh. "So . . . it's time." Time to escape the inescapable; my guilt will get packed along with the rest of my emotional baggage. I take it wherever I go.

It sounds kinda like a sob.

Lacey reaches out and takes my hand.

"I'll miss you." Her eyes search mine. "And for what it's worth, I think it's too soon. And, Brookie . . ."

Her use of my nickname makes a fat tear brim and roll from my swollen eyes.

"Your music," she whispers.

"Fuck my music. I don't ever want to see another piano again," I say with conviction birthed from pain. My voice comes out like a raw wound and Lacey flinches.

I inhale deeply, the cold salt in the air soothing my lungs, invigorating me.

"A fresh start, Lacey. It's what I need. No more music, no more . . . expectations." I fling my hand around at the house.

"You don't have to sell this place," Lacey says in a low voice.

"Why would I keep it?" I ask with heavy sarcasm. "What do I have to come home to?" I hiss, embracing my anger.

Stages of grief, y'know. Of course, the experts don't say how long each stage is, do they?

I think the anger stage will be awhile.

"And school?" Lacey cocks a brow and I cringe inside a little. Even though everyone at the university understands, the tragedy of my family's death has sensationalized the small community of pianists. I am no longer a fellow pianist but tabloid fodder . . . the poor little girl forever marked by a brutal tragedy. Once a top contender for Juilliard, my hard-earned respect is now overshadowed by the infamous killings that seem to define me now.

Juilliard could suck it, there would be another . . . golden girl. Or guy. I fold my arms and Lacey knows when she's lost. Juilliard can't have me now . . . because—I can't have them. Music and the memories of my family are inexplicably linked. It's what I deserve, anyway. Why did I get to live when none of them did? I should have been here. Should have been with them.

"Okay," she says in a quiet voice. "But you promise me . . . Promise me that you'll come back."

Tears of anger masking my sadness run down my face. "I can't, Lace. I can't." How can I play piano when they can't listen? How can I live here again when every space I breathe in has their absence in it? There would never be enough oxygen for me.

"Miss Starr," Marshal Clearwater interrupts us.

I clear my throat, swiping at my wet face, which heats with embarrassment. "Yes," I say.

He pauses, those dark eyes probing my own. "I'm sorry for your loss."

I nod, expecting more . . . then he says the first positive thing I've heard, surprising me. "And good luck in Alaska."

My hands tighten around the small box from Aunt Milli and I give the first smile of this miserable day of memorial for my murdered family.

"Thank you," I say, the damp sea breeze lifting the hair at my neck.

He stares at me a moment longer, looking as if he wants to say more. Then he walks away.

Like everyone else.

My hands slide into that box and wrap around the present inside.

My flesh heats the solid brass key.

I hang on to it like the anchor of comfort it is.

It's hold on or sink.

ONE

~

May
Homer, Alaska

I cover my nose then cough. A plume of dust rises and I drop my hand.

What a dump.

I hear a horn beep and turn around. The taxi driver who gave me the ride from ERA, the local air carrier, waves.

I give him the thumbs-up and he drives off. My eyes shift back to the run-down log cabin. I keep my eyes on the wide plank door as I climb the thick steps, the deep graining and knots in the wood, loved by age, mellowed to amber, greet me. I look down at the key in my hand, wrapping suddenly cold fingers around brass that's stolen my warmth. I slide the gift from Milli into the surface lock and the tumblers slide and click apart. I push the heavy door inward and it opens with a whisper of sound.

The interior is as dismal as I expect.

Everywhere my eyes land is caked in dirt. Years of dust entomb every surface.

It'd take an act of goddamned Congress to clean this place up.

I sigh, trudge out to the cabin's porch and carry in my suitcases one by one, four in all. I swipe the screen of my smartphone and see that it receives Internet.

Amazing.

Back on the porch, I scan the forty-acre spread, as open as it is achingly cloistered. The spruce trees scattered on the edge of a huge cliff accentuate the lonely frontier feel. Wild lupine shows green against grass that isn't awake with the late spring of this northern latitude. Fireweed shoots emerge between patches of snow.

I exhale sadly and haul the rest of my gear inside and survey the interior again.

Yup, it's still shitty.

I set my phone on the kitchen table, disturbing the dust, and put my things on the floor. I move to a crooked cupboard and open it, then open the rest, one by one. I leave them standing open like gaping, toothless mouths.

My eye catches something and I stand up straighter. In the vast nothingness of the lower kitchen cupboards I see a spot of color. I move closer.

It's a quilt. Large circles intertwine with one another, the patchwork reminiscent of the post-WWII era.

I know what kind of quilt it is: wedding ring.

My great-aunt Milli has slept beneath this. When she was younger than I am now.

A tight burning sensation begins deep in my chest and I know better than to contain it. I let the silent, unstoppable tears come.

The wildlife of my property doesn't mind my grief. I stand in the middle of my new home, clutching a quilt my great-aunt made with her own hands, knowing that this cabin is mine through the default of her death.

I wonder if I'll ever be right again.

I don't deserve happiness. Because they can never have it again.

After an indefinite time, I lay the quilt over a ratty couch and lie down.

I fall asleep before my head hits the cushioned armrest.

My nose twitches at the musty smell.

My crushed heart still beats.

Somehow.

⌒

I wake with birds chirping outside the window. The pale light showcases things that though neglected were once loved. My eyes scan the scarred surfaces of antique dressers forgotten, mirrors whose silvered surfaces toss the light around the space. Pale green paint, like untouched sherbet, is crazed on the moldings that hold doors that have faded to a light amber. So much potential . . . so much age. So much. I shiver and roll over.

Potential doesn't keep me warm. I'm freezing my ass off. I sit up on the couch, the sunlight gray as it filters through the grimy glass of the cabin. Divided light windows settle into the center of enormous old log walls that intersect at the cabin's corners, the glass rippled, ancient. It looks like water's running over the panes. It's not, they're just that old.

I look around the interior again and stretch, yawning. My gaze stumbles on an old Toyo heating stove, maybe updated as recently as the 1970s.

Wonderful.

I move to it, arms folded over my chest, hugging my elbows. I crank the knob to *on* then hit a switch at the back of the old-fashioned stove. My eyes follow the flue as it snakes its way from the main body of the stove and plunges through the tall ceiling. It creaks to miserable life, ticking as it wakes up.

I realize that I don't know how it's being fueled and look to a fireplace, open and dark. Rough-hewn logs flank its sides and a matching log, split in half, acts as a mantel. The spruce has aged to a polished soft gold.

Of course, I'm just guessing at the color because everything is vintage beautiful with a layer of gray. And epic dust.

I sneeze and stand by the stove until it's too hot for me to tolerate. I move away.

Well, I guess this answers the question of propane delivery, I think. I move aside a moth-eaten lace curtain, and my eyes immediately peg a rusty old tank in the backyard, peeling paint completing the rustic yard ornament. I let the curtain drop and walk over to the kitchen, which is part of the living room. My eyes move to the pair of doors that line the back wall and I walk over there, my exploring not quite finished. I push open the door to the right, the hinges protest softly and I catch sight of a shower pan with a curtain hanging off of an eye hook of nickel that's worn thin to reveal brass. A steady drip of water falls, the sound exploding in a dull *pop* as it lands in the old porcelain cast iron. The commode stands in forlorn silence in the corner, a small window set high above it. To the right, a wall-mounted sink hangs off the log, with a long chrome chain from the center of the taps that holds a rubber stopper at its end. I sigh, stepping back and shutting the door at the lovely vista. I turn in the tiny open hall, with just a partial wall that divides the kitchen from the small rooms. I move through the door at the left of the bathroom and a small bedroom stands before me. A full-size bed, without bed linen, a small nightstand and two tiny windows, one at the north side and one at the east, open casement style round out the spartan room. A lonely glass kerosene lamp sits in a layer of dust on the nightstand. I back out, closing the door and I sigh again.

This place is nothing like my parents' six-thousand-square-foot home that I've sold. Out in the nothingness of this property, I could be at the end of the earth.

I feel like I am.

I walk back into the kitchen. I swallow hard and turn on the faucet above an ancient porcelain farmhouse sink. Cold water pours out from solid nickel taps, the metal frosting.

I put my hand underneath the rush and snatch it back. It's so cold it burns.

I might as well be in a foreign country, I think.

I shut off the water just as I hear an engine.

I open the door and quickly shut it behind me; don't want that precious heat to escape.

I watch a 1970s Bronco pull up the long winding drive and come to a stop. It's hauling a trailer with the car I just bought, sight unseen. A burly and disheveled guy exits his red-and-white rig. At least, I think it's red and white, but it's hard to tell through the dirt, not to mention the rust that's eating at the wheel wells and edges of it like cancer.

"Hi ya!" he says and gives a friendly wave. I give a little wave back and make my way down the broad split-log staircase to meet him in the center of the driveway, the gravel lost to the weeds long ago.

"I'm Tucker," he says, sticking out a meaty hand, and I shake it as he vigorously pumps mine. I look at him, trying to reconcile his email correspondence with the face.

I've been raised to be socially gracious. In fact, I'm comfortable around most, but . . . the people of Alaska have proven to be an exception.

There's no pretense and I find I miss it. Or maybe it's what is familiar?

Tucker ignores my inspection of him as he takes in my great-aunt's homestead.

I use this opportunity to look him over, from his strange knee-height brown rubber boots to his camel-colored heavy denim pants that meet a beat-up T-shirt that says *Catch More But at Sea.*

What?

When I reach his face, I see his head is partially covered by a cap made of nubby charcoal-colored wool, pulled on haphazardly, strands of dark hair curling around the rolled brim.

His eyes are warm when they meet mine and I blush as he

gives a belly laugh at my perusal. "Like what ya see?" he asks, waggling his brows.

Dear Lord.

"Ah . . . I'm . . ." *Oh God.*

"It's okay." He smiles, letting me off the hook. "I hear you're old Milli's niece . . ."

I nod numbly. *Don't ask, don't ask . . .*

"Brooke Starr," I say, my face heating again. I feel certifiably stupid.

Tucker grins. "How is the old girl doing?"

He's asked.

I give a small squeak and he says in a low voice, "Is she gone, then?"

I nod again and he reaches out a large hand, the whole of it swallows my shoulder. "It's all right, Brooke," he says, his eyes moving to take in the vast property, the sweeping cliffs that hold jagged rocks that meet the sea. "She had a full life, y'know."

I breathe out a sigh of relief. I don't fool Tucker. He studies my expression then inclines his head, not questioning me further.

Suddenly, he grins. "I guess you want to see her."

Her?

He chuckles at my expression. "Cars are always referred to as females."

Not by me, I think. The best I can do is think of my Scion as That Which Runs. A small giggle escapes me and Tucker glances over his shoulder with a cocked brow.

He moves to the back of the trailer that holds the three thousand dollars' worth of metal. With a flourish he jerks off the car cover. My eyes widen, roving over the vintage VW bus. The car does me in. The photo he sent me over the Internet looked . . . different. A caption—*1967 VW bus, needs body work*—had appeared alongside an image of a gunmetal-colored vehicle.

"What . . . how?" I stutter as I take in the huge rainbow-colored flowers over the deep cerulean blue paint, a low glitter winking as the fog departs the property and the sun edges in. I sigh.

"Beautiful, ain't she?" Tucker asks, running his hand over the psychedelic yawn of a paint job.

I want to blend in, exist unnoticed among the huge influx of migrant fishing workers.

This Scooby-Doo bus is not going to fucking blend in.

I open my mouth to rake him over my blazing anger, but his sweet expression stops me. Tucker straightens. "What? Ya don't like it?" he asks.

The primer gray would have been perfect. I bite my lip and he waits.

"It's okay," I say.

"Hell, yeah!" Tucker enthuses and I smile wanly.

"Okay, just let me unhitch her and you can take a look . . ."

Tucker backs the bus off the trailer. He gets all four wheels on the bare stretch of pastured driveway and gives it a start while I move to the side of the house, out of the way. It's then that I catch sight of the outhouse around the back of the small cabin for the first time, and a laugh bursts out of me before I can stop it.

Tucker exits the bus and walks around to meet me. He gives another smile. "That's the shitter?"

I stare at it in disbelief. "The necessary," I reply primly, and he belly laughs.

"That too," he winks.

I step onto the broad porch as Tucker finishes tinkering with my new bus. It's half as deep as the interior of the small cabin. Tucker notices me surveying the deep roof that covers the porch.

"Snow load," he responds automatically.

I look above me, thinking about a seven-foot-deep porch and how much snow would accumulate to necessitate the size.

Only for the summer, only for the summer, I chant in my mind like a mantra. I know the fishing job is temporary. I can figure out later where I'll go next—who I'll become.

Tucker is almost to his Bronco when he turns, his instep on the chrome running board that still clings to the dilapidated body.

"Heard you're on Chance Taylor's crew," Tucker asks like a statement.

I nod. "Yes, I'm a part-time deckhand."

It's his turn to look me over. He shuts the door and slowly walks over to where I stand.

I try not to let anxiety rule me. But I've never been the same since my family's death.

It'll change a person. I'm no longer the free-floating and trusting girl of a few months ago.

Tucker sees my wary expression. "Let me see your hands."

"My hands?" I ask, confused.

He nods solemnly.

I hold my hands out and he takes them, studying them.

"What did you say you do?"

I haven't.

I shrug a little, taking my hands back. I stuff them inside my low-rise jeans, shifting my weight on my feet.

Tucker waits as I stare at the ground.

"I was a student."

"Yup." He gives me a level stare, waiting.

I sigh. "I studied the piano."

"Ah," he says, his dark eyes move to my hands, hidden inside the denim. "They look like hands that have worked . . . but . . ."

I feel my brows rise.

He gives me a steady look. "You'll get beat up out there."

"I need the job," I say. Though not for the reasons he's thinking.

Tucker looks at me again, shaking his head. "It's tough work for a woman."

My chin kicks up. "Yeah . . . well, the pay's good." And the location—the distance. Not to mention that absolute divergence from classical music and everything that defined my life before, I mentally add.

Tucker nods, saying nothing more.

"How am I going to get beat up?" I can't help but ask.

He's almost in his car. "If it isn't the sea, then Chance Taylor will do a stand-up job."

Tucker slams his car door as my stomach knots.

Translation: my new boss is a dick.

He backs up, turning around in the large part of the driveway. I watch his Bronco jostle over the uneven driveway as his hand pops out the window in a one-wave salute.

I lift my hand in return then slowly let it drop.

I have one week before halibut season begins. One week to get this cabin in order and get the tools of the trade and—I look around the dingy space—cleaning supplies.

And three months to forget, my mind whispers.

~

I'm still dragging after the long journey to Alaska. My stomach grumbles, and I'm not surprised to discover that there are barely two crumbs within the four dim corners of the cabin. After Tucker leaves I decide it's time to make a supply run. I unpack my first suitcase and take out the Garmin, a girl's best friend. The GPS navigational system will tell me where I'm going.

I take stock of the cabin. The TP is moldy and lank; a dry sliver of soap sits crumbled inside a cagelike chrome holder screwed above the old sink. My eyes move to the "shower." I move the curtain aside. A huge showerhead, the chrome worn through to the brass casing, drips about every thirty seconds. *Great.* Somehow, I'll have to experiment with how to get wet in there.

I sigh, adding plumber's tape to the list.

I sling my backpacklike purse across my shoulder, head outside, and start up the bus. It zings to life beautifully.

It's colder than a witch's tit on the shady side of an iceberg, I think, stuffing my hands between my knees.

I let off the clutch and the bus lurches forward. I put it in first gear and crank down the hill.

I make the solitary trek to town, which, as I live at the very end of East End Road, requires nearly fifteen minutes of winding driving. And though I'm from drippy Seattle where everywhere you look is a tapestry of greenery, I can't help but notice the majesty this rugged place possesses. I carefully avoid handling the memories of Aunt Milli too intimately but her voice breaks through without my permission.

The mountains are like jewels made of ice, Milli whispers inside my brain.

My eyes move to the Kenai Fjords and their glacial peaks rise to my left, the long finger of Homer Spit, the world's largest natural sand spit, holds its rows of small shops . . . and fishing boats moor to those mountains like an anchor at its feet.

I tear my eyes away from the same view that's just outside that dirty cabin I'm now living in and move into the parking area of Safeway.

I get out of the bus and slam the door. It shrieks as I do, protesting.

Pulling out my list, I write: *W-D 40. Awesome invention,* I think.

I walk toward the glass door and pass some girls who are my age, their long dresses brightly colored with metallic thread picking up the low light of the morning and glittering as they move. Their skirts sweep the ground as they pass by me. One of them turns and looks at me, her deep eyes framed by a vaguely Amish-style cap with thin cotton ties. The girl stares.

Sees something she knows, maybe.

She says something in a language I don't recognize.

I look away. Sometimes strangers will recognize my sadness intuitively, though I try to hide it.

I ignore my feelings of uneasy grief, as per usual, going through the automatic glass doors of the grocery store.

I'll just grab what I need, then rush back to my lonely little cabin where I can breathe, like an asthmatic without an inhaler. Solitude gives me oxygen.

Just keep breathing.

I don't dwell on the precept that existing is not the same as living.

I died that night five months ago, along with my family.

TWO

⌒

I collapse backward on the couch and watch a plume of dust explode into the air, colliding with the dust motes that already float.

Yuk.

I fold my arm underneath my head, crossing my feet at the ankles, and scroll through my phone until my finger lands on Lacey's image. I tap her face and wait as the dialing continues. I'm about ready to tap *end call* when she picks up, out of breath.

"Brookie," Lacey answers in a voice tinged with relief.

"Yeah," I say, a small smile on my face at just hearing her voice.

"I told you to call right away, lame-ass," she chastises, her voice at once distant with a touch of desperation and that "I need a Brooke fix."

I sigh, recrossing my legs as I watch the dust settle again.

"Uh-huh . . . I was totally wiped."

Lacey gives a grunt of disapproval. "Well? How is . . . it?"

I look around at the countertops littered with products from my supply run, the filth in every corner, the showerhead in the bathroom doing a slow, sporadic drip.

"It's . . . a dump." I give a small laugh and it comes out sad.

The open phone line's ongoing buzz sounds during the pause of our conversation. "Oh, Brooke . . . come home," Lacey says in an insistent voice and I clench my eyes, the heat of my sadness burning like acid behind my eyelids.

"No," I reply quietly. The relocation hasn't muted my sadness, my guilt . . . but at least I no longer have to contend with the torment of familiar surroundings that inspire too many memories, that turn my sadness into unbearable grief.

The silence stretches. Finally, I fill it. "It'll be really quaint when I put in some elbow grease . . ."

"Quaint?" Lacey asks in a disbelieving tone and as usual she doesn't think anything's good enough for me.

"Charming?" I add hopefully, though my tone belies my words.

"Those are terms that people use when something could be cute if it was torn down and rebuilt."

Exactly. Out loud I answer, "It's not so bad. There's heat . . . kinda. And there's running water."

More silence.

"Like, was no running water really a possibility?" Lacey asks.

I see the roof of the outhouse from my perch on the couch. "Yes," I say with real feeling.

"Okay," Lacey says, and I can see her shoring up, the mental image of her folding her slim arms across her chest, blowing an errant strand of light hair out of her face as she tries to resolve my chaos for me. Typical Lacey mode; she's always been there for me that way.

I don't want my broken fixed. If I'd wanted resolution I'd have stayed in Seattle and faced whatever music was there.

Instead, I fled.

"Send me a pic of your car," she demands.

I groan. This just keeps getting worse. Sometimes I want to lie. But I don't; my honesty is as brutal as my circumstances.

"God, what now?" Lacey asks.

"Well . . . the guy I bought it from thought he'd do me a favor and give it a quickie paint job."

"Tell me."

"It's his idea of hippie chic."

"Oh for shit's sake, it can't be that bad."

I look through the haze of grime on the windows and can make out the bus from fifty feet away; the bright colors are beacons of tackiness.

Pretty bad.

"Hang on," I say, then slipping off the couch I shove my feet into my Crocs and step out onto the porch. Like some scene from a movie a ray of light pierces the cloud cover, dousing the bus with its strobe of light.

I hold up my phone, click, then hit *send*.

I wait for the inevitable.

"Oh. My. God!" Lacey shrieks in my ear and I take the cell away from my ear.

"Right?" I agree, wincing at her pants of hyperventilation.

"It's like someone puked paint on your car . . ."

"Yeah," I agree.

"Sorry," she finally says in resignation.

"Thanks," I reply, but I'm smiling, thinking about how happy Tucker had been, thinking he's doing me a good turn.

A pause then, "So what do you think? Really?"

I look around at the cabin . . . the open pasture that rolls to the woods as they stand watch over the cold sea. I can vaguely hear waves crashing on the rocks below.

"I think Alaska can get in your blood."

"Huh? Really? Don't you miss . . . everything?" Lacey asks.

My family.

"Not really," I lie.

"Huh," she replies, not believing anything. "Turnouts for Juilliard happened," Lacey says casually.

I knew that. Late April—for entrance in the fall.

I swallow past the painful lump that forms like a soft rock in my throat. The sea breeze tears through the open posts as I stand on the porch. The freshness of the air is indescribable. It's full of sea and green, and it's just . . . clean. I suck in a lungful, my cheeks wet.

I say nothing and the conversation stalls.

"Brooke . . . are you, have you . . ."

"No," I answer in a short, chopped-off syllable. "I told you, I'm not playing again."

More silence.

"Don't stop calling me, Brookie. Don't let what's happened stop . . . us."

My hand grips my cell, that thread of our friendship pulling taut between us. It's from before and it hurts. A million memory fragments swirl in my head like dandelion seeds caught in the wind. I see the Barbies, then the boys, the late-night talks, the tears . . . each one shared, every milestone of our adolescence shared. It hurts so much because when I think of Lacey, my past knocks on the door of my memories. When things were normal. We went from playing dress-up in our mothers' clothes to actually dressing up to growing up, separate but together. Lacey is feeling the sting of my defenses. The barricades I've put up are impenetrable. I don't want anything breaking past them. Even her right now.

I breathe.

"Brookie . . . I love you," Lacey says in a low voice, needy.

Breathe.

"I love you too," I say and mean it. Then suddenly it hits me deep in the gut that she's the only person left in the world I can say those words to; say them and mean it. "Gotta go."

My finger hovers over *end call*, swiping it smoothly.

I take a deep, gulping breath as the wind swoops in, biting at the tears that run down my face. It doesn't care about my sadness—nature moves forward, the world spins. Tragedy doesn't stop the world.

Just my world.

⌒

You wouldn't think it's bright in Alaska. You'd imagine igloos everywhere and polar bears running free underneath a pewter sky that's pregnant with snow.

It's just not like that.

I've been here for three days and still find myself trying

to acclimate to the cold and fiercely fresh bite in the air, the brightness of a sun that sits low on the horizon but stays lit like an eternal flame. I throw my sunglasses on the instant I slide into the bus, the newly oiled door closing almost soundlessly as I get in. I take the mainly dirt road to town.

East End Road is known for its seclusion and beauty.

I watch the fjords run parallel to me as I drive, rising up like ice kissed by the palest blue as the ocean shimmers at its feet. My eyes move to the road, then unerringly they float back to the view. I note the nutmeg-colored sand of the Homer Spit bisecting the sea as the sandbar extends its finger into the ocean depths. Fathomless . . . secret.

A sea I'll be fishing in soon.

I swallow over the sudden dryness in my mouth. It had all seemed so easy a few months ago when none of it was real yet, when one hand gripped the solid brass key that eventually would lead me to Aunt Milli's Alaskan homestead and the other searched through the want ads for work. I remember exactly when I hit upon just the right wording, its vagueness and ambiguity calling to me:

Looking for adventurous, hardworking male/female, age 18–25 for seasonal employment. Must be adaptable.

Murder forces one to adapt. *Check.*

I'd answered the ad and gotten the job. Chance Taylor had asked for my résumé via our email correspondence and I'd lied through my teeth—alarmingly easy to do without face or voice and only the click of the keyboard for accountability. All those summers that Joey stayed with Aunt Milli and I'd come up with every excuse under the sun not to, has come full circle. I feel like I owe it to my family to do what they would have done . . . had they been here. And it cultivates my desire for forgetting superseding my morality in a clean one-two punch. Motivation and evasion are a deadly combination.

Did I have deckhand experience? Why, yes. Did it count that I'd watched people fish in Puget Sound from my family's back deck? Probably not.

Did I get seasick? Hell if I knew.

Did I have problems working in close quarters with others? I didn't used to.

Could I use a gun? A bat? I thought of my family's murders. Odd questions that had caused a low thrill to unfurl like a sail upon a mast.

Yes, I was pretty certain I was up for that.

Mr. Taylor didn't sound too friendly, didn't want my picture, didn't ask why I was moving from Seattle to Homer. Hell, my only truth in the whole thing had been that I was female and twenty-one.

Well, almost twenty-one.

I smile as I cruise up the spit. It looks so small from the top of East End . . . but it takes almost six minutes to drive to the other end. I make a large loop at the gas tank farm, condos standing at its tip like an afterthought, blocking the view of the beach.

The sand of the beach isn't brown, I think as it appears from a distance . . . it's charcoal-colored, like pebbled smoke on the ground. I park the bus and step out, the wind this far out on the spit snapping the color to life on my cheekbones.

I need a hat, I think, remembering the one that Tucker wore when I met him. I understand better now. A wool hat in May. I shake my head in wonder. Summer's almost here but Alaska's bitter hold on winter can still be felt everywhere, the icy tentacles of the season loath to let go just yet.

I walk to the only wedge of beach I can see, the state ferry slapping against the pilings driven into the ground that hold it tight against its moorings. I take in the brutal beauty of the place, and I feel like I'm truly at the end of the earth. I feel the pull of the tide against my body, calling to that fragment of soul that still cries for life, that despair can't snuff out. It's the only part of me that still wants to live. The rest is just pretending. I walk down the gentle slope of beach pebbles, held in rough swaths of finely ground sand that is a mixture of many different shades of gray. Every color in that elusive spectrum emerges in the beach that looks like stormy salt. The sky is blue overhead as the seagulls swirl around their position as stewards over the big ferry. A horn sounds and I glance at my cell . . . noon. My stomach rumbles and I sigh, not wanting to leave the bosom of anonymity that this small stretch of beach has given me. But I feel my list of supplies crinkling in my hand and I trudge back to the bus, reminded of why I drove into town in the first place. I'm pacing myself. One trip for household and one trip for fishing gear. Baby steps. The heavy burden of my guilt-tinged grief makes even minor chores feel insurmountable. I read it for the fifth time, my eyes scanning the unfamiliar garments:

Slicker plus bibs

Xtratufs

Carhartts

Wool hat (I smile at this.)

I start the bus, the heat kicking on as I drive back down the spit to Kachemak Gear Shed, the local catchall of hardware and, I guess . . . fishing apparel.

I move through the doors. My eyes scan the interior where hanging dead animals line the walls. Their glass eyes follow me as I peruse shelves filled with gear for fishing and every other outdoor recreational activity I can imagine, and some that I can't.

Hardy group, Alaskans, I think. My hand runs over the folded stacks of bright orange plastic slickers, suspenders sold separately.

A guy around my age with wild hair and hip-hugging jeans walks up and gives me a quick head-to-toe. "Help ya?"

I nod, handing over my list and he looks at it. Then his eyes meet mine again, a friendly moss green, his errant shock of dark blond hair stuffed underneath a Monster Energy Drink cap parked backward atop his mane. "Deckhand?"

I nod. "Yes . . . How do you know?"

He smiles and chuckles. "It's like the pat uniform for 'but fishing."

" '*But* fishing?" I ask.

He glances over his shoulder with a critical eye, gauging my size even as he responds. "Halibut fishing . . ." he says with a raised brow, already deep into sizing me up. He stacks a set of bibs, size small . . . unisex, on top of a pair of the ugliest brown boots I've ever seen.

"Are those the . . ."

"Xtratufs? Yeah," he replies, kicking up a foot, and I see he's wearing a lovely pair himself.

"Do you fish?" I ask, confused as to why anyone would ever wear them. Voluntarily.

"Nah . . . but they're great all-round footwear."

I look at them again, unconvinced.

He gives a low chuckle and sticks out his hand, shifting my pile. "Evan."

I smile. "Brooke."

"You're not from around here, are ya?"

I cast my eyes down, feeling sort of exposed. "No . . . Seattle."

He gets a thoughtful look, palming his chin, his other arm holding my gear load. "Brooke from Outside . . ."

I laugh. "Outside?"

Evan smiles. "Yeah, people who aren't from Alaska." Then his eyes take in my Seattle mix of jeans with bling, so skinny they're more like leggings, my almost black hair piled up in a messy bun on my head, and a slow grin spreads across his face. "How long have you been in Homer, Brooke?" Evan asks over his shoulder as he walks my gear to the cash register.

"About half a week," I say.

His eyes sweep to mine then shift to the pile of purchases he thumbs through, mentally ticking things off my list. "Size six on the Tufs?" I look at the boot critically, then kick off my ballet flat and jam my foot into the sucking vinyl ugliness. I move my toes.

"Feels big," I reply. Evan squats down, his face close to my feet and I blush. Awkward.

He presses his finger between my toe and the end of the boot.

A sudden swelling grief grips my throat and my chest tightens.

My mom used to do that.

Evan stands, giving my boot-encased foot a contemplative stare. "Looks about right . . . With a wool sock it will feel snug but not tight . . ." He looks up and sees my face.

"What is it?" he asks sharply, his eyes scanning my face.

The pocket of grief rips open, the vulnerable stitching torn. This is the nature of grief. A small, seemingly insignificant comment or memory comes to the surface in an unguarded moment. You're helpless against it. Like the tide, it washes over you and however much you cling to the rocks, the ocean breaks you down with its tireless cycle, until the bits of you are carried away on the current.

"Hey," Evan says in a low voice, dumping the rest of my purchases onto the counter.

I can't breathe.

He sees it. "It's okay, Brooke . . . whatever it is, it's okay." He grips my shoulders, staring into my eyes, and I notice his have flakes of brown like sprinkled sugar, swimming in the forest green of the irises.

I take a great swooping breath. Then another. He breathes with me like we're in a Lamaze class or something.

I regain control then give a shaky laugh.

Evan releases my shoulders, his eyes searching mine. "Did I flip some kind of switch . . . trigger?"

My eyes snap to his. I silently nod. Then blurt out, "My mom used to"—I swallow—"measure my feet like that."

She hadn't done so since I was ten. It's been a decade, but the memory had risen until it burst like a bubble seeking oxygen.

Evan smiles tentatively and his teeth are white; blond stubble covers the square jaw of his friendly face

"Listen . . . you're new here," he begins in a soft voice. Then his eyes move to my face, looking for some small reaction as my breathing settles back into an acceptable rhythm. "Why don't you meet me and a few friends for a bonfire tonight?"

No relationships, no people . . . escape. But in my heart, I know these people don't know me. I did escape. And Evan saw the sadness in me and he didn't bolt. Nor did he push.

Points were stacking up in his favor.

"Okay," I say after mulling it over briefly, and his face lights up. His hand sweeps through his curly blond hair, impossibly long lashes touching his eyebrows.

Evan rings up my purchases, then looks at my face and I blush a little at his scrutiny. He grins back, ignoring my discomfort or choosing to not notice. "Do you have wool socks?"

I nod. There were some universal things that I picked up before moving to Alaska.

He gives me the damage and my jaw drops. "It hurts, right?"

"Hell, yes," I say with a laugh.

"Let me help you," Evan says.

We troop out to the bus and Evan turns suddenly, my packages stacked in his long arms. He barks out a laugh. "Tucker, right?"

I stop, following his gaze as it moves over the bus. "Yeah," I say slowly.

"Looks like his work." Evan opens the hatchback to the bus and puts the packages into the back.

"Does everyone know everyone here?" I ask incredulously. No one knows anyone in Seattle.

Evan nods, slamming the back. "Yeah, population swells in summer for the wharf rats . . ." He gives me an apologetic look. "I mean, migrant workers."

"Wharf rats," I say, putting my hands on my hips.

"Not you!" he says, laughing as he backpedals. "I meant . . . y'know, people that live on the beach and work."

"Like homeless people?" I ask, trying for clarity.

He scrubs his face, the skin warming slightly underneath his palm. "You don't live at the beach, do ya?"

I let him sweat it. Then finally I let Evan off the hook. "I inherited my great-aunt's place."

Evan breathes out a sigh of relief. "Who?"

I tell him.

Evan snaps his fingers. "East End . . ." Then laughs. "The very end." His brows rise to that curly hairline.

"Yeah." I laugh.

We stand there awkwardly for a minute. Then Evan's eyes flick to mine. "So . . . why don't you meet us at the Dawg and we'll go from there."

I give him a blank look.

"Right," he says, then shifts his weight. "The Salty Dawg Saloon?"

I think quickly. Then an image of a lighthouse pops up in my mind. "Is it that lighthouse building?"

He nods. "One of the oldest original buildings."

"Rowdy?" I ask in a drawl, suddenly feeling the need to spend a night out, away from my dingy cabin, away from . . . myself. My self-imposed solitude. I recognize it's a chance I'm willing to take.

"Definitely. We know how to party here in the Land of the Midnight Sun."

"Does the sun never set?" I ask, slipping into the bus and closing the door. I crank the window open and he leans in, smelling like pine and soap. Clean.

I swallow uncomfortably at his nearness and he smiles. The concept of personal bubbles is clearly nonexistent up north.

"We get a twilight of sorts, but the sky just . . ." He pauses, his face turning to the brightness of the sky. It's colored the vacant blue of spring, not the deep cerulean it'll be when autumn comes calling.

He finishes his thought, "It just gets kinda dim."

"The light?"

"The night."

"I guess it's tough on stargazing . . ."

"Nah, we have the aurora borealis."

I've heard of it.

He slaps the window rim lightly with a palm. "So . . . seven at the Dawg?"

I nod, feeling simultaneously hopeful and desolate . . . my emotions wrapping me in a package of uncertainty. But that's the tenor of my life these days—uncertain.

I put the bus in gear, my new fishing gear and a tentative date with an Alaskan stranger set for tonight.

Two days until fishing.

I catch Evan's eyes in my rearview mirror and he gives a single wave as I pull away.

It doesn't stop my sadness, but affords a temporary abatement.

The guilt is always there.

THREE

∾

I put the last of the supplies away and, moving with great reluctance, I turn the faucet to *hot* on the old shower. The pipes
moan as the water moves through them underneath the floorboards and I wait.

Then wait some more.

After about three solid minutes, steam begins to pool then
rise as the water becomes hot.

No temperature gauge on this, I note, fiddling with the faucet
until the water won't melt my skin off.

I kind of have a date, I think as I step into the shower.

Not really, my mind answers as I lather, rinse, and repeat.

I towel off, feeling lucky to have running water in the joint,
then check my phone for messages.

My finger hovers over Yahoo! News, a trap of depression if
ever there is one. Then I tap the familiar icon. I scroll through
the top news stories and something catches my eye.

It's so profound I almost drop my cell when I see the head-
line:

ANOTHER JUILLIARD FINALIST FAMILY
SLAUGHTERED

My heart stutters a savage rhythm inside my chest, my
blood roars in my ears. I sit down on the couch; it's either that
or fall, because my legs are giving out. I skim the article, my eye
stumbling over key words and phrases.

Entire family
Gruesome
Orphan
Ruined potential
Bloody

Those are the words that were in our local coverage last De-
cember. When my family was erased.

Another pianist is suffering like I suffered. Like I'm suffering now. I glance at the newspaper and read the name of the
pianist:

Marianne VanZyle.

The wheels of my memory turn. I know her . . . she's in that
elite group of pianists who live to practice. Juilliard contenders,
students like me who feel playing is like breathing—automatic,
natural.

The notes are like food edification on a tactile level, unlike
eating it nourishes not the body, but the soul.

It's a small group, a handful of musicians whose focus is the music, the art of playing for its own sake. We're all aware of each other, our shared passion unifying us to some extent.

Another pianist has been cut down. Not by a weapon. By grief.

I hold my cell in a loose grasp. *What does it mean?* It is beyond coincidence that both she and I would suffer this dual tragedy. It means something.

Yet it changes nothing.

My family is gone regardless of circumstance, motivation, this second atrocious crime.

I clench my eyes, reflexively squeezing my cell in a merciless grip.

When it vibrates I drop it. It lands on the old wood floor with a clatter, skittering like plastic sleet on the floor as it vibrates and shrieks its ring tone.

A face lights up on the screen. *Marshal Decatur Clearwater.* The FBI agent who's assigned to my family's death. I watch it twitch on the floor, his image blinking on the screen.

It rings and I let it.

Finally, my cell falls quiet and I reach forward, scooping it off the floor. With my finger I move between the details of the news story, then back to the phone icon that signals a voice mail from Clearwater.

I swipe *delete.*

With hands that tremble I turn off my cell and open a tiny drawer inside a little table that sits beside the front door. The small glass pull winks as I slide the cell inside and close it.

I turn away from my phone, the reminders of my past safely sealed off in a drawer. Shut away.

If only I could do that to my emotions.

I pull up to the Salty Dawg Saloon, established 1897. Actually, as I peer at the sign it says that the old one-room cabin was erected in 1897, then went through many incarnations to finally become the saloon of today in the 1950s.

Large whiskey half-barrels hold sprays of nasturtiums, their variegated leaves striped with creamy lemon yellow veins. I run a finger over a fragile blossom that's the color of sunrise and a little hurt starts in my chest again.

I shouldn't have come. I'm not good company . . . to anyone.

"Those are hothouse grown, y'know." I whirl around, hand to my chest.

"You scared the crap out of me," I say. Evan's hooded eyes capture mine as he takes a pull from an Alaskan Amber.

I cross my arms over my chest, my eyes flicking from his beer to his face.

"The flowers," he says without shame, and grins.

I shake my head. "Do you always just prowl up on unsuspecting women?"

Evan looks around, kicking an errant pebble with his ugly brown boot and grins. "Yeah."

"Huh," I huff.

I look at the brilliant flowers, yellow, red, and orange flopping over the bounds of the beat-up edge of the whiskey barrel and smile.

"We have to cheat this far north," he says, his eyes on me, his words referencing the flowers. I suddenly wonder if we're still talking about plants.

He takes another pull from his beer, then he says something I've not heard in a while.

"Y'know, I didn't really notice in the store but . . . your eyes."

I cock a brow.

He steps closer and I fight not to move back. He takes my chin and inspects me, searching my eyes.

"They're not really blue . . ."

I shrug. I've heard it a lot. I have Liz Taylor's eyes.

"They're . . ." He looks deeper as I squirm. "Sort of purple, shot through with blue."

Evan releases my chin.

"Who gave you those?" he asks in soft inquiry..

I breathe in and out in a measured rhythm. "My great-aunt."

His brows rise to disappear underneath his mop of hair. "The one that gave you the cabin?"

I nod.

I know her eyes will never see again. But mine do.

Evan studies me, internally deciding something, then he grabs my arm. "Time for beer!" he says, breaking the sadness that moves in around me like a tide pool.

"'Kay," I say, sucking my bottom lip inside my teeth, my underage status my secret—for now.

He tows me after him and as we move deeper into the small structure. I look around in wonder.

Money is tacked everywhere. Monopoly money. And photos—what look like snapshots of locals. The clutter telling the town's story.

I spot Tucker right away and wave. He lifts his hand, rising from his perch at the bar, the surface deep, thick, and wide, running the length of half the room.

"Hey, Seattle!" he says as he draws nearer.

"I found her first," Evan warns, then winks at me.

I relax a little, trying to shake the sadness that clings to me, trying to enjoy the attention.

Tucker gets close, looming over me. He's easily six feet three and built like a lumberjack, though I know most everyone fishes here.

He claps Evan on the back. "So you've met our little Brooke here?"

"Yeah, she came in." He takes a sip of his beer, notices it's gone, and puts a finger up for another. "For 'but season gear," he half yells over the din of the saloon.

Tucker nods, palming his short, scruffy goatee and nodding, the communion of words understood. "She's going to give it a shot like Joey," he says.

My breath stills as Evan's brows rise and my heart thumps an uneasy rhythm inside my chest.

Tucker explains over the din. "Her brother, remember hearing about him . . . He'd fish the summers, loved Alaska . . ."

Evan shook his head, taking another pull from his beer.

He knows, I have time to realize.

I'm measuring a quick evasive response as my grip on anonymity is threatening, while my guilt and grief encroach. But circumstance saves me again.

Tucker opens his mouth to ask a question when a rippling silence overtakes the crowd. Evan gives a small smile. "Act one," he says quietly and throws me a sidelong glance.

What? I mouth. He jerks his chin to a small corner stage where a guy sits bent over a guitar and a small spotlight filters pale light that's at once bright but with a blue cast that makes him look like ice washed by the night sky.

Tucker puts a beer in my slack palm and I take a solid gulp, my eyes riveted to the stage. It's a virtual sauna inside the saloon, people packed in like sardines, but I notice a small open area around the guitarist as I study him, the crowd giving him room, making a bubble of space for him to strum.

He begins to move nimble fingers over his guitar strings as I sip beer and watch him master the frets.

I recognize the melody instantly.

The piece I would have played had my family lived.

Had I kept my position for the audition at Juilliard.

I'm mesmerized like inert organic material. Girl inside saloon drinking beer while wallowing in secret grief.

Tucker takes my empty beer that I've guzzled and replaces it with another. Notes filter through the stillness of the saloon, as every eye is on the lone player, I stay, enraptured by deeds unaccomplished.

A life aborted.

A path severed.

I study the suppleness of his playing. Tapered and long, his fingers stroke the strings like breathing . . . he's that natural. My eyes travel up an arm taken up with a sleeve, not of cloth, but of an intricate and colorful tattoo. The fine muscles of his forearm ripple with the movement of his fingers playing chords that become increasingly more complicated.

I know where the song goes, where it will take me, and I can't stand another moment, another memory.

I poise to leave, but at the exact moment that I've decide to flee, he looks up, his dark eyes locking with mine.

And I'm rooted to the spot for an instant, staring back into a face that's all hard planes and sharp angles. His bottomless eyes create a magnetic pull, a physical tug that almost beckons me forward.

But as soon as he glances down at his fingers, the spell breaks and I stagger backward until my spine slams into the door.

Evan says, "Hey!" and moves toward me, but my sweaty palm is on the handle, heating it as I push out into the night. It's too much sensory overload.

I flee.

It's too much.

The beer, the new friends.

The heartbreaking song that reminds me of what no longer is. Suddenly my sadness is no longer manageable, my guilt is a drowning tide inside my mind.

I run until I'm out of breath, until the people and noise of the intimate little drinking hole are far behind me. I find that wedge of beach again and underneath a deepening sun, the night held back by a hairbreadth, I pour my sadness out onto the sand still warm from the day.

I'm there by myself for minutes that become hours. When I look up, the sky's a deep pink, my sweatshirt soaked where I've cried against it. Fine grains of sand litter my face like dark sugar. I blink once . . . twice, but it remains. The booze magnifies the fuzziness of my head. A lone diamond in the sky sits unblinking over the fjords.

Venus.

She sits, and in this moment she's the sole witness to my sorrow.

Suddenly I know what I need to do, what I should have done at the beginning. I've been fooling myself that I could start somewhere fresh and just leave it all behind me. The distance brought only a deeper sense of loneliness and isolation . . . an even rawer pain.

I know it's the coward's way.

It's a lie that you can change where you live, embrace anonymity and alter the past.

Yet you just end up with the same baggage, different locale.

I stand on shaky legs as my eyes move to their destination.

The pier.

I move, not bothering to wipe the tears from my face.

The sea will cleanse my grief.

Forever.

Chance Taylor

I retune my guitar before putting it away in its case. I tune it when I take it out too. *OCD for guitarists,* I think with a smirk.

I rub my eyes as smoke rises in a foul cloud, floating like an interior sky inside the Dawg as Evan saunters over, a cold one in each hand. I give a chin lift and he nods back, his wild-ass hair flopping forward with the motion.

"Hey," he says, handing me my beer and giving me a knuckle-kiss palm glide in greeting. My lips twitch; Evan's as laid-back as they come. And with my occupation, I can sure use a dose of that.

I take a long slug of the beer, checking the label that it's not a pussy light flavor or some shit. I'd have to cut him for that. Biggest insult ever: cheap beer.

"Hey . . . chill, Taylor, it's the good stuff."

I stand, nodding my thanks. "Yeah, I like it."

I tear the hoodie over my head that bears the slogan of the saloon and pick up my guitar case. I've got a long day tomorrow, probably shouldn't have played the set tonight, but it gets me out of my head. A head full of fishing quotas, crew, food, weather, and of course, the sea.

That's *The* Sea. My mistress.

I slam back the rest of my beer and dump the bottle into the recycler in the corner, an old wooden water-collection barrel. I think it used to collect rain before running water hit the spit. I smile at the irony of it collecting beer now. Nice.

I give Johnny a nod as he swabs the bar top down after last call and he gives me a one-finger salute and I smirk. Characters . . . all of them. It's my home, where I've spent my entire life, sea and salty people.

Evan and I wade through the deep filth of peanut shells, napkins, and other stuff. He slaps the door open and the fresh air hits me like a wave of purity and I just stand there for a second, taking in the lush crispness of it all. I open my arms and stand there in the middle of the Dawg's tight parking lot and inhale.

"Damn . . . smell that air!" I say loudly.

Evan grins. Then my memory hits on something. Deep eyes, exotic girl. Newbie . . . definitely not homegrown.

My eyes narrow on Evan. Not that I have room for chicks. A fisherman's life is no place for relationships, let alone family. When men do it they always lose it.

But . . . that face floats up in my brain, burning like an imprint.

"Who's the girl, Ev?" I ask.

He tries for coy and misses it by a hundred miles. We begin walking toward my car, a souped-up hot rod, impractical . . . gas-guzzling.

Perfect. Love those stock Hemis in the old 'Cudas. I chuck my lightweight gear into the low-riding backseat then carefully slide in the precious cargo. I shut the door, not bothering to lock up. No one steals in Homer. *Unless we're talking beach rats.*

My eyes shift through the gray of a twilight that won't come, the sun a melting ball of pink at the lowest point it will sink in the horizon. It flirts with night, but this close to summer solstice, it never quite takes. The haphazardly erected two-man tents lean and flow with the wind that comes off the waves, hollowing out the sides as it bites. Not a light on anywhere.

It's 2 a.m., not much is stirring. Good.

"What girl?" Evan asks, a laugh caught in his throat.

"For fuck's sake, Ev . . . the *hot* girl. The one with hair like ink and those eyes . . . and that body. Y'know," I say, my hands miming an hourglass.

"Oh, yeah, That Girl," he shrugs, throwing his beer into a trash can. *Not a greenie,* I think. Of course, I can't bitch too

THE DARKEST JOY   53

much. I use salmon heads for bait when the Coast Guard isn't near.

Smelly ones.

Whatever it takes to trawl, capturing what I can for the age-old commerce.

The hateful part of the job. The frighteningly practical part.

"Fine," I say, scrubbing a hand over my shorn hair, my day-old stubble more than a shadow on my chin. Shit, I am going to have to clean up hard. I have an appointment tomorrow to meet my newest deckhand.

"Don't tell me . . . but you know I'll find out."

Evan makes a mock gun with his fingers and shoots me. "Of that, I have no doubt."

"Besides, don't you always say not to get tight with the ladies?"

I do.

I nod. "Yeah, counts double for you."

"No-oh. I like this girl . . ." Evan says, his face growing thoughtful with some memory I'm not privy to.

"What?" I ask, stepping forward.

Evan shakes his head, gazing at the sky for a moment. I follow his eyes, catching Venus hanging like a low glittering gem in the mixed velvet of a sunset that lingers for hours this far north.

"She seems"—Evan rakes a hand through his hair—"sad."

I put my hands on my hips. "How is that attractive?"

Evan shakes his head. "I don't know, but it gets me," he says, placing his hand on his sternum. "Right here. I feel like I need to help her or something."

Bullshit. That's a chick playing the emotional bullshit card.

I scoff. "Sounds like she's playing you."

Evan stares at me. "Well, if that's true, she's Academy Award material."

I shrug, looking around me.

I decide to walk it off. The day. Sometimes after a hard night playing, and an even harder day fishing, a walk along the pier will bring clarity. Or whatever.

"You walking?" Ev asks, intuiting my mood as always. He's cool that way.

I nod. "Yeah."

"See ya tomorrow," Evan says and gives a strange smile. I wonder at it.

"Yeah . . ." I reply, watching him as he jogs to his car and hops in. I stare until his brake lights become twin red dots as they travel back down the spit. Then I move, one foot after the other, walking the same path they have since I began playing at the Dawg.

They take me to where I've always gone. But something about tonight already feels different.

FOUR

❧

Brooke

I sway, my swan arms balancing me perfectly at the slick edge of the pier. No ferry to block my dive. No well-meaning rescuers to halt what I've been moving toward since their deaths.

I've already drowned emotionally.

The raw smell of the ocean tingles my nose, the breeze lifting my hair as I dangle. One foot in life, the other already in death.

A single image replays in my mind.

The crime scene tape billows even as it's driven by the sleet into the sodden front yard.

I stumble out of my car, the chime rings as I leave the car door open.

Ding-ding-ding . . .

I rush to the door and a cop bars my way. I hear my voice, coming from far away. "No . . . no! I just talked to my mom, she's okay . . ."

I can't breathe, a weight bears down on my chest and he answers, "I'm sorry, miss, this is an ongoing police and federal investigation. I can't have you inside."

My breath hisses its escape like a tea kettle that never boils.

His speech is robotic, an indifferent monologue.

But his eyes tell me about the horror and brutality that wait inside a home I've shared with people I love.

Past tense: who loved me.

We are flawed, we don't always get along. But the love was there, the unconditional devotion.

The cop has a sheen to his eyes when he looks into mine . . . maybe not so indifferent after all.

I shake my head, backing away as the first body is rolled out on the gurney.

The black bag hasn't been zipped all the way and my eyes seek the small sliver of flesh that's revealed.

My mother's hand, defensive wounds on the palm that is turned to the sky. Her wedding ring winks in the harsh fluorescent glare of the crime scene lights as her body is loaded inside an unmarked van.

My knees buckle as they drive into the wet grass, the denim soaking through.

I hear a voice. "What's going on here?"

"It's the vic's daughter . . ." the cop begins.

"Jesus . . . could you have handled this a little bit more sensitively?"

Disdain leaks like cold venom, edging in around my numbing grief.

I hear nothing, see nothing: blind, deaf, and dumb.

There's a whisper of rustling, then strong hands bear down on my arms, ripping me off the soaked dirt and grass. I stand and look up into a tall man's face, and those eyes, like two black marbles drill me with their intensity.

Their compassion.

"Miss Starr . . . come with me." He shoots the cop a withering glare and gently hauls me over to a small covered area outside the loop of cop cars and unmarked vehicles.

"I'm Marshal Clearwater . . ."

I nod as I suck a deep burning breath into my lungs, then burst into tears, covering my face in shame.

It feels like it's happening to someone else. This night, these deaths. It can't be happening to me.

I've lost it in front of a stranger, while my dead family lies in black vinyl.

Unseeing.

Unfeeling.

"How?" I ask in a hoarse whisper, a question posed in abject disbelief.

Clearwater's eyes tell me he doesn't want to give me the details.

I force him.

When he finishes the morbid recounting, I'm shaking.

Like I shake now at the memory.

I never did see their bodies.

Somehow, it's worse that way. My imaginings are worse. This final choice is the only one.

I look up at the sky, trying to focus through my alcohol haze. Night has finally arrived. The moon looks different here . . . *more.* The uncaring man in the moon looks down as he has for millennia.

I am not significant. I won't be missed. Because there's no one left to miss me.

My gaze slides to the churning water. Without sufficient light, it's black. A void ready to engulf me.

I'm a strong swimmer, but I know what hypothermia is. And how long it will take.

For the first time since their deaths, I feel a sense of peace. My decisiveness in this moment will be my first selfless act of atonement for living while my family doesn't.

No more grief from their absence, and the lesser void caused by the lack of music in my life . . . gone.

Lacey will miss me, I think with an ache in my chest.

I listen, hearing the call of the sea like a macabre melody.

I answer.

I leap gracefully, and behind me I hear a shout as if from another world, another time.

The water slams into me like a wall of ice, stealing my breath.

It's so much easier than I thought it would be, I think as I close my eyes inside the watery grave I've chosen.

The water drenches my clothing and I begin to sink, the clothes weighing me down.

Then the chill seeps into my bones as if it has always be-longed there.

Chance

The pale twilight fizzles to night, maybe an hour of true dark-ness bleeds through the ambient in-between stage of a night that struggles to chase out the last of a stubborn day. The moon takes over its temporary shift, casting washed-out bluish-white light at my feet, picking out the white stones that flow through the gray at the beach to my right.

I don't know what causes me to look up at this dead hour of the night; nothing is stirring but the vastness of the sea.

But I do, and that's when I see her, arms arced over her head, as if preparing to dive.

What the fuck?

I'm already in motion, my body responding before my mind can process what I'm seeing, running toward the female figure. If she survives the drop, the water will kill her.

It's a death wish.

I kick off my shoes as I sprint, tearing off my hoodie. My blood rushes in response to the kick of adrenaline that bursts through my system in a single pulse of driving electric numbness.

I watch her lift up on her toes, tense as she simultaneously bends at the knees, and then she's just . . . gone.

I thunder after her, arms pumping as my clothes trail me like birdseed, and rush off the dock. I never pause, my legs and arms piston like I'm still running in midair, the safety of the dock behind me. Then I scoop and lengthen, diving right after her.

I know what the ocean feels like and brace myself, fighting the urge to curl my body in brutal anticipation. Instead I split the water with hands pressed together as if in prayer.

The icy black water hits me like a slap as it punches my body. I'm plunged ten feet under before I know it.

I swirl and instinctively churn upward, breaking the surface, snapping my head around as my eyes search the dim light from the moon that hits the sea, my breaths coming in short bursts.

I never stop treading. I know better.

Can't see her! My mind roars as my heart races inside my chest. Droplets of salt water swing and splatter, hitting the surface just as a lone bubble breaks just five feet from my position. I go after it like a bull's-eye in smooth crawl strokes, diving underneath the water where the subtle ripple appeared.

I plow downward through the icy wetness and catch sight of her.

Like an apparition, her image slams into me, pale skin like alabaster, black hair like a floating spiderweb moving around her body as she sinks.

My lungs begin to burn as I move toward her. *Gotcha,* my mind says as I latch my forearm around her torso and wrap it underneath her armpits, hauling her against me even as I rise to the surface.

She's small against me, light . . . I feel something shift inside me at the unfamiliar feeling of having this fragile burden in my care.

Because I don't take care of anything but myself. And the sea takes care of me.

The moonlight pierces the dark water, the need to breathe becomes a fireball inside my chest. The tingling in my extremities shouts at me that I've run out of time.

I break the seal of the waves in an explosion of limbs . . . hers . . . mine. Our heads break out into the cool air, yet warmer than the blanket of the sea. I turn in one motion to my back as

I do a one-armed backstroke for shore, a sucking gasp of oxygen hitting my needy lungs. I swim backward as a still woman lays on my chest.

Not breathing.

Dear Jesus don't let her die, I think as I hit the sand and drag her onto the pebbled beach.

I turn her on her side and water pours out of her mouth.

She's gonna die, I think as a slow numbing horror tries to assert itself and shake my natural calm.

I roll her onto her back and begin giving mouth-to-mouth. The chill of her lips makes me shiver; I only want to feel the warmth of her flesh pressed to mine, evidence of life. I begin chest compressions. My palms fill her entire chest, she's so small.

I don't want to break her. That thought doesn't derail what I must do.

I watch my hands, crosshatched over that delicate rib cage. They pump up and down, covered in a whitewash of the palest blue underneath an uncaring sky, laced together to prevent her death.

Up.

Down.

As though from a distance I hear a clicking sound.

It's my teeth chattering.

I pump.

I kiss savagely icy lips again with breath . . . with hope.

I repeat.

Though it's cold enough for me to flirt with hypothermia myself, my wet clothes clinging to me like a second skin, I break out in a sweat.

A life in my hands.

I own a moment I don't want to.

I've never given a shit about anyone. I fish, I party . . . and I'm accountable to me. It's always felt perfect . . . right.

But suddenly, it all seems meaningless as I work to bring another human being to life.

She shudders and pukes up more water.

I turn her gently on her side. Then . . . like music to my ears, she draws her first shuddering breath.

I watch her hack more of the sea onto the soft charcoal sand, black as night, the occasional white stones staring back at me like luminescent eyes.

I fall back on my heels and shudder as I plant my hands on my soaked knees.

That was so close, I think as that hot sweat begins to chill on my skin.

We stay like that. She begins to breathe on her own, and suddenly I'm left wondering what I've gotten myself into, what to do next. I suddenly feel the weight of responsibility for something bigger than me, something I don't understand.

Like a girl who doesn't want to live.

Her eyes pop open and I give a weak smile, a tired smile full of relief.

It turns to surprise when I recognize her.

She's the sad beauty who watched me play my set tonight. Her image burned into my skull, pinging around like a ball without a goal.

Well fluke of fucking flukes . . .

But a more important question hangs in the air between us.

Hers is a different one from mine . . . or maybe not.

Why?

Brooke

I open my eyes and notice my body is moving and I can't stop it. I shake until I rattle, my teeth slamming into each other.

I'm a Mexican jumping bean.

A horribly, irrefutably, mortally embarrassed one. I take in the odd scene, the chattering of my teeth and the roar of the waves as they hit the shore the only backdrop of sound. The moon casts strange silver and blue light around me and for a moment, reality and fantasy blend like vision that doubles and I wonder if I'm in heaven, if my goal has been met. Then it hits me like the ocean slapping the beach: I'm alive. The moon, the waves, the cold . . . they bear silent witness to a life that stubbornly clings to me, regardless if I deserve it or not.

Even with his hair slicked back and draped in drenched clothes that cling to his body, showing every rippling muscle fiber, I know he's the one.

The guy from the Salty Dawg, the inked-up guitarist.

Fucking great.

I can't even die right.

I close my eyes as I try to control my convulsions. But I can't shake my horror that he's been witness to the darkness inside me.

Suddenly something scratchy but soft folds over me and I'm airborne.

My eyes swim as I open them, double vision clouding my sight until I gradually focus on his face. This close I can feel the electric charge between us.

If I think it's been tangible when I caught sight of him inside the dimness of the saloon, it's a suffocating inferno now.

"I almost lost ya there," he says in a soft voice, regret lacing his words.

It's not his fault, I think, my mind swimming with the disorientation of hypothermia and a chaser of shock. *I'm nobody's responsibility. Not anymore.*

I open my mouth to tell him that, but instead I croak, "Thank you," my teeth back to chattering.

He gazes down at me as he easily carries me to his car, contemplative and silent.

The gloom recedes as the hour approaches for the sun's return. It gathers at the edges, pale golden light timidly seeping in at the edges of the sky, teasing darkness with its early approach.

He smooths a piece of hair out of my eyes and I see the stubble of his chin. Dark, hard, a shadow of black pepper that moves along the contours of the squareness of it, diving into the pronounced cleft at the center. His eyes are shadowed and sad.

He knows, I think and I close my eyes against the knowledge I see in his.

"Whatever it is . . . it's not worth this. Never," he says and my eyes open to the raw command in his voice.

I want to believe that I can transcend this slow-boiling agony of guilt.

Of bereavement.

I don't know that I can.

"I can't"—I pause to rattle and shake—"talk . . . about it," I finish with a chilled lip clamp, my feelings in turmoil about his rescuing me.

He looks into my eyes. "Promise me that if I take you home, you won't . . . do this again."

We stare at each other. His heartbeat thuds against my cheek, the latent heat of his chest gifts me with vitality, warmth . . . and strangely, peace.

I nod.

Today I won't die.

I don't know about tomorrow.

It's not day by day for me anymore, it's hour by hour.

But maybe, him saving me is the sign I need to move on. Maybe I don't have to die to live.

As if he knows that, he places me in the backseat of his car then tucks the blanket around me.

Like a future butterfly in the safety of its temporary home, I lie there in a cocoon fashioned by him.

He slides into the front seat and swings the heavy door shut with a soft click. I watch silently as he turns around, his muscular arm hanging over the seat.

He looks at me and our gazes lock.

"Where?"

I tell him, my teeth chattering almost gone.

His brow rises in surprise but he starts the engine. It roars to life, a powerful and separate presence, reverberating underneath me like the purr of a lion.

I close my eyes. They're so heavy.

I'll just rest them for a second, I think. Shame, despair, and exhaustion are a heady mix, driving consciousness away like a riptide. I feel it change course toward something that might allow the grief of my despair to lift like fog when sunlight appears even as I spiral into a discomfited slumber.

I don't wake when he lifts me and tenderly places me on my crappy couch. I don't feel when he takes off my wet clothes, wrapping me in the coverlet from my bed.

I don't know that he stays for an hour, alternately checking my pulse and feeling the slow and gradual return of my warmth.

My life.

As my consciousness fades again to black, it strikes me that for the first time since everything happened, at least in this moment, I don't feel alone.

Chance

My fingers drum on the steering wheel, eyes pegged on the old homesteader's cabin at the bum-fucked-Egypt last stop of East End, torn between staying or leaving.

I scrub my face, so tired I feel like I have sandpaper where my eyeballs should be.

The sea doesn't care if you save a girl that wants to die.

How late you stay up.

How hungover you are.

The tide comes, the fish spawn, swim, and wait to be caught in an endless circle of the food chain.

My clients won't be sympathetic to anything either. Fishing waits for no man. And yet . . . I can't bring myself to move. I glance at my phone and remember the girl I've picked from twenty applicants. I'm due to meet her in . . . I look at the glowing numbers on my cell.

Six hours.

Fuck me running.

With one more glance at the cabin, I exhale loudly as I put the 'Cuda in gear and glide down the driveway. The ribbon of grass that bisects the center hisses like a snake as it whispers its good-bye underneath my low-riding car.

I reluctantly pull away as I hope she won't try to do that again.

I swallow hard.

Ever.

I don't want to admit that she's the first real thing that's ever shaken the careful foundation I've laid.

I don't do attachment. It's safer that way. Attachments are for those who have never lost anything, their trust easily given. But I lost something a long time ago. And I know how to steel myself against ever feeling pain like that again.

I belong to the sea, that's my attachment. In that sense, I guess I am a one-woman man.

And I'm taken.

But as my thoughts move back to the girl from the pier, she stirs something within the careful house of cards I've built for myself. And I wonder if that fragile structure will hold.

The image of her rises in my mind. It's not pretty: the purple lips, the chalky skin, the slicked-back, waterlogged hair clinging to her like silken despair.

But those eyes, those haunted eyes, they're burned into my brain. Her sadness has caught me like the fish I net. I've hit her hook without even knowing I'm in the ocean; saving her has reeled me in inextricably.

And I don't even know her name.

FIVE

Brooke

Something smells like ass.

Wait . . . it's me. I crack an eye open, breaking the crust of sleep induced by near death, the dried seawater covering me in a stiff shroud of vileness.

Somehow, it's not as awful as the memory. I stew in my own seawater stench and the night's memories wash over me like the ocean had just hours before. Now that the fog of alcohol has lifted and the melody of the painful tune has faded I feel . . . embarrassed. My heart gives a lurching thump in my chest, pounding with my emotion as I realize I'm not honoring my family's memory through my death. They would want me to live . . . if not for me, at least for them. I lie there a moment longer, hot tears creating clean paths against salt water that's dried on my face in a sticky mess. I think about going to work in the same capacity that Joey did, fishing lazy summers away in Alaska and how that choice has been robbed from him forever. Now I have the chance to do it . . . for him, for me. It's a gift, not something to toss into the sea like I tried last night. I feel my old determination rise within me. It's scary, exhilarating . . . right.

"Ooh!" I groan, throwing my bent elbow over my eyes as bright sunlight stabs its way through the gray glass of my small cabin, spotlighting the grimy interior as I choke back a sob, remembering, my feelings of getting back on track wavering like water running over glass.

The hot guy who witnessed my botched suicide attempt.

My new friends, Evan and Tucker . . . I ditch in favor of despair. Everything is fucked six ways to Sunday. But I realize now, it doesn't have to be.

Slowly, I lower my arm from my face, the sunlight bathing me despite the dirty glass. Vaguely, I can hear the sound of the ocean, a symphony of crashing waves, a ruthless rhythm that's timeless and unending.

I look around, my eyes latching onto the clock. An archaic windup thing with the name *Ben* inscribed on its face I'd found in a nightstand drawer in my bedroom and commandeered to the living room. Its loud ticking jars the quietness. My cell is safely stowed in the drawer, though the low-power beep is like a beacon of alert that it's about ready to die.

There's one right thing I can do: I can phone my new friend and let him know I'm okay. I sit up, the blood rushing to my head, blanking my vision momentarily. I sit there, trying to regain my balance. I haven't eaten in . . . I can't remember. It was a dumbass move to drink last night, considering. And to let everything get to me. I mean . . . I can't listen to a song without it becoming a trigger?

Apparently not. My eyes trip over my damp clothes on the floor.

They damn me on the spot.

Oh Jesus, I think, *he's seen me without clothes.* The nameless hottie cum rescuer has seen . . . shit, everything.

More blood rushes to my head and I fight the urge to put it between my legs, my palms dampening.

I offer myself a lame consolation: *I bet I'll never see him again,* internally promising myself to avoid the Salty Dawg at all costs.

That's it, I determine. *Easy.*

But I should know, nothing ever is.

Easy.

⌒

I make the call, like the walk of shame . . . it's the call of shame. *Never mind me, Evan,* I speak inside my head, *I'm trying to drown my sorrows.*

No, not with booze. With the sea.

Out loud I say, "Hey, hi," my cell light beeping *low battery* in warning.

"Brooke!" Evan says. "Shit, girl, you gave me and Tucker the slip and we didn't know what happened!"

There's an awkward pause in the open line. I yearn to fill it just as I yearn to hang up.

I swallow. "Yeah . . . I, ah . . . had too much to drink and couldn't drive the bus home . . ."

"Don't you have the deckhand job starting today?"

I nod, realize he can't see me, and say, "Yeah."

"I'll rustle ya up!" he says cheerfully.

"Okay," I say in a small voice, feeling like a colossal asshole.

I'm never telling Lacey, I think randomly. Correction, I'm never telling anyone. My mortification is too acute, too private. I've already shared it with a stranger and even that's too much. I tread lightly with my emotions, as my body betrays me with a near panic attack. It knows I almost died even if my intellect's in acute denial.

"Is that okay? Helllllooo . . ."

I'd lost the thread of the conversation. "Yes, please . . . I'm sorry . . . I just caught a ride with whoever . . ."

A man who saved me, who knows how little I value life—my life.

"That's not cool, Brooke . . . I would've taken ya home."

"I know, I'm sorry."

He gives a soft chuckle. "Don't let it happen again," he says in a tone of stern warning.

"I won't," I promise, meaning it. Evan doesn't know how much.

"Be there soon," he says and the line goes dead as I say good-bye.

I look down at my phone and see another call from Clearwater; they're piling up. Shit, doesn't he have a murderer to catch?

Then it hits me: *maybe he does and that's why he's calling me?*

Do I want to know? To finally face that nameless blank individual who killed my entire family? The same menace who I'm assuming killed that other pianist's family?

I should be thinking about calling him back.

I should be giving serious consideration to the parallels here.

I don't. Instead, my eyes burning, I pivot on my heel and make my way to the shower.

The water eases my sadness down the drain, hiding the proof of it as the two mingle, draining somewhere far from the grief that bleeds from me. The seawater still clings to my skin. I reek of the ocean and have to wash twice to get rid of it.

⁓

I clean myself up by the time Evan pulls up in a Jeep that's so high off the ground I have to hop to get into it. Mud is caked underneath the wheel wells like he's driven through a wall of it.

"God, wash your car much?" I ask, immediately trying to talk about anything but last night.

Evan jogs around the front. "I'm from Alaska, we have . . . three seconds of summer, and a ton of it is rain." He shrugs, his blond hair almost ringlets as it bobs with him as he effortlessly swings into the cab, his hand gripping the roll bar like a monkey with a purpose.

He turns on the motor and the engine buries us with its teeth-rattling shake. "Besides," he nearly screams over the dull roar, "it's great for mud-bogging."

Mud-bogging? "What the hell is that?" I ask, almost not wanting the answer.

Evan gives a slow, evil grin, shifting into first gear and bouncing us out of my lumpy driveway. The long grass grabs along the sides of the car like escaped tentacles of wheat. "It's called taking my chances with the tide."

My mind allows that sentence to tumble within the recesses of my skull, polishing it until it shines.

"No way . . . you . . . go out on the ocean floor when the tide is out . . ." I ask incredulously.

He nods, turning up the volume of the head-banger music to a crescendo that diminishes coherent speaking ability. Disarmonia shrieks in the background, with the engine running second in the race of going deaf.

"Yup!" he says, giving a fist pump that hits the ceiling of the Jeep and I jump. "Hell, yeah, it's a blast."

"Riiight," I drawl, but laugh when I see his hurt expression. He's so into it.

The Jeep lurches over every curve and pothole on the tapestry of the road. "Gotta have a way to burn off steam," Evan explains.

"So," I say, crossing my arms, grateful beyond words for the distraction of Evan, "this is your testosterone purge?"

He nods again. "I think there's hope for you, Brooke from Seattle."

I roll my eyes. *Uh-huh.*

Then Evan looks at me, poker face firmly entrenched, the wheels of the Jeep kissing asphalt instead of dirt road as we make our way to the spit. "Don't underestimate the stress reliever churning some mud can be." He waggles his brows and I bark out a laugh. The first natural sound out of my mouth in almost twenty-four hours. My smile fades and he says, "What?"

I answer with the truth, or my version by omission. "I'm just thinking how much of an ass I was last night . . . to just . . . bail on you guys." I shrug. "Sorry."

I look at my hands, feeling my face heat with all that I know and don't say.

"Listen . . . Brooke," Evan says and I look up from my laced fingers. His eyes meet mine, brown sugar floating in the pressed emeralds of his irises.

"Yes?" I ask, and my breath catches at his serious tone.

"I know we just met but, we stick together here." Evan looks out at the sea that froths at either side of the spit, the surf pounding lone logs of driftwood, the wind beating the wharf rats' tents into submission. "We're pioneers," he continues, sweeping his palm around the seascape. My eyes take in the austere frozen beauty all around us. The sea moves endlessly as the fjords rise up from its feet, coming together like two halves of a whole.

Alaska has this feeling of *otherness* . . . like we're somehow together but separate. It's impossible to quantify, but you can almost feel like nothing outside of this place matters.

However, last night is proof that it does. Your past follows you no matter what corner of the earth you call home.

"Alaska gets in your blood."

"You mean . . . the climate or . . . ?" I ask, genuinely curious. I've been here days, he's been here years.

"Everything," Evan says softly, then putting the Jeep into neutral and setting the brake, jolting us both out of our reverie with a loud, "We're here!"

He kicks open the door and slides out with a practiced hop.

I look down at the big fall from seat to ground; the pebbled asphalt looks far away from my perch on the passenger side.

I tentatively put the tip of my All Star sneaker on the running board and then two hands clasp my waist.

Warm.

Vital.

Unforgettable.

My eyes snap up and take in the deep and arresting bluish-green ones, kissed by midnight, that stare intensely back into mine.

I'd seen them from a distance in the Dawg.

I'd seen them look at me with a tender concern that tightened my heart when I was soaked by the sea.

Seeing them up close was an intimacy that clenched my guts. I instantly infuse with heat, the sensation melting to my toes, my heart trying to escape my rib cage.

Somehow I become aware that Evan has come around behind my savior's shoulder.

"Hey Brooke, meet Chance . . . Chance Taylor."

⁓

"Hi . . . *Brooke,*" Chance says with a smile.

I search his face, very aware of his big hands on my waist as he lowers me to the street.

He's very tall, I note, swallowing in a suddenly dry throat.

"Here's Boss Man," Evan says, unwrapping a Blow Pop and shoving it into his mouth.

Of course, I can't even fake indifference. I stand stupidly, staring up into my savior's eyes. I blink.

"Cat got your tongue?" Chance drawls and I flush.

Shit . . . fuck. He's going to . . . what?

"Hi," I croak.

His hands leave my waist. I look up into his face as Chance puts out the hand that was just on my body for me to shake.

The guy who saved my life.

Who I work for.

Who's seen me in my underwear.

As if in a daze I put my hand in his, his larger one swallowing mine, giving a gentle squeeze.

A tingle of pure electricity shoots between us as our skin mingles and my eyes widen as his tighten. I can tell he felt it too. But at his touch, the memory of last night crashes into me and I realize that Chance Taylor, *my boss,* isn't going to want to mess with a washed-up pianist-turned-orphan with a death wish.

"That's the longest handshake in the history of the universe . . . Just sayin'," Evan comments in the background, his voice droll.

I snatch my hand away as though it burns.

Chance's small smile widens to a grin. "Do you have any gear?" he asks, ignoring the big fat pink elephant romping around between us.

Last night.

The chemistry.

Total awkwardness.

My cell vibrates in my pocket and I ignore it. *Maybe it'll go away?*

Chance's eyes dip to my pocket where my cell twitters and shakes. I feel heat rise to my face, his eyes pegged on my hip.

What is wrong with me? I need to get a grip here, I'm not sixteen.

"Yeah, it's in the back . . ." I stammer as he smirks, turning to the Jeep.

He jerks the small door open and pushes the seat forward, hauling out all the goodies I got for the job.

"We start tomorrow," he says, his back to me, and I watch the muscles in his shoulders roll underneath the thin T-shirt he wears and gulp again.

I want to close my eyes against the view but I can't look away; suddenly I'm mesmerized by the ornate tattoos peeking out from under his shirtsleeves, wondering about the story behind them.

I sigh.

He carries my gear to a small lean-to office that is one of many shanty-type buildings that line the beach, an elevated and weathered boardwalk running along the front of the shops, their façades similar. As I follow him I glance at the colorful hand-lettered signs, each one pronouncing a different trade. The tin roofs stand alongside one another in a melody of different hues. Their bright colors appear to stand in opposition to the quiet power that lays just beyond the row of small buildings.

Evan trails behind us, his hands jammed into his pockets, a moody expression riding his face, the stick from the sucker standing at angry attention in his mouth.

We're outside the door as my eyes latch onto a wooden sign, the words burned into the wood: Take a Chance with Taylor. And then below in small print it reads: And Catch Some 'But!

A larger sign stands above the wood sign, which reads: Deep Sea Charter.

A bell chimes as Chance passes through with my gear and Evan stays my arm with his hand. I turn, looking up at him.

He looks down at me. "What the hell," he mutters and swoops me up into a hug.

I hug him back. It feels good to be liked. I soak in the act of affection like a flower starved for the sun.

I know in my head that I should keep people at a distance. I can't stand the mere suggestion of more loss. But I let him hug me anyway.

Evan pulls away and whispers, "His bark is worse that his bite."

Oh.

"Okay," I reply, more off-kilter than ever.

"Catch ya later, Brooke," Evan says and walks off.

I look after him, wondering why his expression was tinged with sadness.

Is it catching? Is my bullshit contagious?

"Brooke?"

I swing around and Chance is leaning against the door frame. The short sleeve of his shirt rides up just enough for me to catch another glimpse of his tattoo.

My eyes drift back to his.

He smiles. It's so real I can touch it, as if it were the sun, sliding through rain clouds.

And I know it then, though I try to deny it. Resisting the inevitable.

I'm falling for Chance. How could I not? I feel like I'm beyond fixing, but in that cold, wet heart of an Alaskan night, he saved me. And those floating pieces of my heart have begun to find each other again. Chance has begun the mending of it. Whether he meant to or not, it's happening.

But he's most definitely not falling for me.

"Let's talk," he says, all business, and my stomach falls like a stone in a lake.

Great.

He pulls open the door and the bell tinkles as I walk through it and pass by Chance, getting the slightest hint of his scent.

It's not rank seawater either.

I find myself wanting to know exactly what it is, when I'm busy seeing where the tat ends. Yeah.

I turn and he sweeps his palm toward the chair.

I sit and hold my breath.

"I've already hired you. However," he spreads his palms wide and away from his body, leaning against the beaten boards of the wall behind him, glass windows flank his form, his ankles crossed. "I think we have to talk about . . . what happened."

I look down at my hands. *I can't tell him*. He can't know . . . if he does I'll have to face his pity, or judgment. Or whatever.

I look up. "Listen, I've been through something and I drank too much last night . . ."

"So you decided to swan dive off the pier?" Chance asks, his brows rising to the short dark hair that frames a hard face: square jaw, cleft chin, yesterday's stubble.

A beautiful face.

Gawd. "Well . . . no. I mean," my eyes flick to his and they're leveled on me. Not going anywhere. "I'm trying to make a new start."

"I can't have you on my boat if you think you're going to"—his intense eyes stay steady on mine—"do a repeat," he finishes softly.

I shake my head. "I don't think so."

There's a long pause and he exhales, raking a hand through his dark hair, those deep eyes nailing me . . . boring holes deep inside me, carving up my soul with the pathway of their intensity.

"You don't think or you don't know?"

We stare at each other and I say, "I don't think."

"Shit, that puts me in a tough spot." He puts his hands on his hips and paces in front of me.

"I know," I reply in a whisper. I just can't lie . . . not to him. I put a hand over my heart. Trying to hold in my misery through the hole that's there. My emotions are all over the place.

He stops in front of the window and gazes out at the sea. The whitecaps look like whipping cream against a green that mimics the grayness of the sky, the water reflecting the turmoil of my day.

He spins around and pegs me with those eyes. "I can't . . . let you go. God knows I should. But I want to try to help. And I think . . . I think this will be a good job for you."

"You don't have to," I say. I don't need the money, I need to heal . . . but he doesn't know that.

But maybe he's not blind.

Chance walks to my chair, his hands wrapping the armrests.

"I know," he says. Suddenly he jerks the chair so close our faces are inches from touching. "I don't do shit I don't want to."

"Then why . . ." I start, my mind filling in the blanks, *do you want to*? My mind finishes my own question.

"Because I want to," he whispers in answer, his crisp, minty breath filling my nose.

SIX

~

Chance

I told myself never to get involved, *really* involved.

And here I am, hiring this beautiful, fragile, emotionally vulnerable girl, just to keep her close to me.

I don't even know why I feel this need to protect her. I don't even know what I'm protecting her from. Maybe I can't protect her from herself?

Not okay. I stand there indecisively for a minute and then Brooke gives me those big doe eyes and that's when I see her, really see her. *God, her eyes are some kind of purple*, lashes like black lace setting them off like jewels of tanzanite.

I stuff my hands into my pockets to keep them off her.

Then, suddenly, all I want is to feel my lips on hers again. Without thinking, I move in for the kill. I place both hands on her face, looking into those deep eyes and feel my own close as I barely brush her lips and Brooke gasps and flinches away. My eyes pop open and I drop my hands from where they've captured her. I see emotions flow over her face, but the one I don't want to see is there in living color.

Gravity. Like a slow-moving avalanche her face shuts down. "I can't," she says in a breathy whisper and I feel like kicking my own ass. Of course she doesn't . . . she just tried to kill herself and here I am, her boss . . . trying to, I don't even know. I straighten, raking a hand through my hair, and back the fuck off. I shouldn't have done that. Knowing it didn't stop it from happening though. What the hell is wrong with me?

I struggle to recover. "I'm . . . I'm sorry . . . I really do want you to feel . . . like you can work these eight weeks of the season without . . . fear of, whatever," I say, scrubbing my face, trying to wipe it clean of my lapse.

"It's okay, Chance," she says and I see a flinty sort of resolution in her eyes. It replaces the soft desire I'd seen before and I miss it as I watch it slide away. But I'd set the tone and she'd followed it.

"I never really said thank you," she says so quietly that I lean forward over my cluttered desk. Brooke isn't looking at me and misses my unguarded expression. I'm glad, since it sorta belies my words when I say *back off* and my face says *I want you*. And it does. My body wants her, the desk being more of a barrier than she knows.

No relationships, my mind reminds me like a threat. *No entanglements of any kind.* I exhale loudly and her eyes snap to mine.

Then I remember what she just said instead of struggling to tamp my awakened libido like noxious weeds. "You're welcome," I reply, shrugging.

There's a beat of awkwardness between us, a clock's tick ringing out in the silence. Then I say, "So, the job . . ."

"Okay," Brooke replies, her shoulders slumping a little. Her expression makes something unexpected constrict in my chest. Feels like my give-a-shit meter just came online. I don't want to care.

The hell with it. "Do you want to talk about what the problem is?" I feel my brows rise, my hands resting on the thick wood desk.

Brooke shakes her head, that black hair sliding around her shoulders like watered silk.

I remember what it felt like between my fingers. I pause, collecting my shit.

"No," then her gaze locks with mine, "ever."

Okay. *Broken I don't need,* I decide. The phrase rings false even when I hear it in my own head, but I power through my bullshit.

Fine, it's all business. "I need you here at 4 a.m." Brooke just nods and I continue. "We put in about ten hours of flat-out, balls-to-the-wall fish time then we hightail it back to the harbor, clean our catch, pack . . . clean the boat . . . then you go home."

I watch Brooke's eyes get wider with each detail of the hard life of a deckhand.

Here's the breaking point. This is when the weak will jump ship.

I wait.

Then Brooke surprises me. "Okay, I'll be here." I watch her small hands clench the armrests of my ancient oak chair.

We look at each other. So many unspoken words remain unsaid.

"Good," I say in brusque dismissal. I've not had much fear in my life. I'll take the swell, the weather . . . beating a two-hundred-pound halibut that wanted to break my leg with its tail.

I'd never felt anxiety of this variety.

The woman variety. It's a singular flavor of *oh shit* that I don't want to taste.

Brooke stands and puts her hand out and I break into a cold sweat. *I want to touch her again.*

Haul her against me and never let go.

The watery memory of her floating below me in the sea rises to the surface of my mind. I blink the visual away, trying to grip the reality before me.

What scares me the most is I want to wipe away that despondent edge she wears like clothes in the wrong size. I want it gone.

Instead I take her hand in mine, and that zing like a conduit buzz of electricity goes off between us.

I shift subtly. My body's such a traitor.

She keeps it together, but I can't. Won't.

"Feel that?" I say, calling it out, the zing.

"Yeah," she admits in a tentative whisper.

"What do you think it means?" I ask, wanting to kick my own ass for posing the question.

Brooke gives a sad little lift of her lips and answers as she turns for the door, "Something I don't deserve."

Well fuck me if that's not a sucker punch. I feel it like she just struck me in the bread basket. Her words are the weapon.

I feel like a dick as Brooke makes her way to the door, her

fingers trembling slightly as she twists the knob and closes the solid spruce behind her.

I want to kick the thing. I want to go after her.

Tell her how I feel.

Trouble is, I don't fucking know myself.

Brooke

I practically run to escape that office . . . my embarrassment.

I veer, taking a sharp right and racing across the busy road, dodging tourists, fishermen. My bright bus stands in the empty lot of the Salty Dawg.

I tear the door open and slide inside, taking great swooping breaths of old car mixed with the sea. The side window, like a pie wedge of glass, was left open and the misty filter of sea air drifts through. The salt of my tears is masked by the thickness of the air, the two mingle like coconspirators.

I can't do it.

You will do it, my mind whispers. That tenacious form of self-preservation will stubbornly not be put to rest.

I place my forehead on the steering column. My mind turns over the last twenty-four hours. I need to come to some kind of decision. I can't continue inside this excruciating limbo. Either I choose life and live as my family would want or I throw in the towel.

I need to learn to love another human being again, though the threat of their death hangs over me like a noxious cloud, smothering my intent.

I have to make the decision to move on.

My tears fall to my jeans, forming dark splotches, speckling the denim with my indecision.

My phone buzzes in my pocket and I lift my head off the wheel, digging in my jeans to retrieve it.

Decatur Clearwater.

A little icon flashes with the ringing—FBI logo. I exhale somewhere between a huff and a rush.

My finger hovers, then I lightly brush over the icon.

"Hello," I say.

"Miss Starr."

Oh my God, that voice. The memories threaten, triggered. They push to get in, demanding to be seen. I shove them away. A light sweat coats my body instantly.

Panic attack.

"Miss Starr?" Concern radiates from his voice, that light accent he has threading through the vowels in my name, and I swallow.

I can do this. I breathe in deeply and exhale slowly.

"Hi." Start simply, work from there.

"Thank God. I've been trying to reach you for almost a week . . ."

I don't respond. There's no lie that will sound like the truth.

He ignores my silence, moving forward. "There's been . . . another murder."

"I know."

A pause. "Okay. I'm certain this is difficult to hear about and I'm not calling to hash through it and drag you through things that are painful."

Then why are you calling? "Okay," I reply listlessly. *When can I end this phone call?*

"There are similarities between these most recent murders and . . . those of your family members."

My chest tightens. I repeat the deep breathing method, disallowing the panic that's a knot of cement in my chest to take over.

I see the rain.

The wet grass.

The crime scene tape; the garish yellow floating ribbon a banner of death forever.

My mother's hand, slash marks like red stripes proof of her efforts to ward off death.

"We need to warn you. You might require protection from our Anchorage division."

The constriction in my chest notches tighter. My breaths are starting to whistle.

"Miss Starr. Please, don't be . . . frightened. I'm just phoning to alert you that this is not the last of these tragedies and we're treating it as a serial."

"A serial?" I ask faintly.

"Absolutely. The VanZyle family was killed . . . and there's one more that took place last month, near Portland."

"Oregon?"

"Yes."

Oh my God. "So . . . is the other family . . . ?" I couldn't say it.

"Yes, all the families were related to pianists. We have a profiler working full-time on identifying who might be responsible for this."

"My family's already gone, Agent Clearwater. This killer can't hurt me more than he already has." It's the truest thing I've articulated since my family's death.

Silence.

"That's not true," he says carefully.

"*What . . . ?* Listen to me, Clearwater. This is worse than death."

"What is worse than death, Miss Starr?"

"My *life*." I enunciate the angry words that seethe between us like brackish water.

Silence.

Then, "Okay." Clearwater sighs. I can just see him nervously tightening the band that holds that black hair of his, discreetly combed away from his face and neatly tied at his nape. The raw scar at his throat is a healing pink slash. It makes me feel like a trout gasping for air. *Or a salmon,* I think grabbing on to the thought with shaky humor.

"I thought you went to Alaska to move forward?" Clearwater says as a flat statement.

"I did, I *am*." I say it like smooth candy, tastes great as you suck on it, but when it's crushed crystals in your mouth you regret that brief taste. *Moving forward won't be without challenge,* I think.

"I'll keep in contact. I just wanted to touch base and let you know that you're not alone. And I will reach out if we feel the need to place protection." He pauses, then continues, each word spoken deliberately, "You should contact Marianne VanZyle and Kenneth Thomas. You can help one another."

Kenneth Thomas. This monster is killing all the Juilliard finalists, I think and blurt before thinking, "It's someone that wants in."

More silence. Then, "We've thought of that. In fact, it's such a glaring coincidence it seems almost too pat."

I rummage around in my addled brain to figure it out. Oh yeah, *too obvious*, I translate.

"If the killer wants to take out the competition, what better way to do it than by emotionally incapacitating us . . ." I whisper, angry that I'm afraid . . . and frightened by my anger that's beginning to boil to the surface.

My heart rate begins to speed. Suddenly, the noise of my environment rushes inside the bus, like a reverse vacuum of noise. I can hear the seagulls, the people, and the white noise of their murmurings. The sun pierces my windshield and splashes its heat against my skin. A layer of numbness peels away and I feel a dim purpose begin to ring like a bell. The Band-Aid I've put on myself is torn away in that moment in a painful, swift pull.

I feel that stage of grief slip away, my sadness replaced by anger. Just like that, I embrace it like an old friend. That small part of me that wants to live swims up to the surface of my consciousness.

The anger is like a call to arms. I'm present and alive, swimming freely in my own skin for the first time in five months.

". . . Reaching out to these survivors . . ." Clearwater says and I realize he's been speaking while I've been Having a Moment.

"Yeah . . . give me their names and numbers and I'll . . . talk to them," I promise.

Clearwater sounds relieved, reciting the numbers, and I write them on my hand, scooping a pen off the floorboard of the bus where it has rolled underneath the pedals.

"I'm glad we could talk, Miss Starr."

I smile; it feels rusty. "Brooke."

"Okay . . . Brooke. We'll keep you posted as updates are needed. And the possibility of protection . . ."

I don't need that up here, I think, but don't say. I look around at the wilderness as far as the eye can see, encroaching my surroundings with its frozen presence.

"Thank you," I say.

"You're welcome."

I begin to say good-bye and he interrupts me. "And Brooke?"

"Yes?" I ask, my mind already running to all the things I want to accomplish.

"You take care . . . and thanks," he says, and I can hear a smile in his voice.

"For what?"

"Your trust."

I sit there for a second and hold a phone that's now dead. I look at the cell battery. *Dead as a doornail.* I shake it. Like that'll help. Dumb thing.

I know it's my fault. I've overcharged it one too many times and now the battery life is a couple of hours at a go.

Well, that's okay. We got to say what we needed to.

I turn the engine on and the bus comes alive like Old Faithful, the classic VW rumble signaling my presence at about half a mile. I back up, pulling away from the Dawg . . . feeling like I have a new lease on life. A little warm light of hope sparks inside me and I allow it.

Maybe I deserve . . . to live.

I drive the length of the spit, noticing every detail like it's in HD. I feel like I'm Dorothy in *The Wizard of Oz*. She leaves a black-and-white Kansas and arrives in Oz and suddenly everything's in color.

It's more true than I could ever know, because that tornado is coming. And it will consume me.

Chance

I use the long-handled scrub brush, because my flake of a cleaner texted claiming sick.

Translation: hungover.

Homer is so small I'll know in the next ten hours if it's a bullshit excuse or he's tossing cookies. Doesn't matter, I'm still out here washing my own boat like the truly self-employed. It's a two-hour job done right, as salt water's like slow-working microscopic acid on a boat's hull. It's a *gotta do it,* not elective in the least.

I hear someone approach on the dock, the floats softly hitting the side of the boat as it rocks with the waves in the protected harbor. I stand, my entire purpose getting the boat hosed off, making myself busy so I don't think about Brooke.

My hand clenches on the hose attachment as I ruthlessly spring it to the left on full throttle and the water shoots out in a fire-hose stream of straight pressure, blasting the debris and shit off in a steady spray.

"Beatin' the hell out of her?" Evan asks like he doesn't expect an answer.

I turn. "Yeah, dickhead Matt didn't show."

"He's a girl about booze."

Knew it. "So what? He's hung?"

Evan nods. "Like half dead."

Shit. "Now I have to find another cleaner last minute," I say, shaking my head in disgust.

"I thought Brooke from Seattle's doing it."

I stiffen without meaning to and Evan gives me a look. "Sore spot?"

"Nah . . . just thinking it might be to much for her." I look at Evan, my friend since middle school, and ask, "You guys friends?" I turn and spray the boat more, turning down the jet attack.

"Yeah . . . but she's hot, if you feel me . . . I want it to be more."

I'm instantly angry. Evan and I are like brothers. But suddenly he's my enemy.

I turn and he looks in my face. I can't hide it.

"Whoa . . ." Evan says giving a low whistle. "You're hot to do her?"

I drop the hose and walk to Evan and he stays where he is, humor gone from his face. "Yeah." And so much more. "What of it?"

Evan gives a low chuckle. "Hello . . . she's your employee?" He taps his head like I've got rocks in it. *Not too far off,* I think. "She's like . . . here for two months . . ." Then his face gets a lightbulb look and he snaps his fingers. "You just want a little . . ." He gyrates his hips and does a few thrusts and it makes me even more pissed. But I say what he wants to hear.

"Yeah, I want to sample the wares. I don't want any commitment."

Evan grins. "That's what I figured. Chance Taylor doesn't take chances," he says, pointing a finger at me, and I frown at his bad pun.

"I take plenty of goddamned risks."

"True," Evan says and I hear a *but*.

I cock an eyebrow, twisting up my hose neatly, wrapping it around my elbow and inside my palm in a large loop. I hang it on the huge stainless C hook off the pier stub at the end.

"I don't know how you close your legs with the balls you got," Evan says, miming basketballs between his legs, and I bark out a laugh. He's always good for one. "But . . ." he says, wagging his finger at me, "not with chicks. Never with them."

I shrug a shoulder. I can have a relationship that's just sex. I'm a guy; it's like a biological directive.

"If she's game, then we'll just sex it out," I say.

"What if I want in?" Evan asks.

I turn, my body squaring off with his. "It's a deal breaker, Ev."

We stare at each other, my eyes hard. His are cautious. The tenor of our years together is shifting.

"Over a girl, Chance?" His eyes search mine in disbelief. "Seriously?"

"Yeah . . . over this one."

"Our friendship is worth more than eight weeks of tail . . ."

I can't respond. I don't want to say things I can't take back. And I will.

"Fine . . . fuck it, have her," Evan says in disgust, his angry eyes looking me up and down. "But, you know the mantra." His eyes meet mine like a challenge. "I'll say it again for clarity's sake: bros before hos, man . . . bros before hos."

Evan walks off and I fold my arms across my chest. I've just risked a ten-year friendship for a girl I promise myself is just a fling. A girl who I promised to stay away from, considering I'm her boss . . .

I'm going to toss everything to the wind anyway, the promises to myself broken.

I can feel it like a slow-moving river in a single direction: toward Brooke.

SEVEN

Brooke

I hit *end* on my cell and shut my eyes. Somehow, the spontaneous calls in the middle of a Homer parking lot makes talking to them less big, less real. But it's oh so real.

I feel like a wrung-out washrag, speaking to the other survivors. Their pain and anger—the same as mine. Their guilt: crushing. But speaking with them ushers in new feelings.

Mainly of liberty. I, Brooke Starr, might finally be free to live. I realize I'm not alone in this. Helping them helps me.

I swipe my sweaty palms on my jeans and take a deep cleansing breath. There are others who've survived besides me. That commonality helps breach the chasm of my grief.

I set the brake and swing the driver's door open on the bus, closing it solidly with my palm. I sweep my hand above my brow, shielding my eyes from a sun that should not be hot or bright.

It's Alaska, right? *Wrong.* The sun's at its zenith, the summer solstice arriving in less than a month. Its cold brilliance bathes the knee-high wheat-colored pasture grass as it whispers in the breeze from the cliff. The waves drive the wind up, bringing it through the pockets of forest stranded like islands around the homesteader's cabin that I stare at.

That, I think, *is a wreck.*

I let my hand fall with a sigh. Time to do a whirlwind cleanup. I've crawled from under the rock of my contemplative demise with determination. I can almost hear the small cabin's grunt of relief as I climb the wide half-log steps, split almost a half century ago by my great-uncle. I wrap an arm around the stout porch log that braces the roof as I reach the top of the short run, my eyes taking in the general disarray with a dash of grime.

With a determination that's been lacking for the better part of a year, I swing open the door, leaving it standing open to the breeze.

The stale guts of the place smack my face. I scan the interior, my eyes hitting the dirty glass windows like an insult and I walk over to where I'd hidden the cleaning supplies I'd purchased like a zombie. I had been one . . . now I'm not the walking dead; I've rejoined the living. Finally.

It's time I begin acting like it.

I bring out Simple Green, a butt load of paper towels, and start in on the glass.

Two hours later, I look up from what I'm doing and bold sunlight streams through the windows, highlighting the bare spruce floors, polished to a mirrorlike shine in the tiny space. I move through the straightened area, not bothering with lights; the late May sunlight infiltrates everywhere there's a gap.

For the first time, I notice a slim narrow door: its five recessed panels, exposing the flat-grain pattern of the wood's wavy pattern on each frame, the small glass knob against it, thick with a film of dust.

I bet that thing hasn't been turned in fifty years.

I use my spray bottle like a weapon, blasting the glass, the brass housing loose around the seat of the crystal. I dry the knob carefully.

Then I turn it.

The small door opens, leading down ten steps into . . . another room.

Have I been so out of it I missed this?

Yup, I answer decisively.

There's a polelike rail of the same wood at the bottom of the steep staircase. I hit it with my hand for balance, the stairwell dim, since sunlight doesn't enter here as brightly as the main floor.

It's so dark when I stand at the bottom, I don't feel like I can go farther. Like the blind, I throw my hands out in front of me and search like a staggering drunk for a light.

A slim cord smacks me in the face and I give a little yelp, jumping back. When I can unglue my hand from my chest, I pull down on the thin string, the end capped with a metal bell, and light bursts in the space as I give a gentle pull.

Oh my God . . . I really am in the Land of Oz

My eyes can't stop moving, roving over everything that's down here.

Aunt Milli never told me, I think in wonder, taking in the framed articles, awards, and photos of glamorous events that cover the stone walls. Of all the stories she told me, none were of this.

Aunt Milli had been a pianist back in the day.

And in the center of the room, the bare floor covered in wide rough-sawn wood planks, is a hulking shape that I know very well.

A sheet covers it like a secret shroud but I'd recognize that shape anywhere.

With shaking hands and a heart that threatens to beat its way out of my chest, I pluck the corner of the sheet with my fingers.

And like that Band-Aid I've thought about earlier, I tear the cloth covering away. It falls away like a ghost . . . a whisper and a breath, disappearing.

Literally, I can't breathe.

Not because of panic.

But unbridled joy.

Hot scalding tears crawl down my face. They're the first I've shed in happiness.

A square grand piano teases me, our distance kissing close, and I move toward it, laying my upper body against the smooth top, the feel of the polished wood under my cheek like a lover's caress. The hardwood heats underneath my wet face, my beating heart the only noise in the stillness of my discovery.

I don't know how long I'm there, but finally, with a reluctant reverence I straighten, cracking my back as I twist from my awkward bow.

When I can, I pull my eyes away from the gift the piano represents and look around the room. I see there are windows.

They line the wall, their frames touching the ceiling but no more than eighteen inches deep, but wide, maybe three feet. Each one has wood molding that separates them from the next. Covered by shutters. *That's why I couldn't see,* I think.

I walk over to the nest of windows and unhook interior wooden shutters and lift them up. There are hooks on the ceiling and like mini garage door panels, they latch there, and I know where I've woken up in.

Where my soul is driving me.

The sunlight swamps the room, illuminating the small basement. The chimney from the first floor is a full Mason, beginning at the foundation in the corner of this subterranean room and rising through the main story and roof. It looks as if it grew up out of the ground. The rustic hearth is flush with the wood floor, old tiles in a deep emerald with a wash of gold cover the floor over the brick and move up the sides to flank a dark hole where wood belongs. A small wood mantel holds a sterling frame.

I know those people.

I move to the fireplace like a person lost in the fog and pick it up.

There is my great-aunt Milli, smiling in the arms of an impossibly young man. She's impossibly young too. I stroke a finger down their faces, feeling more connected to her in death than I ever was in life.

I slowly turn, and every corner tells a story: an old steam trunk holds quilts; large vases adorn small tables topped by aging marble, begging for wildflowers. My hands touch everything, making it mine. Making it real.

I'm stalling and I know it.

I turn and look at the keys of the piano.

Like a magnet I move as though through water to that board of buttery yellow teeth.

I hit middle C and a deep boggy sound, low and wide, resonates in the underground space, the strange acoustics of the stone foundation and wood interior interact.

Perfectly.

A sigh escapes me and I'm on the bench before I know I've moved.

My fingers fit the keys perfectly and they move of their own volition. Not tentative.

Hungry. Starved.

My fingers eat the notes in my head like a person coming awake from a dream and realizing it's been real all along.

My hands crave the feeling absent so long from my life and for the first time, guilt doesn't pierce my heart, sick fear doesn't pump through my blood in an adrenaline rush . . . I play and the music comes.

It begins to heal me . . . if I'll let it.

As I move through my fifth piece, my fingers become fatigued. Yet still . . . I play.

I play until the sun is rearranging itself on the horizon, the low rays flowing over my hands like spilled blood.

Chance

I pull up beside the psychedelic yawn of a VW bus and shake my head. I know Tucker painted that flower-power disaster on Brooke's car. I chuckle, it's just him. Somehow, it doesn't suit her.

Not that I know Brooke. I don't. But I sure as hell want to.

I jump out of my 1974 Bronco. It's the rig I drive in the winter but I don't like it dead for four months so I alternate. It's my baby (which is why I'm rolling up East End, the armpit of rural roads, at a crawl).

Call me desperate.

You'd be right.

I click the door shut gently and take stock of the landscape. I fold my arms and survey the place.

It looks pretty good still, but nothing like it did back in the day. There's pictures in the Dawg from when Brooke's aunt played her rowdy sets on the piano that still sits in the fabled corner. There's even a few of this place. I look it over with a critical eye. The porch still hangs true, if weathered. It's deep and wide as it should be for our icy eight months of winter and four of a summer that's cool and temperate, the sea curbing true heat. I laugh again to myself. It'll be winter again before we know it.

I begin to climb the steps, trepidation weighing each leaden pace.

I told Brooke she doesn't have to worry about any bullshit while she works for me.

Liar, liar, asshole on fire, I think.

I pause, a strange feeling permeates my brain.

Uncertainty.

Fuck it. I raise my hand to knock and see the door is ajar. I push it open and step inside.

It smells like a goddamned lemon exploded, I think, looking around for the contaminant.

Ah, a can of Pledge stands up like a lone flag in the garbage can, a mashed-up graveyard of used paper towels alongside it.

Someone's been busy.

I smile, taking in the spartan digs. A ratty couch with a wool granny's afghan lays folded on top, the squares shouting their color at me from across the small space. A cell phone sits on a tall narrow wood table, sentinel beside the door, a small oil-type lamp perched on top. There's a tiny 1950s Formica kitchen table with a lick of chrome like a belly band holding a surface with gold flecks in a sea of battered white and two mismatched chairs. A great cast-iron porcelain sink with attached drainboard sits in the corner, its brilliant white a slash of brightness in the dim interior.

Sun's low, I note, glancing through the ancient glass. The redness of the sky eases me. *A red sky at night is a sailor's delight,* I hear my mind recite.

I love the sunset when it's red.

Good waters tomorrow, I think absently.

Faintly, a sound moves through the confines of the cabin and it pulls my attention.

I can't find it. My eyes search every nook of the small cabin.

Where is that sound coming from?

There's something about it that strikes me as my eyes hit a slim door.

In the low light of the sun that hangs like a bloody globe at the edge of the horizon, a glint strikes out, facets like diamonds shooting their prisms around the room like rainbow glitter.

I walk to the sparkling thing.

When my shadow passes over it, my hand falls on the crystal knob, turning it.

The door was nearly lost to the eye, looking like the end run of cabinetry in the kitchen.

I open it and the music floods up the stairs like invisible water in reverse.

"Für Elise," my mind brings to me instantly.

I stand where I am and it's then that I realize that maybe she's more than a hot dalliance, someone who I fell into protecting by a coincidence of fate. Her music makes me feel as though I am the instrument and she is playing me. More connects us than that night in the sea, the chemistry we share. Brooke's music fills the space as if she's the melody and I am the harmony. It's not a casual and random connection, I realize. Her music moves me, resonating in that hidden place deep inside me that no one touches, no one sees. I drift down the steep coffin steps.

I catch sight of Brooke as she sits hunched over a piano that dwarfs her.

Yet . . . she commands it.

Her hair falls around her, cloaking her in black as the sun hits her fingers as they move over the keys, bathed in scarlet light. Brooke looks ethereal, perfect.

Hot.

But I knew that, didn't I? No reason lying to myself. I'm caving to the chemistry, end of story.

I've played this piece on my guitar. I stray to the classics when I'm not doing a rock set at the Dawg.

Classical music is pure; Beethoven, Mozart. They weren't distracted back then with YouTube, the Internet, and shit.

It's just music. They eat, sleep, and drink music.

That's what I am watching right now. Brooke doesn't just taste her notes.

She devours them.

I reach the end of the steps as her hands float and stab the notes, the dynamics spot-on.

This is no amateur player, I think.

In fact . . . I know it.

What the hell is a girl with this kind of skill doing as a deck-hand?

The last notes echo into the stillness of the room and a deep breath escapes her. I see her slim shoulders rise and fall.

Naturally.

In relaxation.

I realize I've never seen Brooke relax and almost feel bad that I'm going to bust that awesomeness up.

Almost.

I hope I'm not pissing up a rope here. I'm taking a gamble that she's going to go with what I want.

"Brooke," I say softly.

She whips around, a sliver of sun slanting across her face, making her soft lavender eyes seem to glow in her face.

I swallow. *Fuck,* she makes me nervous. *Excited.* "Remember what I said?" My eyes search hers, gauging her reaction.

Brooke nods, her eyes a touch wide, her hand to her chest. My eyes move to the softness of her mouth, crimson in the illusion the sun makes of her face.

"That I won't have to worry?" she asks with a hint of a smile in her eyes, in her voice.

I nod, all the smooth words I'm going to blow her away with jammed in my craw like sideways toothpicks.

Shit. What the hell is wrong with me?

I stand there in front of her like a dumbass and she slips off the bench, moving toward me. Some trick of the light washes her with gold and a small noise between a growl and a moan breaks free and suddenly Brooke's in front of me.

Jesus, she's so perfect, I think before I fall.

Into her. Her arms come around my neck and my hands automatically are on her ass, picking her up. Intellect grinds to a halt as I look around for somewhere and Brooke pulls my mouth to hers.

She wipes my mind like an eraser. The beat of Brooke is against me and it's the only rhythm I hear. As I deepen the kiss my hands stray to frame her face; delicate—like an eggshell, beautiful.

She's just the living artwork I like.

My fingers splay over smooth cheeks like silk under the brush of my calloused touch, her mouth parting for mine as I slip the tip of my tongue between her lips, breaking the seal of both our mouths. Somehow, my hand finds the back of her neck. Waist-length dark hair is fisted in my hand as I tighten my hold on her hair and neck, bringing Brooke closer, and she gives a soft moan of pleasure and I know I've gone too far. My body tells me.

My mind tries to interfere. How did I go from hiring Brooke, to saving her . . . to devouring her lips like a starving man . . . in the middle of a basement music room? Her presence has stolen my professionalism as surely as a weight on the end of one of my hooks. I let my hands fall reluctantly from her and back away, giving us both breathing room.

Brooke watches my brooding retreat then raises her hand to put it on the lips I've just mauled.

I'd do it again if she let me, if I let myself. In a nanosecond. We stare.

I back farther away.

Then she finally speaks. "That was . . ."

"Wrong?" I admit with a question in my voice.

Brooke shakes her head slowly. "No," she clarifies in a soft voice. She looks at me again. "I'm just surprised . . ."

My eyes scan her face, flushed a light pink, her lips fuller and plump from having been kissed by me and God help me, I want to continue my bout of unprofessionalism and do it again. Instead, I move toward the steep stairs I just came down, making that small distance a barrier between us.

I watch Brooke notice the purposeful distance and she looks so isolated standing there, the sunlight backlighting her with the huge old square grand as a backdrop. I hold my hand out and she looks at it, finally stepping forward. Then she takes it and I tow her upstairs.

Without a solid plan for the first time in my life.

EIGHT

~

Brooke

Chance walks me down the gangplank, hands covering my eyes, and I'm laughing . . . and trying not to think about that stolen kiss in the hidden music room.

But I do.

With my eyes closed and the scent of the sea and Chance inextricably mixed, it's all I can think about.

Chance stops and drops his hands and my mouth falls open, the sunlight blinding me momentarily as the dance of light sparkles off the water. Maybe he's a little more premeditated than I give him credit for. It occurs to me that I don't really know Chance. What is he? Savior, fisherman . . . or maybe, and this could be wishful thinking, a romantic. My eyes devour the sight of the boat, moving over the graceful shape as it appears to break out of the surface of the water, bobbing contentedly in the cozy slip. I'd guess it's close to thirty feet, with *Sea Hawk* scrolled in tiny letters on the exterior of the cabin where teak cleats are peppered in tie-off formation and match the cabin door below. The soft glow of the highly polished wood is a contrast to the whiteness of the hull and the navy stripe that accents the perimeter. The boat is not what I expected. It's not the austere thing I've conjured in my mind, but a thing the water lovingly strokes, at home atop the waves. Suddenly my trepidation about working on what seemed like an alien spaceship dissipates. For an instant, I can almost grasp why Chance looks at it with an expression of trust . . . of companionship. You'd almost have to become one with a ship you sailed. The two are not mutually exclusive.

My gaze travels to the inside of the deck, with a cooler that stands at its center. Along the hull the name of the boat is elegantly scripted *Life Is Chance,* and I smile. A six-pack of Alaskan Amber sits on top and I don't stop the smile from spreading on my face. It feels wonderful, real.

"Gonna ply me with booze, huh?" I ask. Then add, "Sooo professional, Chance."

He gives the scout's honor symbol with his fingers. "That's me, ruiner of women," he says, and winks.

With a kiss like that, I'm thinking anything's possible. "So, what exactly are we doing here?"

"I want to do a trial run on the boat . . . show you the ropes. Y'know, before you come on."

I can't help but be touched by the gesture. "Okay, that makes sense . . . and, thanks."

Maybe he really meant it when he said he'd try to lay off . . . or there wouldn't be any mixing of business and pleasure. But I can't help but wonder if all his deckhands get a picnic on the boat.

Some of my uncertainty and ambivalence must have shown on my face. "Hey . . . Brooke," Chance says in soft inquiry and his hands have my face again. He's disallowing me from averting that intense gaze that rivals the color of the ocean all around us. We stare at each other. "Remember . . . trying here."

Then he gives a full grin, the smile reaching his eyes and lighting them from within and I take a great cleansing breath as his hands drop. I'm confused by how I feel—sad mingling with cautious happiness, nerves melting into the ease I feel around him. I don't know the first thing about fishing, don't know how I feel about starting a relationship with anyone. But the heart wants what it wants. Like a misguided missile it seeks a destination known only to it.

Chance takes my hand and draws me over the side of the boat and I take a visual tour. It looks so foreboding from a distance, but really, when you pace it off, the deck is just an empty square space, sans cooler that sits in the middle. He explains where everything belongs and my eyes fall on the places he names for all the accoutrements of the vessel: interior hull pockets that house everything from small weights, to extra line, to water bottles, and finally my gaze settles on the gaff.

"What is that?" I ask, pointing at a long implement with a barbed hook at its end.

"That's the fish stopper. A gaff," Chance replies with a grin at what's clearly an inside joke. His short index fingernail flicks the point and a drop of blood appears at his fingertip. He stands, shrugging. "Sharp."

"Clearly," I say, taking it from him. It feels too heavy to wield with any kind of finesse and Chance takes it back, easily swinging it around in a practiced swivel. I lean away slightly and he smiles anew.

"The gaff gets the monsters into the boat," he explains.

It looks dangerous to me. His smile broadens into a grin at my wide-eyed expression. "Here's *your* gaff," he says, handing it to me.

I look at the tiny, two-foot gaff and cross my arms over my chest, cradling my breasts and watch Chance try to keep up the pretense of not looking. I smile back. "So I get the girly gaff and you get the manly gaff."

Chance pretends to think about it for about a millisecond. "Yeah."

"Nice!" I say slugging him and he laughs, sidestepping me.

"You're so violent," he teases with that same grin on his face. "Besides, I did hire a *girl* deckhand. That's very forward thinking of me."

"Uh-huh," I agree, but give him my grump face. Girls are born with that ability. Insta-grump. He steps forward and with his thumb he tries to erase the furrow between my brows and I let him, my grump turning to a smile.

"Let's go," Chance says, putting the gaffs back in their pincer brackets and moving to the back of the boat to untie a cleat. He sees me standing there. "Well, get moving, Brooke from Seattle."

I move to the other cleat and when the ropes are inside the deck, I push off from the dock as he's backing out and we head out of Homer Bay.

The bow cuts the water as it sluices on either side, the small whitecaps made by the prow like a dessert on the water, all creamy and beautiful enough to taste. I look inside the cabin where Chance has sequestered himself and think about my own cabin, my new life . . . my choices.

That kiss.

Heat rises to my face as I realize my unguarded thoughts are a classic paradox. It's as though now that I've tasted the bounty my new life can offer me, I don't know if I deserve it. I can't help but feel unworthy. I try to suspend introspection and take in the scenery instead. I walk to where Chance stands, ignoring the captain's chair with the cabin's door no longer swinging but hooked to the outside of the cabin, his strong legs steady despite the churning sea beneath us. I move to the back of the boat and grab fishing gear that belongs in the cabin as I make my way back to the forward part of the vessel. It takes longer than what's pretty as I stumble and grab. Finally, I get to where he stands again, his strong arms rippling with the ease of years standing just like he is now.

Like he's never done anything but this. It's a thing of beauty to watch, how at home he seems on the water.

He feels my presence over the noise of the engine, which has dulled to a sort of white noise, and says, "There's Seldovia . . ." He straightens his arm and points off to the left . . . or, I think about what direction that is . . . maybe east.

"What's there?" I ask, and smell the soap he used that morning. Not as strongly as when he held me for that stolen kiss, but it's there. The sensory memory draws me closer, bravely closer.

I see the tension tighten his shoulders and fight the urge to touch that valley between them where the taut material of his shirt stretches across his muscular back. "It's a place I used to go with Jake when he wanted to fish for kings off the slough bridge."

"You guys fish from a bridge?" I ask, my hand loosely hovering over that spot at his back I want to lay my face against. I can almost see myself doing it with a sigh as my arms slip around his waist. But I remain where I am.

"Yeah, I don't use bait like I do here. I use a lure and see if luck will get that salmon to choose my line."

"So it's by chance?" I whisper and he turns, one hand tight on the wheel as the other slows the throttle.

"Nothing's by chance," he says in a light tone, but his eyes are serious. So serious, and I cast mine down. I can't handle what I see there.

Expectation.

Chance

I watch Brooke shut down whenever I move toward anything more serious than the weather.

That shouldn't bother me.

But it does. It bothers the hell out of me.

Instead of responding, I take the throttle all the way down and set the anchor. I go through the motions, keeping the conversation going about neutral things, pointing out the hiding places for all the apparatus I have on board and Brooke's a quick study. But even I can tell that she's not all there with me. Her mind is distracted by something.

"Let's eat," I say and pray that I got some stuff she'll like. I don't even try to pretend that I'd do a picnic lunch out of a cooler in the middle of the sea on a normal day. Nope. My usual deckhands get only the blow-by-blow and they pack their own grub. My former deckhands are like plants and photosynthesis, left to their own devices to figure it out, water and sunlight filling in the blanks I've left from my minimal explanation. I'm fine giving them the ten-second lesson and they fill in their questions on the sea. Brooke's getting personalized instruction. I don't get all introspective and shit. But I know it's different from my usual modus operandi.

Brooke glides over to the cooler and her lips twitch as she picks up the beer I got and uses the bottle opener to pop the cap.

I watch her face fall, then grimace, then . . . she laughs. Brooke hauls out a canning jar with smoked salmon inside. "What is this?" she asks with clear distaste.

"Ah!" I say, tapping my own jar. "It's the candy of the sea."

"Okay . . . Eww. What is it really? I mean, it smells so strong." Her brow wrinkles between those eyes I can't stop looking into.

"Come on, they have salmon in Washington," I say, feeling my brows rise. "Besides, I canned this myself."

Brooke's brows rise at my admission and her nose wrinkles up in a cute way and I give a dry swallow over the small lump in my throat. She puts me on edge. Among other things.

"Yeah . . . we do, but you guys like . . . worship seafood or something . . ." She guffaws when I bend down on both knees and begin bowing to the small canning jar, my hands slapping the fiberglass deck.

"Oh mighty—" I crack open an eyelid and Brooke's suitably horrified. I bend over again and again, "—salmon!" I use a good zealot voice and Brooke's laughter turns to hiccups.

"Please stop . . ." she says, laughing and grabbing at her ribs.

"You shall not diss my fish."

The smile in her eyes says it all. "God no. I would never diss your fish."

We look at each other and both break out laughing again.

"Try it," I say, unscrewing the lid, and it makes a sharp popping sound as the vacuum seal breaks.

"Can I have something with it?" Brooke asks with a dubious glance at the packed fish.

"Can I have something with it . . ." I mimic in a high, feminine voice.

"Ugh!" Brooke cries and throws the loaf of French bread at my head. It bounces off and I yell, "Bread bludgeoner!"

I stride over to her. "Open up."

Brooke sighs and I say, "No, you're not getting out of it."

She closes her eyes and opens her mouth. I have the fish in one hand as the boat rocks us on the deck, the sunlight warm against our skin. The smell of the sea is the perfume of this small universe. My eyes scan her face, taking in her soft pink, plump lips, and before I can think, I press my lips to her open mouth and Brooke gasps.

"Chance," she says against my lips.

"Yeah?" I say softly, my mouth falling to hers again and again. Her arms circle my neck and bread crumbs slip down the back of my shirt. I break away and when Brooke gives me a small smile, it reaches her eyes, chasing out the sadness I usually see there.

I press the salmon against her lips and her tongue slips out of that mouth I've just enjoyed. She sucks the finger-size piece inside her mouth and I bend down, taking the other half in my own. We chew, our lips almost touching. When the taste is gone, I press my forehead against hers and ask in a whisper, "Was it good?"

I'm not really asking about the fish.

"Oh yes," she answers, and her face tells me it's not about salmon. Suddenly her body against mine feels like a key sliding into a lock.

Brooke holds the beer against her jean-clad knee, her hoodie tied around her waist. The weather on the water during an Alaskan summer is unpredictable. That's why I tell everyone who fishes with me; wear layers.

Her layers look better on her than on all the deckhands I've had before.

I take her hoodie from around her waist and lay it on the deck where we sit quietly together, the sun warming us through the thin tees, our legs crossed. I watch Brooke eat some of the French bread (the portion that's not all over the deck), fresh from our local bakery, half a jar of smoked salmon, and some garlic mozzarella. She suffered through my beer without complaint.

Brooke's eyes hold me back from more. Because I want to do more. So much more. The thick silence swells like the waves lapping outside the hull. I've been fooling myself, telling myself what I want to hear. That this day is about familiarizing Brooke with the boat. But really . . . it's about familiarizing myself with her.

I gather the leftovers and set them inside the cooler, sliding it to the stern and attaching it to the interior stainless loop. Then I hit the switch to engage the lift for the anchor so we can head back.

Brooke doesn't fill the silences with words that would ruin the beauty that breathes all around us, the day on a spinning axis of perfection, letting it spiral around us. The sea breeze lifts her hair as we swing into the harbor and I bear hard to the left, seeing my slip and expertly navigating the narrow passages until it reveals itself for full entry. Brooke stands from her perch inside the cabin and moves beside me.

I could dock the boat in my sleep, but having her this close unhinges me. My knuckles turn white as I abuse the wheel in an effort to hide my obvious nervousness at her closeness. It's much harder to pretend in this small piece of real estate.

"Would you . . . ?" I murmur to Brooke. She's so close I can smell the meal I fed her on her lips and I close my eyes in a long blink.

"Sure," she answers just as quietly. I watch her throw the bumpers over the side of the hull and they sink between the dock and the boat as it bounces softly against the old wood. The long line of her back arches over the side as she gracefully tosses out the second one and I turn off the motor and in a smooth pivot, my feet hit the deck as I watch her, she looks up and gives a small smile.

We don't catch any fish today.

But I think Brooke might be catching me.

Brooke

I say yes when he wants to take me home.

I don't say no when he asks me to play for him.

The sea has an interesting afteraffect: I'm sun kissed and wind tired. The light picnic food settles comfortably in my belly, giving me just the touch of relaxation I need so the keys move under my fingers like they're an extension of me and my music. The notes weave themselves in the tight and swollen air of the underground space, filling it with a melody like a shining breeze of gold captured for the moment, weighted but floating between us. We breathe in the music as it connects us.

When I finish the song and the last note resonates into an echo, Chance remains standing at the foot of the steps that lead into my aunt's basement music room, one muscled arm bracing his weight against the floor joist that holds the ceiling above us, his eyes never leaving me.

He's silent for so long I ask a little nervously, "Did you like my playing?"

Chance gives a slow nod. "I like watching you play."

"Watching me play?" I repeat, swallowing over the tension the music's absence leaves behind while my mind tumbles over the hours on the boat, the sting and bite of salt in the air softened by the fresh sea that carried us in its watery embrace.

"Watching you," he replies simply and walks toward me slowly. My body tenses with anticipation.

But Chance doesn't do what I think he'll do.

What I think I'm beginning to crave like breath.

Instead, he take a quilt that lies on top of the chest at the foot of the piano and lays it out at its feet.

He holds out his hand and I take it as he lowers me to the quilt.

I lie down and he moves to his side, looking down on me. "Tell me about Brooke from Seattle," he says softly, moving a single strand of hair off my face.

I do, my body tense with the emotion of wanting to share yet being uncomfortable with it. Omitting the truth with the precision of a surgeon. Gradually, each muscle in my body becomes less tense, the day sweeping away my reservations even as I hold on to the worst of it in a compartment for later.

For now, I am with Chance and it's enough. It's a start.

Starting anywhere feels right; starting with him feels more right than it should.

I don't even know when I fall asleep, but I dream of eyes that hold the sea, my grief slipping away with the tide.

NINE

Chance

She's lying. I know it.

I watch Brooke's face as her eyes slip from our locked gaze when she talks about things she wants to avoid.

Who am I to bitch, though? I haven't offered her anything solid. Oh yeah, the glam job of cleaning up fish guts and seaweed. Right.

Such a catch, I think with a low chuckle at my bad pun and she doesn't stir.

Sleeping.

I look down at Brooke, her hair, as black as my own, curls around her body like an ebony cocoon. Sooty lashes lay against her pale cheek, residual pink infuses her softly from our . . . kiss, a testimony like a watercolor painting of imagery and tactile sensation that tightens my growing feelings for her in a vise.

Without an observer I stare with an intensity that scares the shit out of me. Brooke's body fits exactly in the hollow of mine, like a human puzzle piece that's found its place. With me. I close my eyes.

I don't want this to end.

I sigh harshly, sitting up on my elbow, knee up, and watch Brooke sleep, trusting me.

God, we've got fishing in three hours.

Damn, damn . . . the sea waits for no one.

I squat beside Brooke, then haul her into my arms, and she doesn't stir, a soft and perfect weight against me. I tuck the quilt around her a little more, and the unbidden tenderness almost pisses me off.

This isn't like me. The picnic on the boat, the quiet inter-lude afterward when I take her back to the cabin and listen to her play the piano. Later we lie together on the quilt. I know I should ask her why she doesn't want to live. But maybe, just maybe . . . she'll decide she does.

Then I remember what she does to me with just her eyes and I exhale again.

And I've called friends who have girlfriends pussies.

Won't be doing that anymore. I'd be eating an assload of crow after this gets around.

I meant to sweep her off her feet and convince her to stay, to work alongside me. I'm always in control, the one calling the shots. I like it that way.

But with her, I never saw it coming. One minute, I was standing, the next . . . I was airborne and in her net like the fish I catch.

I climb the steep basement steps with Brooke tight against me and notice her phone is blinking.

Messages.

I move quietly to her room, navigating the darkness easily. I've always been able to see like a cat in the dark. *Besides, with only forty minutes of darkness per night, it's really just dark daylight,* I think, smirking in the gloom.

I slide Brooke into her bed and she rolls over, tucking her bent wrist underneath her chin.

She looks so young like that. Then I recall how much of a woman she's proved herself to be in that room beneath my feet.

I stare at her for a few more moments, memorizing her, then back out of her bedroom, closing the door softly.

I'll kill her alarm, I think, moving toward her cell. There's no way I'm making Brooke come in for that 4 a.m. shift that starts—I look at my diver's watch—*one hour and forty-four minutes from now.* Fuck that noise. In fact . . . maybe I shouldn't even hit the rack. I might feel like hell either way. It's been my experience that less than two hours of sleep feels almost worse than just burning it and never going to bed.

I rake a hand through my hair, scrubbing it into messy spikes. I scoop up Brooke's cell off the small tabletop next to the front door and thumb through the navigation tiles on the front page. I hit *alarm—silent.*

I move to set it down and a flashing icon from a message catches my eye.

FBI.

I blink. I look again. Yeah, I'd recognize that symbol anywhere.

I hesitate, the angel on my shoulder condemning my next move, the devil fist pumping on the other side.

Horns win over wings on this one.

I read the message twice.

What the fuck is this?

Miss Starr, phone me immediately from a land line. We have a break in the case.

I read the name twice too: Marshal Decatur Clearwater.

I know a little about the FBI. Witness-protection Feds have marshal status. Not your run-of-the-mill bureau boys. Uh-uh. The big guns.

My mind rolls over the "something that happened" that Brooke referenced earlier, the meaning deepening with each passing second. The boyfriend inference is puzzling as hell.

What's happening? What *had* happened?

And who the hell is Brooke Starr, really?

A woman with a past.

Fugitive?

Refugee?

Or . . . worse?

The shadow of her aborted suicide spins in my head, looking for a landing. The more I try to figure it out, the more it makes a grim kind of sense. Who wants to stop living? What is so terrible that you can't transcend it . . . that you feel your only choice is the most final one of all?

I don't know. But I knew enough to save her.

I'm damn well going to find out.

I put the phone down gently when all I really want to do is heave it, then quietly leave.

I stare at the solid wood front door standing partway open, my eyes moving to the square black box with a thumb-latch lock. I've never locked a door in my life.

However, I've never had something so precious to protect.

I move the interior lock until it clicks into place. Then

I close the thick door behind me, hearing the lock engage, and jog down the wood steps and to my car.

I drive down Brooke's driveway, needing time to sort shit out. The possibilities of her past and who she is courses through my brain like a torrent of mud. Messy, slow . . . weighty.

I put the Bronco in third gear, going faster than usual, dust kicking up behind me in a thick cloud.

I don't want to leave.

But I can't stay.

Brooke

I blink awake, surprised that I've awakened before my alarm.

I flop back down onto my lumpy quilt and groan, throwing my arm against the bright sunlight filtering through freshly washed windows. I slowly lower my arm and look around, trying to gauge the time. It looks like I haven't beaten my alarm, I just forgot to set it. And now, clearly I've completely missed my first day on the job.

I swing my legs around on the bed and glance over my shoulder, surveying the quilt, and I'm flooded with the memory of falling asleep in Chance's arms in the basement, the piano our witness.

Against every impulse of regret a small smile lifts the corner of my mouth.

I rise and stretch, noticing the tenderness of my lips as my fingers brush the flesh there.

I can't ignore this, I realize.

Chance is like my dream catcher. I've been asleep, my dreams all nightmares, then he comes into my life and catches the bad ones.

Maybe they'll be better now.

I pad across the cabin in my button-up shirt that moves around my body like a short cape and boy-style boxer shorts. I make my way to the front door and pick up my cell from the small table beside it.

I smile when I see the alarm silenced.

Okay, I guess when my boss decides I get a day off, I can hardly say no, I think as a small laugh escapes like a bubble bursting.

I see a blinking icon and swipe it. *Clearwater.* I read the message, twice.

I don't like seeing it there, mocking me.

I sigh, my light mood turning dark, eyes suddenly burning with tears I don't want to shed. I'm surprised I have any left.

Fuck it, I'll . . . call him later.

Or text.

I nod to myself, shoving my phone into the drawer.

Later, I think, moving to the bathroom, where I take out my emotional grudge on the shower faucet with a hard twist.

I lather up twice and rinse off, thinking about Chance. I realize that I don't regret a single golden moment with him.

As long as he doesn't know about . . . what happened, then maybe we can have something.

For eight weeks, my mind whispers its reminder.

I shove those thoughts away. For once, I want to live in the now.

I grab the keys and head out for a coffee.

I resolutely ignore the butterflies that churn. Their restlessness for absolution from a past I can't alter, that won't free me—to a present that begs for me to engage in . . . to live. They wait.

I'm tired of waiting.

I walk out into the brilliant sunshine, the warmth of the sun possessing a cool press, the northern latitude stealing true heat but lending length to our days here. I close my eyes, lifting my face to the sun, my damp hair in a single braid down my back.

I see the light as though from a crack underneath the door as I reach to open it.

Almost.

Almost free.

TEN

Brooke

I pull the bus into the parking slot in front of the best coffee shop in town. Of course, no place can outdo Seattle. We have coffee beat there. There has to be a balance for all that wet weather, a counterbalance to chase the chill dampness. I wait out the comparison of my two homes, my emotions sorting my internal temperature. It doesn't make me feel too sad and feeling a new confidence, I open the door of the bus and walk up to the storefront.

Latitude 59, the driftwood sign reads as it swings in the sea breeze. The organic chic of rough font with weathered bright coloring makes me smile. It's a vibe that's pervasive in this town. A beachy community of tough year-rounders, part-timers, and summer dwellers, it's an eclectic mix of people.

Of course, then there are the Dreaded Tourists. I look around, spotting them like pink flamingoes outside the confines of their tacky yards and smile.

I've got to argue they have a right to be here and enjoy the uniqueness that is Alaska.

Just like I've a right to my avoidance.

Doesn't everyone escape?

The bell gives a small tinkle as I slip inside, my new wool cap jammed haphazardly on my damp hair, the tail of my braid making a small dot of wetness on the back of my zip-up hoodie.

I walk forward, my eyes already on the menu. I see a cappuccino and automatically think it's the best way to gauge a new coffeehouse. After all, that's what I do with a restaurant: order a cheeseburger. Seems rudimentary, that simplicity.

Since I have a menu of about five things I like, it's all uphill from here.

A bubble-gum-snapping barely teenager gives me the once-over and says, "Can I help ya?"

I smile. "Yes, I'd like a cappuccino with extra foam, one hundred eighty."

She cocks a pierced brow, the earlobe gauge moving in subtle and expressive agreement. "Ya wanna burn your tongue off?"

Snap-pop, smack. A wad of green disappears inside her mouth and she looks like a cow chewing its cud.

I smirk, answering, "Pretty much."

Actually, I'm an expert food-and-hot-drink juggler. I don't want the ass-end of my drink lukewarm.

"'Kay," Bubblegum says and saunters off to make my drink while I look around the place. The roar of the coffee machine sounds, an old dude with a thin braid of gray hair makes sandwiches for the lunch crowd. I check my cell . . . gawd, it's almost noon.

Then I check to see if Chance contacted me.

Nothing.

I grunt in dissatisfaction then feel a stab of guilt.

He's working. Chance probably had to figure out something really stupid to cover for me.

I smile at the thought as Bubblegum hands me my scalding coffee, giving a little shake of her head at the weird summer girl.

How does she know?

She does. They all do. Homerites, as I think of them, seem to have a built-in radar for those who are from Outside. That's anywhere but Alaska, guys.

Yeah.

I sit by the window and cross my legs, sipping expertly through the little hole at the top.

I shouldn't have brought my cell. Its existence teases me.

I should call Clearwater.

Don't want to.

I sip more coffee, looking at that blinking icon.

The door chimes and another patron walks through.

Tucker.

I smile as he stands like a full eclipse in the open doorway, waving him over as I put my cell on the mosaic-topped bistro table, and forget all about staying informed with the FBI.

"Hey, Tuck, stop gaping at the girl and get your ass in here. No flies, bud," the old guy with the gray braid and hound dog eyes instructs in a droll voice.

"Yeah, okay," Tucker says with a grin, swinging the glass door closed.

"Hi," he says.

He looms above me and I look up, way up. "Hey, how are ya?"

"Good," Tucker answers and walks over to the counter. Bubblegum acts like she's just won the lottery.

"Hi, Tuck," she says, fluttering her fake eyelashes.

Pleeassse, I think.

"The usual?" she asks with a wink, then sashays off when he gives a nod.

I must have given a hard eye roll, because as he walks back to the table, Tucker says, "What?"

"That girl . . ."

"Brianna?"

I nod. She has a normal name, just looks weird, somewhere between punk and hipster. "What's with all the—" I swirl my hand in front of my face.

"Metal and shit in her face?" Tucker asks, flicking a finger on his own earlobe to include the gauge.

"Yeah."

"We haven't caught up with Outside."

"Yeah," I say, taking a careful sip of my cappuccino and finding it edging toward warm. "We've got a bunch of dummies that have hanging lobes and holes in their faces now."

Tucker shrugs. "She's great at bagging salmon."

Nice.

He sees my expression and laughs. "I'm not kidding. She can horse in thirty-pound king right off this bridge we fish at every June."

I take a sip again and my brows pop to my hairline. "Really?" I ask. "Horse in?" I restrain myself from braying but give a little laugh at the visual.

Tucker smiles, nodding. "Yeah. It's when you use a heavy-pound test line. It makes the fish easier to bring in, especially from that height, leverage and all."

"Tucker," Brianna squeals at him and he smirks at me as he rises, a mountain of guy muscle, moving like a silent storm to the counter to pick up his java.

He strides back, setting the steaming coffee on the table.

"You been anywhere but here and the Dawg yet?" he asks, taking his first sip and burning his tongue. "Shit," he hisses.

"Ya trying to burn my tongue off, Bri?"

"Hell yes!" she says without missing a beat and gives me a significant look. Do I see some grudging respect? Nah . . . hallucinating again.

He catches the passing glance. "What's that?"

"I get mine at one eighty."

Tucker gives a low whistle. "Hot tongue."

My mind instantly kicks up an image of Chance and where his tongue's been. On me.

Inside.

An ache begins between my legs from the memory alone.

Jesus, I can feel the mother of all blushes coat my neck and climb like liquid heat to the roots of my hair.

"Whoa . . . Brooke. That's a great reaction!" he says, rubbing his hands together with a chuckle. "Can I get lucky and think it's for me?" Tucker asks, blatant hope underlying a question posed as a joke.

I shake my head softly. "No."

"Damn, baby! Someone's already got to you and here you are only two weeks in."

I nod, the flush of heat flaring briefly.

Maybe Chance doesn't want anyone to know?

But I know. And . . . I can't change how I feel and I suck royally at games.

I've never been a player.

"Tell me it's not Chance, Brooke."

My eyes jerk up to his, my heartbeat thudding against the inside of my ribs.

"Ahh. . . . man," he says and gives his face a careful scrub of frustration.

"What?" I ask, but not like I want to know.

It's just a feeling, but judging from the look on his face, I never want to know something like what I think Tucker's going to tell me.

"He's a player," he says, then self-corrects. "Don't get me wrong, Brooke. He'll do anything for anyone. Give the shirt off his back . . ."

Or save a drowning girl.

Wrap her in the blanket of his body with a kiss I still feel tingling on my lips.

My coffee's grown colder and I let it die an icy death in front of me.

"Shit, you look like someone just killed your puppy."

Yup. That's not entirely accurate, but as metaphors go, it'll work.

I stand and so does he. "I'm sorry, Brooke."

I look up at him, not sure what to say.

"He's never been serious about a damn thing but the sea. That's what matters to Chance Taylor. He's been with a ton of girls, but—"

"—never been serious," I finish for him, taking a stab at guesswork, and he nods.

"I've known Chance his entire life and it's the sea and the catch."

Well, he's sure caught me. Now . . . how do I escape the net? I don't want to be one of his many fish.

Chance

I take off my oversize insulated glove at the wrist with my teeth, letting it drop onto the deck; the guts and bait in the bucket can sit there. I dig underneath my bright orange waterproof bibs, finding my cell in my pocket, and drag it out and search for messages.

Nothing.

Huh. I don't take Brooke for a game player. I think I should've heard from her by now. I swipe a finger across my eye and try to rub it out of my head; feels like I've got a film of gritty sand and shit in it.

It's called not sleeping. At all.

"Taylor," Matt calls from behind me.

"Yeah," I say, grabbing my sandwich out of the cooler one-handed while I juggle the cell, avoiding my stinky fish bait by a millimeter.

I turn, taking a huge bite of deli goodness, and packing it underneath my arm, I swig my water out of the bottle.

Matt swings up the condom to head height. "Is this how much of this shit you want?"

I take a critical look at the rubber, judging the gap between the bait mixture I put in there and how much room to knot the top.

Mouth full, I nod. Matt sighs and knots the top. "I hate the stink of this garbage."

I give him a look as my charter fishing client raises his brows at the colorful language of my deckhand.

My reluctant deckhand. Matt's made for finer things, he's mentioned on more that one occasion.

What can be finer than riding the sea? I wonder, taking another gulp of water.

Matt hadn't been happy about the 3 a.m. wake-up call, but he owed me for being fucking hungover and leaving me to clean the boat up. I tear another bite from the sandwich and gulp down half my water. With the sandwich in my mouth I screw the lid on and dump the bottle into the small pocket that hangs next to the cleat.

Bob, the client, comes over, the gentle sway of his line lifting with the swell.

Calm today, I think. Because, God knows, it's random as hell.

Matt hits the switch on the electric reel and the driver kicks in, the *whiz* as it jerks the line up a soft whir in the background. I can see Matt in my periphery, tying off the condom and a partial salmon head on the hook.

As I load my lunch trash in the cooler, Bob asks, "What's in that stuff?" and jabs a thumb toward the rubber filled with what I like to call my "special sauce."

Clients ask a lot. It sucks telling them. Halibut are bottom feeders. That basically means garbage guts. Sometimes my clientele would rather not know that succulent fish they like to mow on eats unsavory shit. Like my special sauce that I put in rubbers.

"Well . . ." I begin, "let's say it's a mix of squid, salmon entrails . . ."

Bob's face takes on a green tinge. Hell, I haven't even gotten to the really interesting part.

He wards me off with a hand.

I grin. "The goal is to combine the most rancid crap I can come up with, then mix it all together," I say, tapping the blender full of the blood, guts, and rotting bits I brought from home.

I hear it before I can respond to Bob. The line zings. . . . singing as it takes a hit from a deep-sea monster.

I know what it is because it bends my hundred-pound test to the water, bowing the rod to kissing distance of the surface.

"Holy smokes!" Matt screams, lurching for the rod. Bob makes a mad scramble to his rod, the end seated in the integral stainless holder on the deck.

"Hang on," I say in a calm voice as I stride to the stern. Taking the rod out of its holder, I jam it against my hip and reel in just until the tension is on the loose side of tight, giving a little lag.

Come on baby, I coax silently, a fine sheen of sweat beading on my upper lip.

The slab of fish takes the line and I jerk back, setting the hook with the smoothness of a thousand before this one. It whines as it goes out and Matt says, "Taylor . . . that's too much line . . ."

"Peanut gallery, Matt," I say, taking the reel up, pointing its bowed end at the sky.

Matt shuts his mouth.

I fight, getting closer, then turn to Bob. "She's all yours," I say.

Bob staggers over to the pole, his land legs still attached. "It's a female?" he asks as I smoothly hand off the pole, positioning his hands correctly.

I grin. Clients—so random. "Yeah, the big ones almost always are."

"How do you know it's big?" Bob asks, hopeful. His legs are spread wide for balance, sweat running down his forehead. He swings salt-and-pepper hair out of eyes that are a shade too wide, keeping the sweat at bay.

Matt pipes in, "It's gotta have a mouth big enough for the bait."

Bob's eyes get impossibly larger. "Damn, that was almost an entire fish head." I can see he's doing the internal reckoning on scale and coming up . . . big.

"I used a king," Matt says casually, then gives an excited yelp. "Holy shit in a sack!" he yells, going for the solid hickory bat latched to the interior starboard clamps.

I begin to move up as Matt shouts, "Barn door, two o'clock!"

I jerk the gaff from its clamps next to the empty hold for the bat and move to the stern with it, a hook like a person envisions Death himself carrying. I watch the white belly of the fish float to the surface through the glacial clear surface, the water parting to reveal the purity of the meat.

My heart races as I see my prize rise from the depths of the chilly sea. This is the critical moment for escape.

I bark, "Back!" and with a practiced swipe of the gaff, I nail the sharp barbed end into the meatiest part of the fish and heave it against the side.

It begins to thrash the boat.

"Matt!" I bellow.

"Here!" he yells from beside me and I trade the gaff for my gun.

"Oh, Lord," my client says softly as I cock the hammer and aim for the head.

One bulbous eye rolls to meet mine, buggy and muddy brown.

I pull the trigger and the bullet hits true, smacking into the white flesh of the head and the eye explodes, taking a chunk of what we can't eat with it.

I'm stoked the cheeks remain, the best part.

I throw the safety on and slam the gun into its holster in the interior pocket of the stern. Matt collects the other gaff and we work the halibut into the boat. It flops onto the deck and like a chicken with its head cut off, the tail moves.

"Stand back!" I say in a loud voice as my client, who is a handsome shade of baby-shit green, lurches to the starboard and heaves his lunch into the sea.

No time to comfort the queasy, I think. The 'but's trying to take out Matt's leg with its tail.

Nothing another bullet won't cure, I think. However, can't have a hole in the boat. I swipe the hickory bat from Matt and whale on the halibut, leaving the best of the filletable meat untouched.

The tail stops thrashing—finally.

I stand, the dead fish at my feet, my heart racing, my shoulders and every muscle in my body employed during the catch of one fish.

I swivel my head to the client as blood turns my white deck red.

Bob wipes a thick hand against his mouth, his skin a little gray. "Remind me never to piss you off, Chance Taylor." He gives a shaky laugh, but his eyes are serious.

"I'm not really violent," I say, my large hand gripping the wood like an old friend.

Matt smiles at my comment.

"Could've fooled me," Bob mutters as I bend to put the halibut in the hold.

I wink at him. "I'm different on land."

"Right," Matt says so low only I hear.

I don't say anything. The dead fish gives me an accusing glare from a sightless eye, a black hole where it had been. I let the hold door slam shut and move to the cab to return to Homer Bay.

I have a set to play at the Dawg and a two-hundred-pound fish to fillet.

And a girl who makes me forget the sea.

A first.

ELEVEN

Brooke

I say the appropriate things to Tucker, but I'm not fooling him. He knows he's landed a bomb on my head with the info about Chance.

I get into the bus and just stare at the black steering wheel, the only neutral color on the thing, and fight defeat—again. It's not Tucker's fault. He can't know I've barely begun to live again. I turn on the air-cooled engine and it starts faithfully. It won't begin to heat up until I begin moving. A sad little smile perks up the corners of my mouth as I shift to reverse and slowly back out.

I think about the prior night and sigh. It's just what I needed. I want to feel again, live . . . breathe. Chance brings that into my life.

He also brings an income, a change of pace, and . . . clearly, not much else.

It's not like Chance is asking me to marry him. Tucker says he's only committed to the sea, not women.

And clearly he can fake tender like no one's business. Is Chance that good an actor?

Can I risk another emotional bludgeoning?

No. I can't take the risk. It's my job to protect myself. As much as I want to keep letting him in, let his presence chase the nightmares away, I can't open my heart up to even more hurt. Each new relationship I allow is on a case-by-case basis. I know better than anyone how fragile those ties are, how easily things beyond my control can tear them away.

Like a horse that knows its way home, the bus moves down the spit at a plodding forty miles per hour, the seas are calm, the sun is a pale yellow ball in the sky as I make my way to Chance's shanty office digs.

I pull up, and the faded rustic sign with the colorful writing swings in the light wind like it's greeting me.

I get out, slapping the door closed, and walk up the wide weathered steps to the door. Putting my face against the window, I shield my eyes as I gaze inside. No one's there. I move my cell out of my pocket and see that it's three o'clock. I know by what Chance has told me that he should be back by now. I roll my lip into my mouth, giving it a light nibble.

Where is he? I need to set things right . . . I need, I suck in a deep breath, to walk away. Let him go. The exhale leaves me like a deflated balloon.

"Missy?"

I whirl around, hand to my heart, and look into the eyes of a wizened old man. He puffs on a pipe and a fragrant spiral rises around him like devil's horns, his hat hanging cockeyed like a strange beret on the tufts of the hair that remains on his head.

"You scared me," I say as a lame introduction, my heart hammering beneath my palm.

"Did I now?" he asks with a soft cackle; one brow raises like a gray caterpillar on his forehead.

"Yeah," I say in a shaky exhale that escapes me in a low huff.

"Who you lookin' for, doll?"

Doll?

My face scrunches but I reply, "Chance Taylor."

His brows raise together in a comical arch. "He's down at the dock, cleaning his catch, as always."

Right. I look around and he unclamps his dentures from the end of his pipe, swinging the chewed and beaten stem toward the boats at the pier. "Just follow that sign that says Homer Marina, missy."

"Ah . . . thank you," I say, unable to hold back a smile. He's like a little troll.

A troll by the sea.

I burst out laughing and he frowns, his eyes disappearing in the flaps of skin that hold his brows. That somehow makes it worse and I rudely begin to howl.

Nervous energy.

"Crazy girl!" he barks at me good-naturedly and I agree, nodding swiftly.

"Yes . . ." I hiccup as I laugh. "Definitely crazy!" I hold my sides and stagger across the street.

I turn and wave at the old man, "Thank you!" I call out when I can control myself.

He nods, raising his pipe like a flag.

I'm pretty sure I can hear his snort from here.

I turn, a smile plastered on my face and a case of wicked hiccups.

I see the sign and cross beneath it, my feet landing on an odd sort of woven metal grating with little barbs of metal.

That'd hurt like hell if you slipped on it, I think, my eyes seeing through the grating to the churning tide below. It's a long sloping walk on the carpet of metal that hangs over the water as I make my way down to the docks. Noise explodes all around me, a trick of the wind and my position as it's carried to me while I make my way down to the docks. I reach the wide floating boards of weathered wood and people rush by, pushing wheeled carts full of large white-bellied fish. My eyes scan the pier, where boats are lined up like colorful sardines. Various modes of dress abound and I'm amazed I can already pick out the tourists.

I'm becoming a Homer snob. And it's official, my aunt's homestead puts me in good standing. Even though it's inherited, somehow I've become part of that core group. I've never been so close to a group of such isolationists. An oxymoron for sure.

It's pretty obvious as I begin to identify who the fisherman are. Then I catch sight of Chance and my formerly cool skin heats. I watch his automatic and supple movements as he guts fish.

You can't think for a moment that a job like that can be sexy, but it's a testimony to Chance that he is . . . no matter what he's doing.

I gaze at him as he continues to work, unaware of my presence. People filter beside me like I'm a floating piece of driftwood and they are the sea. They part and I stand there.

Watching.

His forearms ripple with fine muscle and the ink of his tat undulates like the twisted snake it represents, the tongue of the serpent appears to move as he flips his fillet knife around, the metal winking in the sun, turning it to silver fire as he slices through the whiteness of the fish then deftly removes what he needs to, the colorful scales of the ink appear iridescent in the light that slants over him as he works. He steps back, his tanned neck bent as he picks up a hose and sprays off the white marred surface of the cleaning table. Large orange bibs billow around him like a clown suit, rubber and waterproof, but they can't hide the deep valley between shoulder blades that house a broad back from honest work.

I swallow, my throat tender and dry, and I realize I've been breathing through my mouth in a doglike pant.

This isn't going to be easy.

Chance moves all the fish to one of those carts with four wheels and a bar, neatly stacking the meat inside coolers with layered ice. He swivels from the hips, giving the fish surface an-other final hose-down, then shuts it off with a flick of his wrist and hangs it on a large stainless hook attached to an electric pole.

He looks up and our gazes meet.

Chance Taylor steals my breath.

His open smile melts me.

I walk toward him.

It feels like a death march.

Chance

There she is, I think, grinning like a fool. *You're playing it so cool, dumbshit,* I tell myself.

I can't shake it and go for aloof. It doesn't fit. Not after last night's kiss. Not after waking up with her in my arms. I can't go backward; it keeps getting deeper. With each new intimacy, the bucket fills up. It's more than a kiss. I hate to admit shit like this, but sometimes everything isn't physical, and that's what I'm feeling now.

I watch Brooke come and my smile fades. She doesn't look happy. Immediately I get in my head, sifting through what's happened.

Did I let the moment get away from us?

Yeah.

I can feel my face frown. But, as I recall, Brooke was a happy camper after our impromptu make-out session.

I rub my eyes again. I'm tired as hell. Maybe I'm reading shit where there isn't any.

"Hey," I say, my eyes searching her face.

God, she's gorgeous. I can just stand here with only my catch between us and look at her for . . . about an hour. My lips curl thinking about it, those lavender eyes looking at me. They look like the wild lupine that will bloom around her cabin next month. I open my mouth to tell her that when she throws the wet blanket on my mental party.

"Hey . . . we need to talk," she says, eyes steady.

Nope, not imagining shit, I decide. Effing wonderful—the dreaded "we need to talk."

I nod, my feeling of a great day slipping away with the tide. Damn.

"All right," I reply slowly. "I need to get this catch up to the office. Client's picking it up."

Brooke looks down at the fish dolly and then her eyes meet mine. "I'm sorry about missing work today."

I hear: *I'm sorry I made out with you last night.*

I stand there stupidly. I'm not used to a chick rejecting me. Usually, I can kinda have who I want. I keep them at arm's reach and my life moves on.

I like it like that.

I don't like this.

I wheel the fish with the coolers toward the grated plank. My eyes travel it and it's steep. Terrific, tide's low so the fucker's sky-high.

Brooke follows my gaze. "Do you . . . can I help?" Brooke asks, throwing out an olive branch.

I lick suddenly dry lips. "Sure," I say. Even to my own ears I sound like I'm going to puke.

"'Kay," she says and sidles up beside me and we push the cart up together. It's a bitch without help but I like her beside me, even if I won't want to hear what she says later.

We make our way to the street, wait out the tourists and cross at the crosswalk. I look at her small hands on the bar of the dolly next to mine.

I remember how they felt when they dug into my shoulders when we were pressing against each other like we were the last solid things in the world.

Vividly.

Suddenly, I'm thankful as hell for bibs. The mighty conceal-
ers of wayward hard-ons.

We park the dolly just as Bob the barfer makes his way to
the front door. I write out a receipt for his fish and direct him
to the place that will pack his fish for the flight back to the
Midwest.

I'd love to be a fly on the wall for his fish tales told where
there isn't any sea. I give a small shudder at the thought of living anywhere there's no ocean.

Bob gives my hand a hard shake, his eyes momentarily sliding to Brooke. "He's a keeper . . . You sure the hell don't have
to worry about your safety around Taylor here!" he says with
frightening enthusiasm, and I give a low chuckle.

Brooke offers a puzzled smile, looking from my client to
me. "What?"

I smile and tip Bob a wink. "What happens on the sea . . ."

"Stays at sea," Bob finishes with a wave as he walks off, a kid
taking the coolers for him.

"What's that all about?" Brooke asks.

I wave a hand. "Same old, same old." I smile.

"Another day fishing?" she asks with a smile. But I think it
looks sad. I nod, my face getting serious.

I want to kiss the expression off her face. But something's
changing and I don't know what. I don't want to blow it.

It's scary as shit when the first girl you feel something for
is playing Russian roulette with your emotions. Hell, I didn't
think it was possible for me to get this kind of entanglement.

Wrong.

"So . . . what's on your mind?" I ask, bracing for the blow.

Brooke surprises me, her hand touching my forearm, wrapping around it she covers my ink, a pale stripe against the black symbols that climb up the dark skin of my arm.

I don't even know how it happens, but I raise hands cold from the water and cradle her face, kissing her lips so gently they barely touch. "Don't say what I think you will, Brooke." My voice is barely out of the range of begging.

"Don't," she whispers, kissing me back.

"I can't stop when you're in my hands . . ."

She steps back and I let her. Our eyes meet and I feel like I've been kicked in the guts. Twice.

My hands fall to my sides.

"What is it . . . what? Last night?"

She shakes her head, stray coal-black strands of hair curling around her jaw. "No . . . last night was . . ." She looks at me, really looks at me. "Beautiful."

I can tell she means it. Totally. I'm confused as fuck, I gotta admit.

"Okay." Thank God I didn't fuck that up, hurt her . . . do the wrong thing. I scrub my face, looking at her over my hand.

Brooke looks down at her feet. Then her eyes rise to mine, piercing me, and I reevaluate the color of that absorbing gaze. It consumes me like a violet river.

I'm drowning.

"I can't . . . do this."

My chin comes back and my eyebrows jerk up. "What? The job?"

Brooke puts out a palm. "No! No . . . I want the job . . ."

"Me?" I ask, swallowing in a dry plow down my throat.

She looks me dead in the face and nods. "I can't do both. I need the job but we can't . . . go out," she finishes.

"You're fired," I say without a forward thought and knee-jerk reacting all over the place.

Brooke's face falls, her lower lip trembles.

Oh dear baby Jesus. "Brooke," I begin.

A slow tear struggles out of her eye and something small in me dies at seeing that tangible bit of sadness. "I was kidding."

I'm not. I'll can her ass in a second if that's the stipulation for being with me. In a second. But I don't want her hurt. It goes against everything I convince myself I want. In the end, now that I've met Brooke, it seems like a lie that's no longer true.

I'll never forget her near drowning, and I'll never forget jumping in after her, saving her. Ever.

"Okay . . . thank you, Chance."

I put my hands on my hips, her scent . . . her presence off limits now and it makes me ache. I'm running on no sleep, low food, and a sexual hangover I can't shake. In a word: hell.

"Why? I mean . . . why is it so bad that we made out?"

Brooke looks at me. "It's not bad . . . I just, I'm not ready."

I call the pink elephant out of the closet where it's been hiding. "Is it about your suicide attempt?"

She's quiet and I know she thinks about lying. Brooke takes a deep breath, letting it out slowly. "Some of it."

I probe her with my eyes, but my scrutiny doesn't even make her flinch. Brooke isn't telling me everything.

I look at her and understand she doesn't want to.

Well, tough.

"We're going to talk about that, Brooke," I say, meaning it.

She meets my eyes. "I know," she says softly. "But not now."

"Soon," I say.

Brooke flushes at my demand and I don't back down. I care . . . Hell, I'm already half in love with her.

"Okay," she says.

I smile and she smiles back tentatively.

"Let's go!" I say, letting her off the hook.

Brooke's confused. "Where?"

I turn, grabbing my civvy clothes off the hook beside my door.

"Bonfire, babe," I say with a smirk.

"Wait . . . I thought . . . we have it figured out."

I turn, nodding slowly. I stalk up to her and Brooke backs up against the door, palms flat against the wood.

I search her gorgeous eyes, intimidated and inquisitive— both, a paradox. Like her.

"I figure we're friends," I state, my fingertips a millimeter away from the silk of her hair. I fight not to touch her.

She nods her head. "Yes." Brooke squeezes her eyes shut then opens them. "I mean, I think we agree on that."

"We're friends all right."

I step away, holding out my hand and after a few awkward seconds, Brooke takes it. "Let's go . . . friend." I say that last word with just the right amount of heat.

I never give up.

TWELVE

~

Brooke

If possible, I feel even guiltier than I did before. Chance moves expertly over the shifting sand that surrounds a towering stand of driftwood. Guys keep chucking the awkward pieces, one on top of the other, until it resembles a pyre instead of a bonfire.

Bonfire my ass. I look around, expecting the fire department to two-wheel it around a corner and put the blazing inferno out. My eyes scan the twilight that passes for nighttime at latitude 59. Nothing but a suspended Venus can be seen, caught in gauzy clouds like cotton candy.

Chance waves and I flutter my fingers in response. He looks away and my heart squeezes at his indifference where intimacy had ruled just twenty-four hours ago.

It's what you want, I remind myself.

I feel my back pocket vibrate and sigh. I'm sure it's that Fed Clearwater.

I pull out my cell and break out in a grin as Lacey's image fills the tile, her middle finger stiff with a puffed-out lip smooch. I swipe her image and thumb in one ear, I hold the cell to the other.

"Hey stranger," Lace says after I say hi.

"Hey."

The commotion, sparks sizzling from the fire, and the crashing waves make hearing her a chore.

I persevere, she's the one tie from before I keep knotted. It makes something disjointed and loose inside me settle.

"What the hell's all that noise?" I can tell that Lacey's nose is out of joint because she might be missing something.

"I'm at a bonfire," I say, cupping my hand around my mouth.

"You mean party?" she asks, all-knowing.

I look around, where every hand holds a red cup like plastic poppies in bloom.

"Yeah," I reply.

"Wait a sec . . ." Lacey begins.

Here it comes, I think.

"You've met somebody."

Yes. No. "Not really." Jesus, we've so met.

Silence. Then, "Definitely." Excited, "Who is he? Is he hot? Wait . . . how distracting is he? Is that why you haven't called . . . ?" She huffs this part out in an indignant half yell.

"Lace," I groan with a smile.

"He's definitely hot. And no, I'm not dating him. And yes, he's like major distracting."

"Who. Is. He?" she all but yells and I pull the phone away from my ear. Her typical demand for every ounce of information rings in my ear.

"Chance Taylor," I whisper into the phone as my eyes sweep the group just twenty feet away. Chance is talking animatedly with Tucker as he throws his head back laughing and puts his hands about three feet apart from each other.

Regaling with fish tales, I guess, then swing my attention back to Lacey and her shock.

"Holy fucking crow, you're doing boss man?" she says incredulously, and I can taste her disappointment.

Shit.

"Not right now," I defend.

More silence. "That's not really a denial, sister."

Right, she caught that.

"No, I guess not," I say, resigned.

Silence fills the phone. Finally, Lacey says, "'Kay, so you've got a fucked-up conundrum there . . ."

I snort into my cell. Well put. Lacey's always had a way with words even if she's a little controlling.

"So, and don't freak out . . . pull up a piece of driftwood or something."

My heart begins to speed and I plant my ass in the charcoal sand, warmed by the sun of the day, the heat of the fire reaching even where I sit.

Chance looks over at me, a small frown forming when he sees me by myself, on my cell . . . with a funny look on my face.

Don't come over, Chance, I beg mentally. *Please come over Chance,* my heart overrides my mind's last command. I'm so screwed.

He begins moving to where I'm sitting and Evan intercepts

him. His eyes are on mine for a long moment then they shift to Evan.

Thank God. Or not.

Shit.

"You there?"

I nod, realize Lacey can't see me, and say, "Yeah."

"So Marianne VanZyle's family—"

I interrupt. "I know."

I can hear her palatable relief on the other end. But God love her for trying to tell me.

"Who told you?"

"The marshal."

"The Indian guy?"

I smile. "The Native American . . . Clearwater."

"Has he . . . Do they have any more information?"

I look at my feet, my toes buried in the warm sand, the wool socks their only covering, the ugly boots thrown to the side and flopped over the top like they're asleep.

Chance is breaking away from Evan and coming my way.

"I don't know, I've been avoiding talking to him."

"Why, Brooke?"

"I just . . . I want to move on, to forget. I don't want their protection, I don't want to know anymore."

"It's gotta be a competitor," Lacey says with conviction. "I mean, why else would someone take out two families but not the Juilliard candidates? And why the hell haven't the Feds tagged who it is already? Duh."

Why indeed? I agree mentally, feeling a frown form on my face. Lacey sure connects the dots . . . Why can't they?

Ten feet. Chance is almost here.

I whip my face away and say, "Listen I got to run . . ."

"Is he coming . . . beefcake with a side of taters?" she asks, and I can hear the smirk in her voice.

"Yes . . . I'll call you back, " I answer, my hand cupped around the mouthpiece.

"Uh-huh!" Lacey says with a huff. "Ta-ta for now . . . but remember, you owe me my Brookie time!"

Gawd. "Call you tomorrow," I say, ending the call with a swipe of my index finger over Lacey's image. The tile disappears and the cell blackens to hibernate.

Chance stands in front of me, his back to the sun, now hanging like a bloody ball at the horizon's edge, turning the water scarlet and black. His hands are jammed into his pockets, those fine muscles I'd admired earlier in full rippling display, the tattoo of the black snake with the rainbow of scales wrapping his left arm and disappearing underneath the short sleeve of his tight tee. I breathe out slowly, taking charge of my emotions.

Lacey's call has stirred up the hornet's nest and they are buzzing inside me in an angry swarm.

"You okay?" he asks.

I nod, noticing how his eyes look as black as the ocean, though I know they're a seawater blue. I look down at my cell and stuff it into my back pocket.

"Who was that?" Chance asks as he holds his hand out to me. I hesitate.

"Can't take back the pause," he says, shrugging. "It's no big thing."

"Lacey," I say.

He waits.

"She's my best friend."

"Oh . . . from Seattle?"

From before. "Yeah," I say, my throat tight. I have the most powerful urge to tell Chance everything. It's a ball of *tell all* caught in a lump in my throat. All of it: the murder, my missed Juilliard audition, my fear . . . my claustrophobic grief. More than anything, I want to take back what I said earlier and drown myself in what Chance offers. The call with Lacey leaves me with an aftertaste of self-doubt.

He waits with that quiet and intense expression, his eyes darkening to a midnight blue as they search my face.

Then my self-preservation instincts kick in. Nice to know I have some.

I can't be with a guy who will always put something else before me. Now more than ever, I have to come first. I can't be second to the sea.

"She's just checking in on me."

Chance chuckles, cocking his head to the side, and the deep sky and all its colors swim around us, washing our clasped hands in a smear of pink, tangerine, and orange. "Do you always look like you're getting a root canal when you're talking to your friends?"

I shake my head, slanting a smile his way. "No . . ."

"Come on," Chance says, his voice saying he won't press, his eyes telling a different story.

Eventually I'll have to tell him everything. It's not something I can just ignore. Somehow, it's disrespectful on some level to dishonor my family by omission.

He hauls me to my feet and we walk to the bonfire. Evan's eyes latch on to our laced fingers and I let mine slide out of Chance's large strong palm. He doesn't react but Evan smirks and I suddenly feel bad. I've blown it. Why can't I do anything right?

Then Chance smiles at me, a real slow, deep grin, his expression telling me that my weirdness is something he can deal with, move past.

If only I could.

He picks up his guitar and perches on a driftwood log that's far enough away that his strings won't melt from the heat of the fire.

Chance begins to strum a melody I know well. It's my tryout song. Of course.

I'm not a real believer in coincidence so I feel myself do a slow squat to another piece of driftwood and Evan walks over and sits beside me. Whatever force is pulling us together makes me come alive like the music emanating from the guitar that Chance strums. It's part relief and part uncertainty that grief is not the only emotion I feel anymore. But throw into the mix my conviction to keep him at an arm's length, and suddenly I feel exhausted by the emotional cocktail.

"Hey, Brooke," he says, his moppy hair looking orange in the dying light of the sun. I meet his eyes for a heartbeat then look away. I pull out my cell and it reads midnight.

"Hey," I say.

"You got somewhere you gotta be?"

I shake my head no, then rethink it. "Actually, it looks like I need to go. I'll have to show up to fish tomorrow."

Evan cocks an eyebrow. "Yeah? You mean," he waggles his eyebrows, "Chance'll fish and you'll get the bat and gun ready."

That gets my full attention, the soft chords of the melody pulling every string of my heart. I try to shut the music out, though it feels like Chance is playing it just for me.

My mind conjures an image of the gaff and I have a vague recollection of a bat, stained brown. "What?" I ask, feeling a furrow of confusion knot between my brows.

"What do you think happens when he pulls in those mammoth halibuts?"

I haven't thought about it and lift a shoulder; can't even guess. However, the mention of a gun and bat does make my imagination run.

Evan looks at Chance playing the guitar. "If they're big enough, they'll need to be subdued." Chance laughs. "It's like dear old Dad always says, 'Nothing a good piece of hickory can't cure.'"

"He beats the fish?" I ask, my mouth popping open.

Evan nods. "Hell yeah. Those big boys will break a leg." His eyes droop into a classic half-eye position. "Or big girls. Usually the fat fish are girls."

I pop him in the arm, using my knuckles. "Ow!" he howls.

"I meant curvy. Curvy fish."

"Stop. Don't even try to save yourself, you ass."

Evan grins. "Guilty . . . but you should've seen your face."

The music stops and Chance gives me a full look, his eyes shifting to Evan's, and I feel him stiffen beside me as he stands.

"What?" I ask, my hand plucking his brightly colored tie-dyed T-shirt.

Evan looks down at me, those sparkling eyes hooded by shadows. "Ya don't know?" he asks, then plants his thumb in his chest. "I've been warned off you."

My face turns to Chance, who is tuning his guitar. I turn back to Evan.

I do a slow blink. I didn't realize Evan was interested. "Why?"

Evan shrugs. "You. He wants you all to himself."

"I thought he's kind of a player," I say a little uncertainly.

Evan nods, unwrapping a piece of candy and popping it into his mouth. "Totally." His jaw moves over the morsel as I think about his comment.

More confirmation . . . that's good. Kind of. Not really. Shit. "Okay . . . so why does he care?"

"Beats the shit out of me." Then Evan looks at me and some trick of the light darkens his face and I suppress a small shiver. "But I wasn't going to test it." He's quiet for a moment then says, "Hickory isn't always just used on fish, y'know."

We look at each other and I look back at Chance, who's stood and begun to collect his things.

I watch him, thinking about how tender he was with me. Is there more to him than I'm hearing, or is what I'm hearing all there is?

"Ready?" Chance asks, his gaze pegging Evan with a cold stare.

And this after I've called things off.

"Yeah," I say then add, "I have to work tomorrow, right?"

He keeps his eyes on Evan a heartbeat longer, then turns that laser stare to me.

We look at each other, the chemistry between us making the air thick.

"Yeah," he says. "I'll walk you to the bus."

What can I say? "Sure."

I move away from people I haven't met and give a little wave to Tucker, who waves back, his eyes on the two of us. He's probably thinking how dumb I am for not listening to him.

He's right.

So dumb.

Chance

Watching Evan make moves on Brooke made me want to punch a guy I went to kindergarten with, and friends for the last decade. What's happening to me?

I know there's something deeper than not wanting to commit. I've been with a lot of girls and gotten pretty good at reading their signals.

I thought I had Brooke's down. Last night . . . fuck, it was amazing. I remember the fit of her body against mine with a recall so vivid I have to leave the image or embarrass myself on the spot. Like some kind of lovesick chump. Yeah.

I didn't like the look on Brooke's face when she spoke to her friend and I don't much like the open trust she's showering on Evan. Like he deserves it.

Shit no.

I shove my shit around in the guitar case and grab the rest of my gear, breathing through my anger as I walk over to

Brooke. She's like a flighty colt ready to bolt. I'll play it cool. Something I've been expert at.

Pre-Brooke.

I fucking love how I look at things as Before Brooke and After Brooke.

I cast a glance at Evan that clearly says *back off.* He smirks, enjoying my off-balance existence now that Brooke's a part of it. I'm no longer cool but one of Those Guys. That's me, pussy-whipped central.

I look down at her upturned face. The perpetual twilight of Alaska lingers until true night, about three hours away, and washes those startling lavender eyes with a pink cast. I realize I'm staring. Shit, I'm so buried.

I ask Brooke if I can walk her to her car and she nods.

I grab what little bit of stuff she has and haul everything to her colorful bus. I give a laugh when I see it. It's like an auto response.

Jesus, it's ugly.

"What?" Brooke says, folding her arms underneath her breasts, which draw my eyes automatically. Swell.

She frowns, dropping her arms to her sides. "The bus . . . it always makes me laugh."

"Humph," Brooke huffs, tearing the door open with a shrieking squeak and I grab it before it can make any more noise.

I lean in real close and Brooke gives a soft little gasp.

Without taking my eyes off her I say, "I've got oil to fix that."

"My door?" she asks softly, her forehead wrinkling with a puzzled expression as she gives the offending hinges a dirty look.

I stare into her eyes. "Yeah," I say. Our noses are inches from each other. I move even closer, the line of our bodies so close it would've been easier to touch. Still I keep us apart. My forehead dips to touch hers and she sighs.

"I better go, Chance," Brooke says, retreating from me. I feel the loss of her limbs as they untwine themselves from around me, the soft feel of her mouth beneath mine as my lips moved over hers. The scent of her, so new yet so familiar.

Gone.

Just gone.

I'm through lying to myself. I can't go on pretending that my life is meaningful just as it is, the sea and fishing the only sustenance I need. The realization of being with Brooke completes something inside me I don't know I've been missing. Seeing her with Evan is like a slap in the face of my denial. I can lie to him, and make her out to be a novel distraction. But in this moment, with Brooke standing there looking at me . . . self-deceit won't work. I can't fight the inexplicable chemistry that's been there from the beginning. I don't want to and make a promise right then. She'll be mine. Somehow, sometime . . . I don't know when, but soon.

"Okay," I say, backing away when it's the last thing I want to do.

Brooke softly clicks the door shut and gives me the ghost of a smile as she puts the noisy bus in gear and lights out of the parking lot.

I watch her taillights until they disappear.

Tucker comes up to me, both of us watching where Brooke had been.

"Listen . . . Taylor," he says.

"Yeah?" I keep looking at the hole where Brooke disappeared. Wondering if I can make it the four hours until I see her again.

Don't know.

"I like Brooke."

I turn and look at him. "Yeah . . . Your point is?" Tucker's a big dude, a couple of inches taller than me, which is saying something. I look slightly up at him.

"She don't need your brand of lovin', pal."

"Yeah?" I ask, spoiling for a fight. "What the fuck brand is that, Tuck?"

He regards me silently, taking note of my tense body, my hands in fists. "The player kind."

My shoulders drop. "That's not the plan, Tucker."

He nods, his face solemn.

"What?" I ask, my eyes scan his face. There's more; I can feel it like that itch I get when a monster is moments away from hitting my line.

"Why don't you do a little Googling, Chance?" Tucker gives me serious eyes, then claps me on the back. "Knowledge changes shit, right my man?" His eyebrows are arched in question. He ambles off without an answer from me.

I nod at his retreating back. *Yes it does.* My head spins with what Tucker implies.

He gives me a nod and walks to his Bronco, the orange and white stripes burned by a sunset that never comes.

What past is Brooke hiding?

A better question: what is she escaping?

THIRTEEN

~

Brooke

Okay . . . I'll admit it, it's kinda narcissistic, checking myself out like this. The hell with it. I do another slow turn in front of the only mirror in my aunt Milli's cabin.

It's silvered and dotted with age, and my reflection is peppered and distorted.

Not that it matters, because my reflection is as ugly as it can get. I'm wearing Levi's 501 button-up jeans I snagged at a thrift store on the way down through Anchorage, a microfiber long-johns-type shirt layered underneath a long nubby wool sweater in olive green. Topping off the horrible look is bright orange bibs, the waterproof scrubs of fisherman. I look like Ronald McDonald without the face paint.

I groan. So shoot me, I want to look good for Chance. I might deny the intensity of our attraction, but he's on my radar whether I want it or not.

I sigh, stalking out to the front porch where the ugly brown boots wait. I open the door and there they sit, mocking me. I plunk my butt down on the solid log bench to the left of the wide plank door and tug them on. I look up at the sky as I shove my wool-encased feet inside the solid vinyl of the boot.

It looks like it did at midnight . . . still twilight. *Maybe I miss the dark,* I think, seeing stars fading as dawn approaches. I stand, jog down the broad steps, and open the noisy driver's-side door on the bus, the oil I gave it dried up. I frown at that, hop in, and turn the engine over. It starts with a galloping stutter.

I back out of the driveway, one of the tails of my loose braids whipping over my shoulder as I glance back. For the first time I look at the cabin with a caress of care instead of an eye that signals a place to hide from the memories that had followed me here.

Because now I'm done hiding.

If I'm going to push Chance away, then I'm going to have to find another method of chasing off the nightmares. And that means *doing* something. Something I love. Which, today, is my job. I don't have to grasp at straws anymore. I can embrace my new life here, now. Automatically, I begin to tick off what my tasks for the day will be on the boat and find myself smiling, looking forward to my life. My life. Then my thoughts shift to playing the piano. I haven't played for two days.

But I will. And I feel my smile become a grin.

As I jostle over the ruts and potholes of East End Road, I think about Clearwater and Lacey. Independently of each other, they suspect a Juilliard competitor. Mentally, I tick off the small number of candidates. It seems too easy, predictable.

A female and one male.

My mind circles to the guy, Kenneth. Could anyone be talented enough to play at that level and stupid enough to cripple the competition through murder? Something about it doesn't make sense. I wonder how Marianne is coping? Kenneth Thomas? Probably as great as myself.

Shitty.

A huge pothole throws me into the door and I correct the wheel just as the Kenai Fjords rise to south above the ocean, the spit dividing the water like a bony finger of sand.

I remember the therapist Lacey had scheduled for me to visit. I didn't go. Instead, I came to Alaska. I wasn't ready to talk to someone about my family. I'm not so sure I'm ready now.

I take a cleansing breath through my nose and out through my mouth. I crank open the little V-shaped window and wipe first one sweaty palm on the granny square afghan that covers the old cracked vinyl seats and then the other.

I can do this.

I drive onto the spit, people jogging and riding bikes atop the ribbon of pedestrian blacktop that runs parallel to one side of the road.

I'll talk to someone. Maybe if I share what happened, I won't have to relearn how to breathe anymore.

Maybe I'll be able to give Chance a break. He's the closest thing I have to a real friend here. And if nothing else, the murders have given me a perverse sense of strength. What more can hurt me, right?

I pull in front of the marina, already full of people, and get out my small backpack with my lunch and the gear that Chance had listed in his email.

I slowly walk down the strange grated plank above the sea and make my way to his boat. I stare at the name on his boat.

Life Is Chance.

Yes . . . *yes it is.*

"Hey," Chance says, casually wiping his hands off on a brightly colored green towel.

"Hi," I say, my heart thumping inside me like a caged bird. I feel the wings brushing the inside of me and it makes me tingle.

Or maybe it's just Chance that makes me tingle.

I cast my eyes down, look at my toes inside the boots and look back up.

Awkward doesn't cover it.

"Ready?" he asks, a brow cocked neutrally.

Uh-huh. No. "Sure," I say, jumping as a flock of seagulls trumpets overhead.

Chance smiles at my startle and extends his hand. I scramble on top of an upturned crate and sling an orange vinyl leg over the back of the boat, my bibs crinkling like cellophane. A couple of slick types look at me and then at each other. They're maybe mid- to late twenties. I know I look younger than my almost twenty-one years and one of them folds his arms across his chest, giving me a skeptical look.

"This little girl is going to be what?" he asks, his eyes roaming my hidden figure.

I'm suddenly thankful for the bulbous clown bibs.

"Deckhand," Chance answers dismissively and I feel my face heat up as he concentrates on easing out of the slip, making his way out of the crowded harbor.

The client makes a humphing sound in the back of his throat and I scoot a little closer to Chance, who is treating me like the employee I am.

Like I want.

Fishing is unfamiliar to me, but as Chance patiently shows me how to bait the hooks, where all the supplies are located a second time, and how to run the electric reels, I begin to feel more confident.

Until the swells begin.

The water rises, lapping the sides, begging for entrance into Chance's boat. The square deep back deck holds integral chairs with pole holders, and the two clients, Sam and Lucas, are holding their poles so hard, their knuckles blanch.

Chance gives a small smile, checking the lines, his legs spread, feet planted as the wind moves his short ebony hair around his head, his knees dipping slightly as the swell of the waves increases.

"Can't stay at anchor much longer, guys," Chance says, his serious eyes, a match for the churning waves around us, peg first on the water, then move to the sky, a deep, roiling pewter.

"Why? Damn, man! We're from Arizona, we shelled out the moolah for this deep-sea shit."

Chance frowns as Sam gives him a look. "I appreciate your perspective, believe me, I do . . . but better safe than dead. Just sayin'," Chance explains as the guy glowers at him.

Asshole, I think as a hit from a bottom feeder smacks the line and I yell, "But on the line!"

Chance guffaws at my quip and we race to the line together. So much for going back and safety first.

Fish on.

I try to be careful, but the seawater slicks the deck and even the grippy soles of my Xtratufs can't stabilize my uncertain land legs. I go to my knees, sliding across the deck in an ungainly rolling tumble that brings me into the client's chair. It spins his fishing perch, putting him facing the interior of the boat instead of the sea.

"Holy fuck!" Lucas shouts, making a mad scramble for the rod.

But Chance is suddenly there, jerking me up by my elbow and dropping me on top of the large cooler on deck at the same time he grabs the reel and slaps Lucas's hand away.

"Hey!" Lucas shouts, pissed.

I'm a slack jaw with scraped knees, an interior rug burn by denim stinging . . . along with my pride.

"Don't want to queer the bite, Lucas."

"Fuck," Sam says in awe.

I watch Chance battle the fish, the swell rising like a small tidal wave across the bow.

We're taking water.

I'm scared, the boat's rocking side to side as sweat beads on Chance's upper lip, his audience of two clutching the sides of the boat.

Chance's face changes and I know from his expression the fish has arrived. He flicks the sweat from his eyes as he whips to face me. "Gaff!" he barks at me and I stumble to get it. It looks like a barbed grim reaper's hook.

Chance gives me the reel and says, "Hip."

I put the ass end of the reel against my hip bone and pray.

His muscles bunch in readiness as a great mottled fish of many shades of brown and gray rises toward the surface of the water. One second the water is a vast nothingness of blue shot through with green, then the fish rises like a speckled pancake with a creepy bulging eye.

Chance's bicep balls up as he swings the gaff upward. "Heads!"

Lucas and Sam back up. The gaff strikes the fish with a meaty *thwack* and he jerks it against the boat.

"Not real big," Chance comments casually as my heart races.

Big enough, I think, my hands shaking from exertion.

Sam smirks at my obvious fatigue and doesn't offer to take the reel. *Dick.*

"Lucas, take the reel from Brooke," Chance says. And he's not asking.

Lucas gingerly takes the reel and my tired limbs fall to my sides in a grateful slump.

Chance's arm wings around like crazy, the fish at the other end treating it like a living noodle. "Brooke," he says softly. "You trust me?"

Yeah . . . I realize I do and for some reason, the realization makes me want to cry. I don't know why.

I step forward.

"Get the small gaff." *Girl gaff,* I translate.

I pick it out of the interior stern pocket of the boat. "Hit the other end and on three let's bring this 'but in together."

"One . . . two," his low voice vibrates through my body like an instrument. "Three!"

He flashes a grin as I hit the fish, setting the barbed end, and Lucas grunts in the background. I ignore him.

We bring the fish in. Actually, Chance brings the fish in and I balance his effort, hefting it in using my body weight.

"Brooke! Step back," Chance says, his face tight, as a baseball bat covered in brown stains rises, and with the fierce grace of long practice, Chance swings it in an arc and lands on the head of the halibut.

The tail flops, then slows . . . finally it stops.

It's like a combat zone.

Lucas and Sam look at each other warily.

Clearly, they're not in Arizona anymore.

I sit down again on the cooler. Actually, it's more like a graceless fall.

Chance slides the halibut into the hold, a fiberglass trapdoor in the middle of the deck, and the stainless ring pull rattles as it slams shut, the huge fish filling the hold. His eyes sweep the horizon and the turbulent waters, tightening imperceptibly.

He nods, almost to himself, and says, "Let's make our way back."

Sam just looks at Chance. "Yeah, man, this fishing trip was like a war."

Chance grins suddenly, seawater clinging to the blackness of his hair, the orange bibs making his eyes bluer, the green retreating. The backdrop of the gray sky makes him look alive, on fire.

"It's sure not high desert," he comments.

Chance winks and I cover my mouth when a giggle threatens.

Chance

I ride the waves home, the route back from Flat Island as familiar as walking to the bathroom in my dark house as the two-hour journey stretches before me. The swells get worse as I move into the open water. Usually, they don't bother me, but now there's Brooke. I can't stand the idea of anything happening to her.

And as a special bonus, I don't like the way the clients treat her.

Look at her.

I sigh roughly and lift my hand from the wheel, plowing it through my sticky hair.

It's different when Matt worked for me last season. He's a guy and can trade insults, swear like the sailor he wants to be, and act generally borderline derelict and it's all part of the colorful experience the clients expect from their paid Alaskan fishing adventure.

Brooke's different. Her eyes haunt me, her inexperience moves me. Her existence is distracting as hell. Then there's that comment Tuck made.

Googling Brooke would be hard-core. I still haven't mentally committed to what is almost a stalker move. But I can't leave it alone. The suggestion pings around in my head like an escaped pinball.

"Chance?" Brooke says, and I turn from the wheel, taking stock of my two clients, slightly green around the edges, and I smirk. Two full-ride scholarship seniors from Arizona University . . . wrestlers. Who can barely move their wrists after five hours of fishing. It's amusing as hell.

"Yes?" I ask, taking in her bright cheeks, windswept by the day and the sea, her light eyes, somewhere between blue and true violet. Tendrils escape from her plaited black hair and curl around her jaw. Looks like her hair would be wavy in the right conditions.

I notice Lucas and Sam looking at Brooke, their eyes trying to dive beneath the unisex bibs that sport tiny droplets of fish blood mixed with seawater.

I tramp down on the jealousy that swells higher than the waves that hit my boat.

"I have everything stowed," she says.

God, Chance, get a grip, I tell myself. "'Kay, take a load off, we'll be in Homer in about ten minutes."

"All right," Brooke says, and I watch her face, her eyes sifting through the enclosed cabin. It's called an Alaskan Bulkhead for a reason. A small kitchenette and a not very private bathroom are accommodating to clients, though I'd been raised without it and thought it was for sissies.

We cruise in semisilence, the guys talking between themselves, and Brooke is quiet, in her own head. I wonder what she's thinking about. I'm irritated I don't know.

I'm pissed I care.

My eyes take in the harbor as I round the bend, avoiding the state ferry easily. I hate ferry days, they're always a pain in the ass. I put the boat in reverse as I go to park, sliding her in close to my slip.

"Hey . . . Brooke," Sam says and I don't turn but I'm listening pretty hard, keeping my focus on the park job.

Forward . . . tiny throttle. Reverse . . .

"Yeah?" she asks, but even I hear the reservation in her voice.

I know what's going to happen before she does. After all, I'm a guy. *Almost there* . . . I see the dock buoys and maneuver the boat close.

"Why don't you meet Lucas and me at that tavern on the spit?"

There's a beat of silence. Except for the creaking of the wheel under the grip of my hand.

"Oh . . . the Salty Dawg?" I hear her ask slowly. I can almost feel her eyes on my back. I maneuver the boat into the slip and the sides bounce against the buoys.

"You know it?" Sam asks and I can't stand how eager he sounds.

Bastard.

"I do . . . but," she flounders and I step in. "Brooke's gotta work at 4 a.m. Every day . . ." I let my sentence linger and then almost thrust the boat into reverse, plowing into the dock when Brooke says, her voice tight. "Chance is right . . . but I can meet you there early and leave early."

"Awesome," Sam says and I want to hit him.

How can Brooke say yes to having a beer with these yahoos when she said no to me?

How the fuck does *that* work?

Short answer: it doesn't. But I know she's just trying to shove me away. She already told me as much.

I grit my teeth as Brooke and I walk out to secure the cleats. I toss the rope to her and she catches it deftly. My gaze locks with hers and I want to kiss her . . . mark my territory, show these dipshits that she's *my* girl. I want to shake her because she's agreeing to meet with these guys to spite me.

But Brooke is not my girl. She's her own person and I have to watch her from afar.

When I've wanted so much more. I almost wish we'd never kissed. Wish we'd never spent that night together. It's like having the best thing ever then being denied after you've had a taste of it. Better to never know.

Almost.

This isn't done—not by a long shot.

FOURTEEN

Chance

We clean up in awkward silence. I quietly show Brooke how to master each step. She's clumsy with the fillet knife and it's a challenge not to just land my hand over hers and guide her through the meat. Instead I show her and she painstakingly goes through each step. The water at the fish-cleaning table is colder than hell and I watch her bite her lip to keep her teeth from chattering.

I want to warm her.

I don't.

My clients who want to bone Brooke hang at her elbow like the fish lice that still cling to my catch. Makes me want to do a less thorough job of cleaning.

I wash them all off anyway.

Like Bob the puker, I give them the same set of instructions as we push the fish cart up the gangplank, the wheels making music over the louvered and sharp metal grating.

"So . . ." Sam looks around and catches sight of Brooke beginning to rinse down the boat. "Where'd you get that nice little honey?"

Client, client, client my mind chants as my arms strain to make the last five feet of the sloping platform above the sea.

"First . . . *Sam,*" I begin sarcastically, which beats feeding him my knuckles, "she's not a 'little honey' . . . she's my deckhand."

"Right," Lucas says with clear disbelief. "Don't tell me you haven't tapped that?"

I step right into his space, our noses almost meeting. I don't give a shit if he's ranked first in the nation for wrestling. "Like you want to . . . Lucas?" I say with soft menace coating each syllable.

We stare at each other, taking the measure of the other. The age-old question is: if we go in with fists flying, who will come out the victor?

"Lotta heat for a *deckhand,*" Sam comments from behind us. Then he says, real quiet so only I hear, "You act like she's doing more than your deck, pal. Just sayin'."

"Yeah," Lucas says with a smile that doesn't reach his eyes. "We can go"—his eyes lock with mine in a combative stare—"but don't lay claim to some piece of tail if she's not your girlfriend. If she's just an employee, why do you care who bangs her?"

I see red and have his shirt in my fist before I know I move.

I can hear a running clank and don't turn, my fist rising above my head.

"Chance!" Brooke screams and I turn to look at her, black braids streaming behind her, lavender eyes wide.

Then a fist smashes into my temple and the world spins.

I stumble and as I got down, I kick my leg out and take out the knee of the one who hit me. With a howling wail he goes down beside me.

I've never hit a client in my life.

Lucas moves in to take me on, my vision in trembling triplicate while his pal bellows and holds his knee.

"I'm here . . ." I hear Brooke say as the fish cart acts like a barrier of sorts and she moves behind me. Too close to not get hurt. "Step back," I slur and meet Lucas with my fists as Brooke shouts, "Help!"

I watch Tuck come out of nowhere and take the wrestler by the scruff of the neck and toss him about five feet.

Hell, he's Johnny-on-the-spot, I think.

"Little trouble, Taylor?" he asks, turning to meet the bull as he charges.

"Just a spot!" I say with a cackle, spitting out some blood. That bash to the head wasn't dead center, but my teeth feel like they're floating.

"Chance!" Brooke says at my elbow.

"I'm sorry . . ." she whispers.

I pull her against me as Sam staggers to his feet. "I'll sue your ass . . . You fucking dislocated my knee!"

"Uh-huh," I nod, tucking Brooke against me. "Just as soon as you explain that cheap sucker punch you threw."

We look at each other for a drowning moment of slow-moving hell and he sighs, planting his hands on his hips. Stalemate.

We glance at Tuck and Lucas. Lucas is maybe five feet eight inches and 170; Tucker towers over him, but it's not enough.

He's trying to take Tucker to the ground. He'll lose, they're just that good.

"Tuck!" I yell and he steps back, avoiding a flying fist.

"Yup!"

"Call it off," I tell Sam in a low voice.

"Lucas!" Sam says, looking at me, his words for Lucas.

Lucas and Tucker look at Sam, glance warily at each other, and back away.

I watch their chests heave with exertion as I thank Tucker.

"Don't mention it," Tucker says, keeping his distance, his short beard catching the sweat from the fight.

"Take your fish and get the fuck out of here," I say to Sam, my eyes sliding to Lucas to include him.

I've never cursed at a client before. *Lots of firsts today,* I note.

"Chance," Brooke whispers.

"Shush," I say. "You didn't hear what they said about you."

Sam turns accusing eyes on Brooke. "Should've told us you were doing Taylor. We wouldn't have asked you out . . ." He says it like it's obvious.

It's not. Brooke pulls away, turning her own accusation on me, misunderstanding the universe. A female talent, that.

"You told them *that?* Your clients?" Her expression of shock and betrayal make my stomach drop.

"Fuck no!" I yell, coming toward her, and she shakes her head, clearly miserable.

She looks at Sam and Lucas, then at Tucker. Regret and outrage laced with hurt cross her face like a rainbow of emotion and I want to die. They've made a leap of logic and now Brooke assumes the worst. I can't say anything to correct it without burying myself further.

I just unintentionally screwed myself six ways to Sunday.

"God!" Brooke says, turning wounded eyes to mine. "I trusted you." Her voice sounds so raw with regret I flinch from the sound of it. "And it never mattered to you, did it?" Turning on her heel, she strides off, leaving me with two enraged clients, a dead fish, and a friendly acquaintance with handy-ass timing.

I watch her stalk off and exhale loudly.

"Nice, Taylor," Tuck comments.

Shit yes. "Yeah," I agree in misery.

"You could've just told us you were bagging her," Lucas says.

Dick. Head. I turn to glare at him. I can totally go again. This I know.

Tucker glares at him and he throws up his hands, palms out. "Hey big guy, I don't want to go again."

"Fuck. Off," I say. And I'm not one bit charitable. I mean it from the bottom of my boots.

"Right, yeah. Thanks for that great trip, Taylor," Sam says, putting his hands on the cold bars of the fish cart. "Let's roll, Lucas. Leave these fucktards in hicksville."

I snort. They wouldn't survive a minute here. They've got the wrong attitude. Clearly it's all take, no survival, no teamwork where they're from. It's like they've taken a pass on learning how to work with others. Goal oriented without compassion. Hope their plane crashes on the way to Arizona.

Tucker chuckles, breaking my dark mental fantasy. Palming his beard as his cheek swells he says, "Well . . . that was fun."

I make a sound inside my throat partway between a grunt and a snort. "Brooke hates my steaming guts, I beat up a client, and you call that fun?" I begin to walk away. "Fuck me," I mutter.

"Hey, Taylor . . . hold up," Tucker says, his checkered wool flannel button-up a solid blanket of material over his girth. He's one of those guys who wants to be fat but that layer can't negate the muscle underneath.

"Yeah?" I ask, shielding my eyes from the glare of the sun off the water.

"You're welcome, dumbass."

I pause and a reluctant grin breaks over my face. "Thanks."

"Did you Google Brooke?" he asks suddenly.

I shake my head. "Just spit it out, for Christ's sake." I put my hands on my vinyl bibs and frown at him.

He shakes his head. "Make it a priority, pal." Tucker walks off and I look after him as I had Brooke.

Brooke

I brush angry tears out of my eyes and tear open the bus's door. Realizing my gear is fish gutty and reeking, I take the suspender straps off my shoulders and carefully roll it down my body. I give an angry kick as it reaches the end and it flies like a discarded orange carpet.

"Hey now, missy," a voice from behind me says.

I gasp, hand to my chest as my heartbeat tries to burst out the open hole of my mouth.

"You again," I say with a hoarse sort of shout. "You . . . scared the hell out of me."

The old man gives a real smile, his cheeks cracking with it. "Nice that I didn't scare it into ya," he says, taking a puff of his pipe. His observant eyes quietly study me.

I blink.

"I didn't take ya for a dull tool in the drawer, darlin'."

Right. I wake up. "No . . . you're just like a—" I roll my eyes skyward, thinking—"like a jack-in-the-box or something."

He slaps his knee, laughing. At my expense, I'm sure. I sigh, picking up my fishing bibs and head around to the back of the bus to stow them inside the vinyl tote in the bus's "trunk" above the engine. I close the hatchback and peek around the bus and he leans to look back at me from the front.

"What?" I ask, disconcerted.

"Looks like you could use a friend. Or a word or two of advice."

Holy . . . no. Just no. I don't even know his name and I raise my brows at him like, *go away.*

But he's not a subtle guy, the old codger.

"It's Kashirin, Jake." He holds out his knobby hand, the pipe clamped between flattened lips.

He waits and I come forward. Slowly, against my express will, I give the old man my hand.

It's dry and warm and I feel my throat seize up, the day boiling up inside me, threatening to overflow. His unexpected kindness threatens to break the carefully constructed dam that is holding back a torrent of outrage and grief.

I won't cry. I won't break down.

But then I do. In the middle of the Homer parking lot in the company of a 105-year-old man.

"There now, honey." He pats my head as he holds me awkwardly in his skinny old arms, somehow smoking that pipe as it juts out to the side of our embrace like a twig on a tree.

He pulls away, his eyes pale and wise.

"You got some talkin' to do, don'tcha?"

I nod, the wetness on my face like the ocean I just came from.

He gives a chin jerk to another little shanty.

The sign reads: Jake's Treasure and Other Trash.

He walks away from me like I'll follow him.

And . . . I do.

Jake pushes open the door to his little shop with a hip and holds it open for me. I pass through the dim interior, a lone window letting in the light. But the view!

I walk to the middle of the shop, stacks of everything a person can imagine in every corner and piles six feet high in every direction. It smells like old books and tobacco with the faint hint of wood.

The most surprising feature on his small scarred desk is a sleek Mac laptop. What's an old guy doing with a laptop?

I turn and watch Jake turn the little sign on the front door to Closed.

"Take your pack off, Brooke."

My brows rise.

He nods as he studies my expression. "I know who ya are," he says, nodding some more as he relights his pipe with a cupped hand and an expert pull and puff. The fragrant smoke fills the room and it makes my heart heavy again.

"No more waterworks," he says in such a serious way it's like scaring a hiccup into silence.

"Right," I say softly, thinking I should go. What am I doing here in this musty shop with an old guy I don't know?

"Talk first. Then go. But not before we make our acquaintance."

I smile at his antiquated speech. He speaks so differently from anyone I've ever heard. It's sorta charming.

I sit and he circles me, then runs a finger along his tiny desk, tapping a chapped and red finger on his silver laptop.

"Chance Taylor doesn't know who he hired for his sidekick, does he?"

I stare at him, my eyes skipping to the laptop under his finger.

"Does he?" Jake repeats. "Brooke Elizabeth Starr."

Oh my God.

I can see it in his eyes.

That dreadful knowledge. They all have it, that look. I'm normal until they know what's happened. I stagger to my feet like a reanimated corpse, my arm striking out and connecting painfully with a huge stack of books.

"No," Jake says with low authority.

"What?" I croak.

"Stop running."

"Who . . . who are you?" I ask, my breath a dry wisp of oxygen in my throat. It's not enough. Not nearly enough.

A swollen few moments of silence beat the air between us. Then, "I was your aunt Milli's . . . lover."

I flop back into the chair with an unladylike drop, my ass

bones protesting against the solid oak chair. But I'm beyond caring.

Aunt Milli.

I swallow hard and stare at Jake Kashirin.

"Ya stayin'?"

I nod slowly. I'm too shell-shocked to contemplate moving.

"It was a different time then . . . a wild time," he says in a matter-of-fact way. His pipe smolders as his gaze burns through the glass of the window to the ocean beyond.

"Back in the forties you couldn't just date whoever ya wanted. Caucasians stayed with their own, Natives and Russians could intermarry . . . hell, that'd been happening since the Russians took Alaska." His eyes met mine. "But a mixed-breed Russian Native? With a Caucasian woman? Never," he says. The last word is a bitter drop in the potion of his tale.

"She was beautiful, my Milli," he says so softly I strain to hear. He turns those pale bright eyes to mine and I fight not to squirm under their piercing scrutiny. "I knew you were hers before I verified it here," he says, tapping the Mac again.

My heart is thumping, I can barely hear his words over the roar of the blood in my ears, the drumbeat of my heart.

"Tell me . . . tell me what happened, Brooke."

I'm halting at first but it pours out of me in the end. I choke on the last words, this old man the priest to my confessional. "They took my mom out in a body bag that wasn't properly zipped and her hand . . . her hand was just there with her wedding ring."

I close my eyes and the winking gold is an image behind my eyes I can't erase. I can't.

I dissolve into tears and Jake stands in front of me silently, his hand on my shoulder, letting me cry it out. It doesn't feel anticlimactic and unnecessary like I think it will. Sharing the memories brings the greatest relief I've ever known. The weight of my family's death has been crushing me . . . and now, it doesn't. I don't break apart with the telling. Instead, I feel like I'm finally moving toward being whole again.

Finally Jake sits in front of me and says, "You need to face this mess head-on or it'll never leave ya."

I search his eyes, wiping my own with the back of my hand. "Speaking from experience?" I ask quietly.

He gives me serious eyes back. "I am." He takes another puff from his pipe.

We're quiet for several moments and it's a comfortable silence, not awkward.

"She gave you the gift of music, Brooke," he says like a statement and I nod.

"You still tickling the ivories?"

I shake my head and say, "Twice." Chance as my audience, I remember.

He smiles, his yellowed teeth large in his mouth. It's infectious, and I grin back. "Did ya find the grand down in that daylight basement?"

I nod. "I did. It's wonderful, but how does it stay in tune? It plays so beautifully . . ." I catch his eyes and he winks.

"You?" I ask and he nods.

"Yes, ma'am. It's me. I've been tuning that old girl for years."

It's like Milli's ghost caused us to meet. I open my mouth, then close it.

"Do you believe in chance, Brooke?"

I startle slightly at him using Chance's name as a noun.

"Destiny? Fate? Coincidence?" he elaborates.

Oh. "I don't know . . . I guess." It's sort of creepy, the double meaning.

Jake nods like he knows I'm not all there with his thought process.

"Well . . . you better, because it's one and the same."

"What?" I ask, my eyes roaming his features, trying to pick up clues.

He raises his brows. "Do you think you're here by luck? That coincidentally you just happen to be in Alaska?"

I guess not. I elected to come here. It's a choice. Now that I've been here almost a month, I can't imagine someone coming to Alaska by accident. They'd have to be purposeful in the decision. . . . not be led around by a random ring in their nose.

I shake my head no.

"So take a chance, Brooke," he says.

"A chance with what?" I ask.

"With the Taylor boy, of course," he says, then winks.

I burst out laughing. He's so clever and I utterly miss it. His eyes sparkle at me with mirth. I feel about a million pounds lighter having told someone here. This is the first time I've told an old truth in my new life.

It feels good . . . but still. "Will you keep this to yourself?"

He frowns and his eyes do a disappearing act within the folds of his face as he blinks and I feel bad about my earlier comparison to a troll. Now he looks like a wrinkled kind old man. Which he is.

"Be still my heart," he says, putting a gnarled hand against his heart. "Do I look like the kind of fella who'd rat out his new friend? Milli's flesh and blood?"

He doesn't, his eyes as sincere as any I've looked into.

"No," I answer softly.

"Not the vote of confidence I'm looking for but I'll take it."

I stand and Jake does too, the eerie light from the stormy sky giving a haloed affect around him, and I suppress a shiver.

"I'll be watching," he says.

Like he isn't already, I think. He has the pulse on, well . . . everything.

His comment strikes me as weird. "Why watching?"

Jake leans forward, his voice lowering to a near whisper and I find myself leaning forward as well, catching his soft words.

"Because that nut job is still on the loose."

He couldn't help me even if the murderer came here. He's just a weak old man.

Jake sees my expression and interprets it, laughing.

"Sometimes physical strength isn't everything. Someone like me"—he jabs a thumb into his chest—"no one sees. It's like being invisible."

I blink again. He's surprised me twice today.

The second surprise is Jake's acknowledgment of my deepest fear since I arrived here.

That it's not over.

FIFTEEN

~

Chance

I move up the gangplank, thoughts of a hot shower sharing room with those of Brooke.

I've blown it, I know it.

Not only did I lose my cool with a client, I did it in front of the only girl I've ever given a shit about. Nice, Chance . . . Smooth.

I push my hair back off my face, relieved I don't have a set tonight. Thank God. I'm way too in my head to strum shit from Shinola.

I get close to my 'Cuda and catch movement in my peripheral vision.

Old man Kashirin comes over, his cane indented where the ivory bows underneath his hand. Have to be a Native to own ivory, work it. I know because I am. Even though I'm "white Native" and don't live in a village like Seldovia or Port Graham, the full-bloods never let me forget it. Only the coal black of my hair speaks to my ancestry.

"Chance Taylor," he says by way of greeting, smoke escaping out of the dual sides of his mouth, a pipe clamped in the center. I stride to Jake, palm first, and he fits his hand to mine like a glove.

"Hey ya, Jake," I say with a smooth pump that's met with his; hard as nails, like it has always been.

"How's the catch?" he asks, those wizened eyes buried in a face like raisins in putty. He has the eyes of his Russian ancestry, pale blue, like a sky that's heading toward autumn but hasn't made up its mind. His cane pegs the ground at his feet and he does a practiced lean, his face tilted up to mine.

"Ah . . ." I scrub my face, then put my hands on my hips, the vinyl hot and slimy from the day. "Not so great."

"Humph!" he says in disbelief. "I saw those desert folk taking their catch." Jake takes his pipe out of his mouth and points the end at me. "That 'but was two hundred pounds of fish if it was an ounce."

True.

"Yeah, but I sorta lost my cool . . ."

Jake guffawed. "A mite, I'd say."

"You saw?" I ask and Jake nods.

"Shit."

"There's only two things that get a fella riled up like a cat in a room full of rockers." He waits expectantly. It doesn't matter if the worldwide apocalypse is here: when Jake Kashirin has a pearl of wisdom to bestow, you listen.

"Women . . ." He pauses, his index finger briefly touching the one on his left hand. "And"—he sticks his finger straight into the air—"money!" he says with an air of certainty.

His eyes narrow and he says, "I know you don't need the money, Chance."

Gotcha. "No, it's not the money. But I screwed up so—"

"Never too late," Jake says, interrupting. "She's a fine filly that one." He puffs on his pipe, his eyes on me.

Somehow . . . Brooke doesn't seem like any version of a horse but I don't say. Nor do I ask if we're talking about the same girl. I think Jake knows every person in Homer. No one can miss Brooke. She draws all eyes to her when she enters a space.

"You guys done any chatting?"

I clamp down on my expression, my memories crowded with my hands on her body . . .

Chatting. No.

I smile and he gives a sly grin. Then it disappears like the sun sliding behind a cloud.

"You be careful with that girl."

"What do you mean?" I ask, taking an unconscious step forward.

Jake shakes his head. "It's not my story to tell but . . . she might need . . ." He shakes his head again.

"What?" I can hear how irritated I sound and try to dial it back, but the cloak-and-dagger shit is losing its shine.

"Careful handling."

Fine. Fuck. "Okay, thanks, Jake."

I walk away, glancing behind over my shoulder at an old man who knew my parents—hell, my grandparents too. He ought to—he's my second cousin.

I add a Google search as a requisite for tonight. Shower,

stalk Brooke on the Internet like everyone before me . . . try to get her to listen to me.

Easy. Riiiight.

I pop the trunk on the 'Cuda, tossing my bibs into my long and narrow tote. It reeks and I sigh, adding a bleach wash to the list.

The list grows.

I drive home to my log cabin. Even the sight of something I built with my bare hands doesn't do anything to suck me out of the foul mood I'm in. I'm a rare Alaskan: I have a garage. I pull the 'Cuda to the wide wood door and hit the button on the remote opener. It slides up smoothly and I pull my car inside. It's an extravagance in a region that has a short summer like Homer. I drive my Ford Bronco when the weather turns; sometimes I even drive it in the summer on battered roadways. But for now, it's about connecting with something I like.

Too much.

I grab my tote and dump the bibs and the rest of the gear onto the concrete driveway. I walk to the hose bib and give a sharp swipe on the mixer to the right and hot water flows inside the hose. I twist the faucet and after spraying the bibs with a bleach, I hose them down.

They sit steaming and I let them, walking away from the mess of my profession and going inside.

After a shower that's as hot as I can stand, I plop down in front of my laptop, the picture window in front of my solid oak desk showcasing the ocean beneath the steep cliff my cabin is perched on. I can hear the waves crashing as Google lights up my screen.

I type in Brooke's name.

Nothing relevant, no matter how many pages I scroll through.

I add her middle name: Elizabeth.

Suddenly the screen fills with hits that feel familiar. There's plenty of reading about Seattle pianist Brooke Elizabeth Starr.

The more I read the worse I feel. It explains so much. My eyes move over the horror that was her life.

Words like *slaughter* and *instant orphan* spring from each page.

These are things you read about. They don't happen to people you know.

I lean back, my eyes scanning the story from the *Seattle Times* a second time. Then, in very small print it reads: *see related search.*

I move the mouse to hover over that highlighted phrase, then click it.

As I read the story I sit up straighter, pieces falling into perfect place.

The FBI hasn't apprehended the killer. There's a third family that's now dead.

Another Juilliard pianist is out of the running. Who can pursue any passion when their family has been ripped violently from them?

No one.

How convenient for the other candidates, I think.

Which I am sure is what the other candidates thought too.

I close my computer and it sleeps.

It'll be a long time before I can.

It certainly changes how I feel. I realize I've waded into a mess like a bull in a china shop. A little finesse won't hurt.

I rub my chin, my fingers eventually finding my tired eyes, which feel shrink-wrapped inside my skull.

I've got to see Brooke. I know she's pissed at me.

But I can fix this.

I hesitate, thinking. *He who hesitates is lost,* I decide.

I grab the small pistol I keep in the downstairs window seat and slide it into the pocket of my leather jacket, the one I wear when I'm taking my bike. The sawed-off shotgun will remain in my bedroom on the upper floor where it belongs.

I don't like that the man who killed Brooke's family is still out there.

The gun is a cold comfort where it lays within arm's reach.

It's better than no comfort at all.

Brooke

I pull up to the Homer post office and stare at the stately brick building. I've been here almost a month and this is only my second trip. I look at the post office box key in my hand, closing my palm into a fist around it. I step out of the bus, then jog up the wide steps of the building.

I move to the older section of post office boxes. I pass the modern ones and wind my way to the very back of the building. The old boxes come into view, forming a loose U and at the very end, housed in brass and glass, is Aunt Milli's box. I slide the key inside the slot and pull out the mail. I look at it as I walk over to the Paper Only recycling can, chucking junk mail in as I go.

At the bottom of the pile is a notice to sign for something.

I look up and see the line backed up to the door and sigh. I'm totally not waiting through that mess. No way. I look down at the slip: registered return receipt mail. In small letters I can just read the return address:

Federal Bureau of Investigation.

I hesitate between the long line and the short walk to the glass door. I see the colorful VW bus waiting for me outside.

No contest.

Whatever document I have to sign can wait. I stuff the slip into my pocket and walk out the door.

It's pathetic that signing slips for the FBI is their only contact with me. I mean, my God . . . did they need permission for something else? Some other possession of my parents' has been discovered and cataloged in some great cavernous place with an uncaring number slapped on for inventory? A sudden memory of Agent Clearwater's text and voice mails piling up rises to the surface of my brain.

I squeeze my eyes shut against it. The heat of the sun's low position on the horizon washes over me like bathwater and I let the soothing feel of the clean air and the warmth of the almost-summer air lull me for a few precious moments of forgetting.

Then I open them. With a sigh I hop inside the bus and back out, then make my way to Aunt Milli's cabin.

I get a text. I keep a hand on the wheel and look down.

Lacey.

I swipe her image and her words read: *another family.*

I stop the bus. I text two-handed, my left leg jammed like a pirate's peg leg into the brake.

Another Juilliard candidate's family?

Yeah. Then: *I'm scared for you, Brookie.*

Well, I'm scared too.

I reply: *yeah, me too.*

I look up at the crumpled slip on my dashboard and realize that I should have waited in that line. Even if I didn't want to.

Should've, could've, would've.

Didn't.

Crap.

I reply: *call me.*

I wait for Lacey. I jump when my cell vibrates and my damp palm loses control of the cell and it falls to the floor. I retrieve it around my pedals.

I swipe her face on the glass surface and put the phone to my ear.

A shadow, a feeling, an instinct . . . I'll never know, causes me to turn to my left, the bus noisily idling on the soft shoulder that leads to the deepest part of East End Road.

Two eyes greet mine, a hand raised to rap on the glass.

I give a low panicked cry and drop the phone again.

I can hear Lacey from the floorboards of the car.

The door is torn open and two strong arms pull me out of the car. I raise my face to a tall man, his face shadowed in the gloom provided by the spruce tree cover that lines the dirt road.

Adrenaline shoots from my center to my extremities, causing them to tingle as my heart launches itself into my throat.

"Brooke Starr?" he asks, his eyes a flash of the whites in the shadowed road, filtered sunlight a dream as I try to adjust my eyes to the ambient light provided by the dense tree canopy above us.

"Ye-es," I whisper, my bowels clenching, every muscle tense.

"Agent Luke Haller," he says. "Anchorage division."

I feel slightly faint. He steps away, his hold loosening on my arms, and I lean back against the bus. The solidness of it is wonderful. Concrete.

"You scared me," I say.

"I apologize . . . I was sent by our Seattle division. You didn't get the communication?"

Oh yeah. The note.

"Ah . . . hang on, 'kay?" He cocks an eyebrow and nods.

I scramble to my car, feeling for my cell that's emitting Lacey's banshee wail.

"Hey!" I say in a breathless gasp.

"Jesus! What the hell happened? Are ya okay?"

"Yes!"

"Who's there? Did you get in a wreck?"

I put up my palm. "No . . . listen. The FBI is here."

"Well thank God. I talked to Clearview . . ."

I grin so fast my face hurts. "Clearwater," I correct.

"Whatever." I can see her wave her hand dismissively. "Hottie in Fed suit," she replies.

"Anyway," I enunciate slowly, "he startled me. I think he was on the way to Aunt Milli's cabin and I was on the side of the road . . . I just wasn't expecting it, is all."

"Uh-huh. Well, here's the thing: let them do their job, Brooke. This sackless maniac is on a killing spree."

"Who . . . is dead now?" I ask, not wanting the answer.

"The guy's family." Which I'm aware of from Clearwater's earlier call.

I'd been speculating. It seems ridiculous now, but maybe he is responsible. After all, women were never serial murderers. Hardly ever. Now another Juilliard contender family has been stolen from them. Not a competitor, not a pianist. It blew my speculations out of the water. I can feel myself frowning.

"Miss Starr," I hear the agent behind me say.

Kinda forgot about him. "Gotta go, Lace."

"Check his ID," she whispers into the mouthpiece.

I get a full blanket of gooseflesh over my body. "Okay . . . right." I swipe *end*.

I turn around and there he stands in the standard black suit. God, talk about stereotype squared. But the tie throws me: bloodred. Then he smiles and I relax. Just out for a ride in FBI-issue uniform in the middle of nowhere . . . no need to freak out.

"May I see your ID?" I ask, shoving my cell into my pocket and wiping damp hands on my jeans.

"I'm sorry, I should have presented that first off."

He smoothly reaches inside the interior pocket of his suit and the pebbled butt of a handgun reveals briefly, then is swept behind his jacket again as he hands it over to me. I flip open the walletlike ID. A card is there, with a gold embossed emblem. Above that is a holographic superimposed image over the capital letters of the acronym: FBI. His signature appears above his photo ID. My eyes flick to his, color unknown in this light. Agent Haller is tall and fit, moves gracefully, and seems confident. One of those people who are comfortable in their own skin.

Must be nice.

I know the ID because I've seen them a hundred times since my family's death. I suddenly feel lame for asking.

I press on anyway. Staring your own death in the face tends to make a tenacious person even more so. "Who sent you?"

"You mean the field assignment?"

I cross my arms under my breasts, cocking a brow.

"Decatur Clearwater," he replies, sliding his ID back into his pocket and pushing his hands into the pockets of his slacks. Unperturbed, nonchalant.

I let him off the hook. "You stand out like a turd in a punch bowl here, Agent Haller."

He gives a snorting laugh and sticks out his hand. "Just call me Luke." His eyes meet mine.

I let him shake my hand, which is warm and dry against my damp palm. He gives me a slow pump and I smile. "I guess I'm glad you're here."

He cocks his head to the left, slanting his eyes in my direction. "You shouldn't be. I'm not the only agent assigned to protect the surviving family members."

I don't know what to say to that.

"You headed to your place?"

I nod, getting back into the bus.

He looks the car over. "Some paint job."

I laugh at his expression. "Yeah . . . it was a surprise."

"I'll bet."

He taps the window rim where it's rolled down. "I'll follow you home."

I let out a breath I don't realize I'm holding and crank the window up. I guess I didn't know that I've been stressed out. I have. Now that I'm feeling everything again, it's more than I can bear. The emotions are like a perfume you think you'll miss until you wear it again and realize you never liked it.

I nod and he moves to his unmarked SUV—all black.

I wait until his lights come on, piercing the back of the bus and roll away from the shoulder.

We make our way toward Aunt Milli's cabin.

It's been a long time since I've felt safe.

SIXTEEN

Chance

I catch the sun glinting off the windshield of Brooke's vintage bus. You can't miss its clash against the backdrop of the wooded acreage that encroaches around her aunt's cabin.

I move off the deep porch when a black SUV comes into sight.

What the hell is this?

I've always had pretty good instincts, having relied heavily on them on the sea . . . and on land. They're never more crystalline than at this moment.

My mind flashes instantly on the message from the Fed I'd seen by accident. The dots connect that fast.

If the Feds have shown up, the decision's been made that the stakes are too high. My eyes roam the sleek ebony lines of the SUV, the satellite antenna, all-weather wheels, and the mound of a mountable light on the dash are the main clues. My hand falls to my gun, hanging in a solid lump inside my jacket, then falls away. You don't need a concealment permit in Alaska to carry; it's like a rite of passage.

But I bet the Fed will get excited if he notices one on my person.

I watch Brooke step out into the twilight that Alaska has for half the hours of the day and see the guy unfold out of his rig, FBI stamped all over him.

I don't like him on sight. I study him: the dark suit, the un-needed sunglasses that hide his expression. Mostly I don't like the way he carries himself. He has that sense about him, that male potential that makes another guy stand up and take no-tice: dangerous.

I do like what he represents. Then I remind myself that Brooke doesn't know one critical thing: that I understand why she's here, even if she doesn't. A part of my past that mimics her in consequence, even if the circumstances are different. I've had to face that particular demon, or the power of the past never lets go. She's running from a past that doesn't have a statute of limitations and the long arm of the FBI has come calling to remind her. Brooke needs someone other than herself; it's big-ger than her. From what I read, this killer has murdered three families so far. All in a bid to what?

I begin walking to where they stand, Brooke's face register-ing first surprise with a heel-biter of anger.

Great.

I look to the Fed in his suit, a thing that's as foreign to the Alaskan landscape as Brooke's wildly painted bus. Somehow he doesn't jibe with that thumbnail photo that'd come up on her phone number list.

No, this is a different dude.

I walk within arm's reach, my conclusions forming.

"What are you doing here, Chance?" Brooke asks.

Ouch, frosty.

I shrug and go for the truth, since I've had moderate luck with that in the past. "I didn't like the way we left things, wanted to straighten things out." My eyes slide to the witness to our personal shit and frown at Suit Man.

I watch Brooke fold her arms, the classic stance of *you're not getting anywhere with me.*

Fuck me.

I sigh, pegging my hands on my hips, my eyes shifting to Suit Man. I hate not seeing someone's eyes, I can't gauge shit.

"Agent Luke Haller," he says, holding out his hand. I shake it like I'll crush it and he gives good press right back.

Strong.

But my hands are strong from fishing; it's not artificial but acquired. What are his hands strong from?

Before I can give it too much thought Brooke says, "This isn't a good time, Chance."

Agent Haller throws up his hands. "Listen, you two have something to discuss, I was really just surveying the lay of the land, so to speak."

I look at him again, he speaks differently. "You say you're from Anchorage?"

He smiles. "I didn't."

Right. I wait. Silence can be useful.

"Chance . . . he's been . . . well, that's a discussion for

another time," she says quietly, casting her eyes down, hiding some of what she's thinking.

If I hadn't been with Brooke so intimately, I'd swear her indifference is real. But I know better. Brooke's hands twist together in knots, a fine sheen of sweat decorates her upper lip.

She's nervous. Brooke doesn't know I know. She's looking at all this from my perspective of presumed ignorance. Yeah, it'd be damn weird for the FBI to show up.

I look at Haller and he stares coolly back

"I'm going to take off now," he says, turning to Brooke. She starts, her gaze moving from her feet, to me . . . and finally to him. They shake hands and he gives me a measured look. "I'll be around," he says to us both.

No, *nice to meet you,* no pleasantries exchanged. I nod back at him and he hops inside his rig, turning the engine on and smoothly backing out as if he has a hundred times before.

Brooke and I watch him move down the driveway, dust plumes following his tires as they crunch over what little gravel remains.

Brooke takes a deep breath, her soft violet eyes find mine, her full bottom lip trembles, and I watch her roll it into her mouth, nibbling on it, and God help me, I want her. With the weight of everything between us . . . the imperative to work out the mess of her recent history, to apologize for my caveman turn of events today, and now the FBI showing up. . . . I just do. My need to protect her, shield her from all of this, takes over . . . just like it did that night on the pier.

I want to press her up against a hard surface and take her to the moon.

"Chance . . ." she begins, shaking her head.

I say it. I'll figure out the logistics later. "You're fired."

Her eyes snaps to mine and her mouth drops open. "What?" she asks in a breathless whisper, disbelief dripping from that one word.

"You're officially let go. Canned. No longer employed . . . terminated," I say with quiet intensity.

"What . . . I didn't do anything . . ." she says in a plea, her palms out in supplication, her eyes welling with tears.

"Yeah you did," I say, coming so close it would have been easier to touch her.

Her eyes search mine. I touch my hand to my heart. "You made me care more about you than the sea, my boat . . . whatever life I had before you."

Brooke gives me wary eyes and I know there's explaining to do. "I'm sorry," I begin and dip my chin to my chest, letting out a sigh, then meet her eyes again. "I shouldn't have lost my shit back there . . ."

She gives a soft shake of her head, her black hair sliding around her shoulders. "You made them think we'd . . . you and me . . ." Brooke glares at me, her face wavering on that fine line between righteously pissed off and tears.

"We haven't, I didn't . . . they're fucktards. They were just talking out of their asses, not knowing the facts—anything. Hoping for something they'll never have." I look at her, willing her to hear me. To listen. "Something I hope to have." I let my arms fall to my sides and cautiously step closer. "I'm so goddamned sorry, Brooke." I mean it so hard my body physically reacts to my own words and I watch her eyes widen at the emotion she sees there.

Her face cracks, the anger sliding away, and with a gasping sob, Brooke throws herself in my arms and I wrap myself around her. The altercation's like a trigger her recent past, Brooke can't handle a hint of betrayal from anyone. Her small strides to get back to center will be swept away by insensitive bullshit like what went down today. "Shush . . . I know, it's okay."

Brooke pulls away from me, her face wet, lavender eyes pools of sadness as they look deeply into mine, searching. "Know . . . what?"

God, *I can't say it*. Then I do. "I know about your family, Brooke."

She backs away like I've hit her instead of held her.

No . . . this isn't the way this is supposed to go. I move toward her.

Brooke retreats. "No. Just go . . . just leave," she says, warding me away with her hands.

I clench my hands into fists. "No."

Her face shows her surprise.

"You need to face this. You tried to kill yourself, Brooke. You're running. This cabin"—I swing my palm around to encompass the small homestead—"your job working for me . . . it's an escape. And if you haven't noticed, you're still a prisoner."

Her face crumples as her hands drop to her sides. I don't wait for an invitation; I stride to her, wrapping my arms around her again and pressing her face against my chest. I speak without thinking. "Let me help you, Brooke Starr."

I put a finger under her chin and tilt her face up and our eyes meet.

"I can't," she whispers.

I press a soft kiss against her mouth. "You can . . . you will," I say.

She squirms and I loosen my hold on her but don't let go. "Tucker told me you're a player . . . that you'd rather be married to your job than be with someone."

I don't lie. "That's true."

Her face tightens, and a sob that's part gasp bursts from her, then she covers her mouth with her hand. "I can't do this. I can't be used and played. You've *got* to know that."

"I do."

I cradle Brooke's face with my hands, bringing it to me, and she doesn't resist. I kiss each eyelid, tasting the salt of her tears, and close my eyes.

When I open them I make my first promise to a woman. One I want to keep.

"It's all true." My eyes grind into hers, never leaving, holding steady with the weight of my words. "I was sleeping through my life. Fishing, playing . . . going through the motions." I suddenly hug her to me then pull back, a smile I can't help breaking out over my face. She's startled and gives a tentative smile back.

"Then I hired you. And suddenly, I didn't want anything more than I wanted you. I was just existing before, Brooke."

Brooke looks at me, so solemn, so ancient in her eyes. "And what about now?" she asks quietly as I wipe the tears from her face, kissing her lips. Once, twice . . . then she kisses me back, the silk of them moving against mine, and we're where we always are with each other—entangled.

I lift my mouth from her lips and plunge my fingers through her hair, pulling her head toward me again, so close my mouth hovers over hers, answering her earlier question, my breath warm on her face. "Now I'm living, Brooke."

Brooke

I'm not ready to be loved, but I'm ready to be with Chance. Those I love have been stolen from my life, numbing me. Yet . . . I feel like I've been ready to let this man into my life since we met. And now I can no longer think of a reason to resist that feeling. I move into his arms like it's my home and Chance wraps me against him. I feel his heartbeat through the thin tee he wears. His leather jacket bunches inside my fist as he moves his mouth over mine and I know I'm lost the instant he touches me.

I feel reality take a nosedive before our need for each other. I forget about the killer, the FBI . . . my sudden lack of employment. I just feel.

Be.

Chance moves his hands to the small of my back, gripping me as he spreads his fingers over my heated skin. My body yearns for him, my nipples getting hard through my lightweight shirt.

"Please, Brooke . . . be with me," he begs with his words, with his mouth, and I know I'll cave. I want to be with him as much as he wants me to. Even if he knows the truth.

Chance saved me in that water just over three weeks ago.

He's saving me now. All I have to do is let him. Let Chance rescue me. Again.

"Yes." I say the word, but he's already picking me up, his hands on my butt, my legs wrapping his waist as he moves us to the cabin's front door. He bumps it with his hip and it scrapes open, the bottom catching on the wood floor. He kicks it closed behind him and moves toward my tiny bedroom, my arms wound around his neck and breathing in the scent of the sea that clings to his skin.

"The bed's fine . . ." I murmur, wanting him . . . wanting this. Now.

He lays me on top of the old quilt and steps back to stare at me. I see it in his expression: his eyes hold heat and intent, his willingness is like unspoken foreplay.

Chance takes off his sea-green tee, the color matching his eyes. Those deep orbs never waver from mine, so serious, so intense. He rips his shirt off at the collar, swinging it over his head and into the corner of my room. I see his body for the first time in the unadulterated sunlight that streams through my window. The tattoo on his left shoulder shows two salmon fighting each other, a yin and yang of fish. Tribal symbols work their way down one muscular arm, joining in a band that encircles his wrist in a thick bracelet of ink.

He sees me looking. "I'm Native American," he says, gesturing to the symbols.

I didn't know . . . but as I study his face, the high cheekbones, the black hair like spilled ink, and eyes that have a slightly exotic shape, it's obvious.

To me he is so handsome it's like beautiful visual pain. I gesture with my finger, crooking it, and he smiles. Taking off his button-fly Levi's with a single tearing pull, the metal buttons pop open like a reverse accordion and the bareness and length of him stands at attention.

Commando.

It makes me catch my breath as I drink in the sight of him, all sense of caution is lost in the shattering chemistry between us.

Chance reads my mind and he kicks off his jeans, which slide to a heap on the floor as he crawls across the bed. I watch him move, his penis a swinging pendulum above me, and my eyes roam, not landing anywhere but feasting on the wealth of his flesh above me.

"I want you so bad I can't think," Chance whispers as he bends down to kiss me again. I reach out, grabbing the smooth hardness of him, and he groans at my touch, wrapping his hand around mine. "You're going to make me . . ."

I kiss his nose, then his lips, and squeeze him once, hard— and his hand tightens on mine. "No . . . not yet." He begins to pull away and I let my fingers trail down the length of him as he shudders at my touch. I put my hands under his balls, rolling them in a tender juggle, and he laughs and pulls away. "Tickles."

His face turns serious when I sit up on my knees and we face each other. He grabs my belt and releases it from the loops that hold it. It makes a soft sound as it moves through the loops and my hand strays back to him.

Chance pulls his hips away. "I want to undress you, Brooke."

He puts a hand at my nape, then pulls us so close I can't get at him anymore, though I feel him hard and ready between us.

Chance kisses me, stroking his lips on mine, lifting his mouth long enough to take my shirt over my head. It flies into a corner and his arms go around me like steel bands as he unhooks my bra and I lean back, my breasts falling out of their lace pockets. Chance bends to suck my nipple into his mouth and pulls me closer with a hand on my back. I spear his hair with my fingers, clenching the blackness in my hand as he laves the sensitive tip. My head's thrown back, my hand buried in his hair as his left hand wiggles the denim from my hips and he pushes me backward. I fall, my breasts bouncing gently as my body settles beneath him.

I lie there in nothing but my panties, a strip of lace running up my ass and a peekaboo front letting him know I'm completely bare.

"I want to kiss you . . . here," Chance says as he presses his fingertip to the sheer panel that covers the front of me and I jerk in response, the pressure of that one touch wet where it makes contact.

I can only nod. It's more intimate than sex for me as I watch his face lower to where I want to feel him inside me.

Still, his deep eyes beg permission as he looks up the line of my body, one hand on my breast, one finger underneath the sheerness of my panties and I whisper, our gazes locking, "Yes."

He smiles but I don't see his mouth, his eyes crinkle at the corners before the color is lost as he closes them and his tongue pushes past the lace that his fingers move aside and the flat of his tongue presses against my clit.

Chance drags his tongue up the center of my sensitive slick nub of flesh and my hips rise off the bed. He plants his forearm over my hips and holds me still while he licks and presses a finger inside me. I begin to lose focus, the delicious rhythm is hard and fast, smooth and perfect, and I get so caught up in what he's doing, moving against him, the first orgasm crashes into me like a wave, leaving me gasping and panting.

"Breathe, Brooke," Chance says from between my thighs and blows warm breath against my entrance, and a strangled cry leaves my lips, torn out against my will, a release of everything, no more thoughts, only sensation crests and falls over me.

"I want you," I say between harsh breaths and Chance takes my ankles and pulls me down to kiss me on my lips. I taste me on him and he keeps pushing his finger inside me as he lets me taste my pleasure on his mouth. I let my legs fall open. I'm still throbbing . . . in pleasure, in anticipation.

I can't breathe for wanting him inside me.

He sinks the hand that was just inside me into my hair and turns my head so my face is in profile, letting his penis find my wet heat where I wait to be filled with him.

I feel the tip of him at my entrance, and his knees split my legs farther apart from behind even as he enters me slowly, each hot inch sinking deeper, and I let out a hoarse cry, pressing myself back against him. My hips rise and he puts a staying hand on the back of my head and the other at the small of my back, pinning me in place, and I whimper in surrender

How does Chance know I need to be controlled right now? That finally I have chosen something and it's happening with my permission when so much has happened without it? It's a release that's more than sexual.

My body lies still as he buries himself to the throbbing end of me. I feel the pulse of his penis as my sex grabs onto him in response. Chance lifts his hands off me and puts one on each side of my body in a push-up. Then he rolls his hips forward and my body moves with him, the front of me rubbing back and forth against the rough quilt as he shoves into me and I grunt with the pleasure of the deep penetration.

"Brooke," Chance says and softly lowers his solid weight on me, his front presses against my ass and his hard chest flattens my breasts against the bed. I'm trapped and it's an exquisite mix of fear and pleasure. I can't get away and I don't want to. We're joined as he kisses my temple then he moves inside me again and I gasp, thinking he can't go deeper.

Then he does and I groan as he touches me deep inside, an itch that's getting scratched to perfection.

"Come for me," Chance says, rolling his hips in and out, and a delicious heat begins to build. He does it again and again and that fire inside flares, bursting out of my core. It spreads and as I begin to pulse around him in crashing waves, I feel him grow harder inside me, his release coming at the peak of my own as we shudder together.

We're suspended in the synchronicity of the moment. It feels too short but like forever in that bubble of time. Finally, Chance gently pulls out of me and rolls me over onto my back, boneless and spent. All my earlier worries retreat to the back of my mind. I gaze at Chance and only the deep flush underneath his perpetually tan skin lets me know how much our coming together undid him. Undid me.

Chance lays on his side, feet dangling off the bed, solemn

and quiet. I watch him look at my body, his hand moving, the constant motion of his fingers tracing my curves and lulling me into a comfortable silence.

We lay like that for several minutes, quietly enjoying being together . . . his hands seeking every crevice of me, finding what he needs. Chance fills the gaps of who I am, the wells of loneliness and walls of defense crumble before his tender exploration. I've found something new with him that's all mine. Separate from what's happened to me that I couldn't control. I'm the master of my feelings, my motivation, my life. I can choose how I feel. I'm not a bottle in the ocean any longer, going wherever the current takes me. I have a path now.

Chance.

His navigation of me is complete and I whisper the bravest thing I've done since my family's murder. My future shimmers before me like a lone star. I grab on to it as my feelings of happiness and rightness swell.

"I love you."

Chance rolls me into his body, kissing my forehead. "I held out in hope," he admits, a smile touching his lips.

I watch him look at me with his heart in his eyes as silent tears slip down my face, crawling through my hair and soaking my pillow.

He wipes each one away with a care that can't be possible.

Now I realize anything is.

SEVENTEEN

⌒

Chance

I wake, hearing a soft melody, and run my hand over the empty spot beside me, finding it bare and warm.

Brooke's gone.

Her notes tease me from below and I slip out of the bed, naked. I grab my jeans from the floor and pull them on, making my way to the bathroom. I hit the toilet and sink, brushing my teeth with Brooke's toothbrush, and walk to the kitchen. I rummage around as I listen to her play from the open basement door. I figure out how to use the ancient coffeepot and set it to brew.

Looking down from the top of the basement stairs, I notice the chipped gunmetal paint revealing slivers of amber spruce that bleed through on the solid treads that lead down to where we'd first been together. I walk down the flight of steps, ducking so I don't hit my head on the ceiling above.

I reach the bottom and watch Brooke play . . . listen. My

hand grips a floor joist above as one foot dangles above that last step I don't take.

The final note swells in the strange subterranean room, the low windows flooded with bright light as the sun slants through them, coating everything in a tangerine glow.

Brooke presses her head against the top of the piano, running long slender fingers over the keys reverently, and my gut tightens at her raw expression of sadness. That sick fuck didn't just take her family.

He stole her dreams.

Killing someone's spirit should be as illegal as murder. I swallow the ache caught in my throat.

Some sixth sense makes Brooke turn and she finds me standing there, her face breaking into a smile so broad, so real, it makes my chest tighten at her expression. Having that much love from a woman aimed at you is like a weapon. But only when you feel the same way about her.

And I do.

I walk to her and Brooke stands as my arms slip around her waist.

"Hey," she says in soft greeting. I put my head against hers, smelling the fresh scent of her, and underneath that—the smell of us.

"I made coffee."

Brooke tilts her face back, the sun caressing her eyes, taking the guesswork out of the color.

"I smell that," she answers, standing on tiptoe and nuzzling my neck. I take her face in my hands and stare into her eyes. "You have purple eyes y'know," I comment, running a finger from her temple to her jaw. I search her precious skin, thinking about where I want my mouth to be.

She blinks, then without flinching says, "That's why my middle name is Elizabeth. My mom"—she takes a painful swallow—"thought I looked like some actress . . ."

I snap my fingers, the name on the tip of my tongue. "Yeah, an old gal . . ."

"Elizabeth Taylor." Brooke shrugs and I watch the sway of her hips as she begins to move up the stairs. I chase after her and she giggles as I grope her from behind. The violet eyes, my last name. It's not until we're at the top that I realize she really could be Elizabeth Taylor.

If she were my wife.

"I saw that Fed guy on your phone," I say casually, grabbing the stack of mail off the table beside the front door and bringing it to her as she closes the basement door I left standing open.

Brooke's eyes move to mine. "What . . ." she snorts, then laughs, "going through my cell?"

I smirk. "Not exactly." I place the mail beside her and sit down at the small kitchen table. I rake my fingers through my hair, causing it to stand wildly. "I didn't want to wake you up after . . ." I move my hips forward and backward as I sit on the chair, making it groan with the motion. Brooke's lips curl.

"Nice . . . classy."

I lean back in the chair and lace my hands together on top of my head, giving her a speculative look. Holding back my grin hurts. "That's me, babe, all the way."

"You're a class-A slouch is what you are."

My eyebrows rise and the legs of my chair strike the floor. The grin takes possession of my face. "Take it back or I'll tickle you until you scream for mercy."

"No, sir, you should be fishing today," Brooke says in a coy voice, the table skittering as I grab her and she shrieks. The mail I'd carefully placed floats around us and lands on my head as I lower her to the floor gently. My thumbs are in her armpits and Brooke holds her breath.

"Don't you dare," she warns me, those cool lavender eyes glitter like diamonds shot through with violet fire.

"Ha!" I yell, working my hands into her sides, and she yelps, twisting and squirming.

Suddenly I'm eating at her lips, those noises of excited escape becoming contented moans.

We don't make it to the bedroom.

Brooke

I feel the weight of his lips like an echo of pressure and let my hand fall from my mouth as I remember our lovemaking.

And try not to feel guilty.

I don't feel worthy of this soaring happiness . . . not after all that's happened.

I fight with myself, the contrary emotions warring with each other. I'm not at peace. Yet . . . I want joy. Even if it is dark, I yearn for it.

The darkest joy is better than none at all.

Imperfect, vital . . . it comes like a thief in the night and robs your heart of its energy to resist the love that has been offered.

I watch Chance come to me, tenderly . . . brutally. The hallmark of consuming me with tenderness is a slow erotic devour.

"What are you thinking?" Chance asks, kissing his way from my ankle to my mouth.

I can't think . . . I'm barely breathing, but I answer. "I don't know if I deserve it . . . this," I say in a low voice, not meeting his eyes.

"Hey." Chance raises his head from my bare body, which he's just had every way a man can have a woman. And just the thought of what he's done makes heat rise to the surface of my skin like a brushfire.

He reaches out from between my legs, his face level with my belly button and cradles my chin, not letting me escape that seawater gaze. "You do . . . listen, Brooke . . ." Chance sighs and sits up, pulling me up to my knees then swiveling me around to be on his lap.

"Toss me around, why don't you?" I say and he smiles, but he's gone all serious.

"I thought we already did that?" He quirks a brow and my blush deepens.

"I love that you do that . . ." Chance says, kissing my temple.

He keeps his mouth on the side of my head, his lips moving against my skin. "You *do* deserve this. You're not responsible for what happened to your family, Brooke."

Then he takes a deep breath, saying the worst part of it. "You would only be dead too."

A crushing weight lifts from my chest, like I haven't been breathing before and now I can.

"I know," I whisper, admitting the deepest guilt of all. I want to live. I always wanted to.

"Don't feel guilty for surviving, for finding some god-damned happiness," he says in a fierce voice. "They're gone, Brooke. But we're alive. Here. Right now."

I look up at Chance and he meets my gaze, full of conviction, sincerity. "I never needed anyone until I met you."

"Okay," I say. And finally, I might mean it.

"You all right?" he asks.

I nod. "I'm going to clean up."

"Yeah, I've made you dirty . . ."

"You have," I say with a wink.

The hot water feels good as I open my mouth, letting it fill and slide down my chin. I lather my hair and wash my body, every part sore, tingling with that pleasant ache that follows great sex.

Mind-blowing sex.

I hear clattering around the cabin and step out of the anti-quated shower pan, small little hex tiles grabbing the water in the thin grout lines as I towel off.

I get dressed in jeans and a light tee, then pull over a wool sweater. I pad out to the kitchen and see muscular forearms buried in suds and say what I'm thinking, "That's sexy . . . Just sayin'."

Chance smiles and finishes with our chipped coffee mugs. The old speckled-blue enamel mugs drip on the antique por-celain drainboard, the handles curled to the base of the cups as suds and water slide down the integral ribs of the board and swirl into the basin.

"I do dishes," Chance says, wiping his hands off on a bright hand towel. "I save damsels in distress . . ."

I approach him, putting my palms on his chest for balance. "And you give great orgasms," I say.

"Yeah," he agrees, and swats my ass.

"You've got mail," Charlie says, pointing to the stack he straightened on the table after our interlude and I give a small frown. Did it get buried somewhere? I'm sure I've only got junk.

I see the Juilliard logo and my heart stutters. My head whips to Chance and he's grinning so hard I swear he'll chip a tooth. I grab the envelope, pressing it against my chest.

"What do you think it is?"

Chance just shakes his head. "Open it, Brooke."

I tear it open, then hesitate. Why would Juilliard be sending me mail? I've formally bailed on my scholarship, the final audition—missed.

I feel my heartbeat thump where the envelope is pressing against my chest.

The hell with it. I open the letter, scanning the contents. As I read I get more flustered, hot, agitated.

Happy.

I look up at Chance and he knows from my face.

"You got in," he says as a statement.

I slowly nod. "I don't know how . . ." Then a strange idea occurs to me. Or not so strange.

Lacey.

That turd.

I jog over to the table where I keep my banged-up cell and look at the messages. Jesus, there's ten from Clearwater. What's got his government-issue boxers in a twist? I ignore those, getting to Lacey and swipe her image. I wait as it rings.

Chance raises his brows. I shake my head, putting up a finger and he walks over as it's hanging there in the air and in a long pull . . . he sucks it into his mouth. Our eyes meet and Lacey answers.

"Hey ya!"

I startle and Chance begins working his way up my wrist with his lips.

Oh my God, does the man have a mouth? It should be illegal or bottled for sale. The thought makes me smile.

"Hello?"

"Hey Lace," I say and give a mock frown to Chance. He gets to the bend of my elbow and I melt. *Stop it,* I mouth and he releases my arm, stepping back.

We stare at each other.

I turn away or hang up on Lacey. Those are my choices.

"Are you okay? You sound like you're in a daze or something . . ."

I nod then realize she can't see it. "Listen . . . I know what you did."

Silence. "What'd I do?" she asks innocently.

She's so conniving, I know she did.

"You put my name in for Juilliard."

More silence.

"Please tell me you're not pissed, Brookie."

I wait, biting my lower lip, glancing at Chance, who's watching me across the room. I know why they call them bedroom eyes now.

He's got them. Uh-huh.

I look away again, hoping for concentration.

"No . . . not really."

"Are you okay? I mean, I know the FBI is there and . . . well, I've been worried."

"Why? I mean, besides the obvious. I know I was a mess when I left. And some stuff is happening . . ."

"What stuff?" she asks.

Stuff I don't want to talk about right now, over the phone, with my new hot boyfriend listening to it all. "We'll talk about it later."

"Oh dear baby Jesus . . . Have you, are you with *him*?"

Gawd, we're gonna do this.

I step outside and Chance gives me the space.

"Yeah," I say.

"Why are you whispering?" she asks in a whisper.

"I'm not."

"Right. Well, it sounds serious if you're whispering."

I huff and she ignores me.

I wait and so does she.

Fine. "I did . . . he's . . ." How do I begin to describe Chance?

"Hot?" she prompts.

"Yes." Hell yes.

"Good with his hands?"

Oh yes. "Yeah," I breathe out a syllable that sounds like an answer.

"Lace . . . I think." I stop and take a deep breath. "I think I love him."

"Your boss?"

"Yes."

"I don't know . . . Is this like insta-lust and you're getting all your parts all mixed up? Like your vagina and your brain? Sometimes those two switch places."

"No." *She has a point but she needs to simmer down . . .*

"Huh," Lacey says. A pause, then, "Okay, spill. Describe Alaskan Man."

I do.

"Wow. Okay, so he's your boss . . ."

"He fired me."

"God, that's hot. He wants you so bad he fires you. I can go with that."

"It had occurred to me as a good point."

"What about a job now?" Lacey asks.

I blow out air, the wisps of my hair floating then settling around me. "I think I'll have to use some of . . . my parents' money."

"It's about damn time. They'd want it for you, Brooke. You know they would. And they'd be so excited about Juilliard."

She's right, but I can't escape the knot in my throat.

"Oh!" she squeals and my heart skips a beat.

"What?" I ask.

"Agent Clearsign—"

"Clearwater . . ."

"Pssst . . . yeah, okay. Agent Dirtywater is starting to get on my last nerve."

I roll my eyes. "Starting to?"

"Okay, he's using it as a trampoline, 'kay? Just call him back. He said he sent you registered mail, left ten kazabillion messages. He's threatening to come up there."

"Or send someone here," I say, thinking Clearwater should back off now that an agent's here.

"He's just worried, Brooke. This freak is running around, killing families . . ." She trails off in the well of silence her reminder wedges between us, but finally finishes, "of Juilliard competitors . . . He wants the surviving family members accounted for . . . protected."

I think about it. I'm pretty well protected, way out here in the middle of nowhere, a state so far removed from the others they call it going "Outside" when anyone travels to the Lower 48.

I peek through the window at Chance, his head bobbing in a soft rhythm as he strums his guitar. My head turns to his vintage Hemi 'Cuda and it occurs to me that he must bring his guitar everywhere with him. I wish I could do that with a piano.

"Brooke!" Lacey's voice cuts through my mind fog.

"Huh?" I ask.

"Are you sleeping?"

I giggle and she sighs. "You're boning him to death, I get it. Pay attention," she says, snapping her fingers next to the phone. "I'm coming up there. I want to meet the stud muffin. I can't have someone replacing me, y'know. I must be Queen Bee in your affections."

That's it. I choke on my laughter, howling. That's Lace, so full of herself.

"Gawd, ya horndog. I'm coming. You're an unemployed

flake now, so when? You have no schedule and I live the life of leisure so I can breeze up there."

"What about your job?"

Silence.

"I got canned."

That's weird, I think. "Why?"

She sighs again and I get a mental image of Lacey blowing her pale hair off her forehead.

"Texting during work hours."

Imagine that.

"Yes, do come and meet"—I throw my hand over my mouth, lift it, and say quickly before the gales of laughter can take me away—"stud muffin."

"That's right baby, somebody's got to be in charge of the two of you."

I frown at that. I don't think Chance and I need any supervision. "Oh bullshittery, you just want to see if there's any more muffins in the bakery."

"True."

I laugh.

"I heard about the ratio. Lots of dudes, no chicks."

"That seems logical but so wrong on about fifty different levels."

"Uh-huh. Just the way I like it. I gotta run, but Brooke?"

"Yup?"

"I love your guts."

I pause, swallowing past the second lump today. "Me too."

There's a small silence, then, "Call Clearwater before I have to take his ass out."

"You got it right," I say in amazement.

"It happens . . . Bye, Brookie."

I listen to her click off. Turning around, I push through the front door and Chance leans the neck of the guitar against the handle of the fridge and pats his knee.

He gives himself away when he offers that crooked smile that warms me straight through to my toes.

EIGHTEEN

⁓

Chance

I've rescheduled my clients for today, but since they're out-of-towners like all my summer clientele, their time is limited and they didn't just smile and leave, they went away pissed.

Brooke's bad for business but a balm on my soul. She came in with the news that Lacey's coming for a visit. I say the more the merrier. Lacey's been there for Brooke, especially when she was unresponsive after her parents were killed, even as far as to anticipate when Brooke might be ready to attend Juilliard. From what Brooke says, Lacey must have poured on the charm to get Brooke excused from the rigor of protocol required for admission auditions. Of course, with the death toll rising, it's a no-shitter that a few of the competitors would be impacted.

It's worth manipulating my schedule for a day or two to be with Brooke. I look at her across the seat, my air freshener swinging from the radio's old-fashioned knob, the familiar red-tree shape an iconic staple of car owners everywhere.

She walks her fingers across the center console and laces my fingers with hers. "Where are we going?" Brooke asks.

"You'll see."

We're ten minutes from her aunt's small cabin and just about to my driveway when I see an SUV not so subtly tailing me.

It's that FBI dude.

Fine.

I turn into my driveway and cruise up the long curving asphalt driveway. Like my garage, it's an unusual component to Alaskan residency. But I have a unique existence created by circumstance, carved out through hard work.

My eyes move to the rearview and brazen as brass balls, Haller parks, sliding out of the car. His glasses are firmly in place, the tie knotted, his formality as strange as his presence.

Brooke gets out of the car and stands silently by it, not moving closer.

"Hello," I say and Haller moves forward, his eyes scanning my log cabin. If *cabin* is the correct descriptor. It's a five-thousand-square foot palace, some of the logs twenty-four inches in diameter. I can see him trying to make sense of it.

It's whatever, keep 'em guessing.

"Nice home you have here, Mr. Taylor."

"Thanks."

His eyes slide to Brooke and I move around the nose of the 'Cuda and stand beside her. This guy puts me on point faster than a hit on my hook.

"What's up?" I ask, my tone light, my words serious.

He cocks his head to the right, thinking. "I just need to

know Miss Starr's habits. If the killer decides to go after her, it only makes sense I'd want to anticipate when, where . . . how he plans to do so."

Sounds reasonable, I think. I can still feel a small frown overtake my face. Maybe sensitivity isn't high on his list, him just throwing out *killer.* Yeah, that shouldn't freak Brooke out. No-oh.

"You report directly to Clearwater?" Brooke asks.

He nods. "When there's need." The twin dark lenses of his sunglasses turn toward me. "You two dating?"

Subtle guy. I nod. "Yes," I answer, curling my arm around Brooke's shoulders and she leans into me.

Haller keeps staring and I keep saying nothing. Finally he nods. "How's your security on this place?"

"State of the art," I reply. Then, "Let me see your ID, Agent Haller."

He smirks and reaches into his breast pocket and my hand itches for the phantom gun that's no longer there, just instinct. Extreme, but there.

"I checked, Chance," Brooke whispers and I nod. "Humor me."

We meet halfway. He's tall too, our eyes meeting perfectly. Haller unfolds his billfold-style ID and I scan the holographic FBI emblem, his signature, and photo. My eyes catch on his picture, lingering. "Would you take off your glasses?"

The smirk turns into a condescending grin. I don't have to see his eyes to know. That's fine, he can't make me believe anything I don't want to. And right now, I'm skeptical as hell.

Haller removes his glasses and I stare back into a familiar face. He's Native like me, local. "Haller?" I ask in disbelief, every alarm bell going off. That's not Russian, it's not Native American, but he's local, but not from our region. I'm not liking pulling his teeth to get info.

"You're Native?" he asks, though he must know. His eyes, naked of the sunglasses, tell me what he thinks. "Not much blood quantum . . ." Haller comments with that condescending tone matching the smile that never reaches his eyes.

I feel my blood boil. "Enough," I answer in a terse word. I have enough to recognize him and I've certainly been through enough to know that I am. Regardless of my European bone structure and blue-green eyes.

"Chance?" Brooke asks, looking uneasily between the two of us.

"It's okay, just a little brotherhood discussion."

Haller smiles harder, no doubt taking in my coal-black hair and vaguely almond-shaped bluish-green eyes. Finally, he sees something that gives validity to my claim and he nods, rolling his shoulders into a dismissive shrug.

"I'll be around."

"You said that," Brooke says and he gives her an unfriendly look. "I do my job, Miss Starr. Nothing keeps me from that objective."

Dick.

Agent Haller give a nod to us both, sliding on those black lenses, shutting him off from our scrutiny as he gives a last look at my house and leaves as he came, in a contradiction of bold stealth.

Brooke waits until she can't see his car anymore then says, "God, what was all that posturing? You guys were like a couple of roosters or something."

"I like peacock better," I say absently, tightening my hold on her.

"You just wanted to say *cock*," Brooke says, fluttering those black eyelashes.

"Huh," I grunt. "Sounds like someone needs more tickling . . ." My eyebrows drop over eyes gone half-mast with bedroom thoughts, or anywhere she is up to.

"You just want to christen the place . . ." she says and laughs.

I nod; she's got me there. "Yeah," I reply, kissing the tip of her nose. We turn to walk through the garage and I catch myself glancing over my shoulder to the empty spot where Haller's car, as black as his unseen eyes, just disappeared.

So it's confession time. I can see it in Brooke's eyes, the curiosity killing the cat. She's not from around here, she doesn't know. What she does know is my place is not a typical fisherman's shack. I haven't asked her the details of the tragedy that's put that haunting look in her eyes, though I think she really needs to talk about it. Maybe giving her details of my life will bridge that gap.

"So," she says, running a finger down the glossy granite slab that covers my kitchen island, every surface mirrored, black and perfect. Knotty alder cabinets run standard height above the counters and touch the ceiling where pendant lights drop from deep amber logs to hover above the island where Brooke's eyes travel every surface. "Nice place," she says with dripping coyness.

I bark out a laugh. "Yeah."

"Drug dealer?" she asks and I laugh harder.

I manage to rein it in. "No." But my eyes sparkle.

She moves around the island, where I'm perched on a stool, and pushes between my legs. I get hard as she presses between them and my breath squeezes in my throat. "Pimp?" she debates softly.

"No," I reply just as soft, tucking her in tighter, pressing her against me with my hands at the small of her back. I groan into her hair. "You're killing me . . ."

"Not yet," she says. Then Brooke pulls away, her eyes back to serious. "Tell me where all this came from. It can't be fishing." She sweeps her hand out at my place.

I take her hand out of the air, looking at the short nails, clean and bare of polish, perfectly shaped. It's amazing to realize what she can do with those hands. I look up. "Fishing's a good living."

Brooke waits and I don't fill in what I don't want to say. "I hear a *but* . . ."

"We had a family business. Taylor Charters." I look at those perfect hands again, inhaling deeply. I don't want to hurt her, but the parallels won't be missed. Brooke becomes quiet, our bodies no longer pressed together but our hands are still intertwined. Her eyes are steady on mine. Encouraging.

"I was left behind because of my . . . age. My parents were longlining near Flat Island and got caught in a storm . . ."

I don't finish and she knows; her weighted silence fills the space. Just like that, Brooke knows. Tears fill her eyes, rolling a wet pathway down her face. They splatter on our linked hands. I release her and move my hands to her face, cradling it between my palms, the bottom of them meeting at her chin. "Hey," I say softly, forcing gentle eye contact with her swimming lavender sadness, "it's okay. It's been a long time."

Brooke takes a hitching breath. It sounds like a repressed sob. "How long?"

My hands drop and I tow her between my legs again and she lets me. "I was three."

Her eyes search mine for the grief but my parents' absence is what I remember, not really them, only the memory of their loss. "Who raised you?"

I laugh, I can't help it. "Well around here, sometimes when people are lost at sea . . . a lot of adults just pitch in." My eyes swing to hers again. "But I have a second cousin . . . you might have met him . . ."

Surprise pours over her face like a cup filled. "Holy shit." Brooke says the words in a whisper of breath. "Jake."

I nod confirmation.

"I love him," she says with a small laugh.

I chuckle. "I won't be offended, everyone does." I smile and she gives me a watery one back.

We sit silently for a few moments then I tell her the rest. "My dad was insured to the hilt, and Jake . . . well, you've met him. You notice how smart he is after a while—"

"But not right away," Brooke finishes for me and I nod.

"Yeah, he was the executor for my parents' estate as the next of kin and he invested it. When I turned twenty-one, the trust was released."

Brooke looks around again, taking in the high-end surfaces everywhere and laughs. "So you went hog wild?"

"Kinda," I say, pulling her so tight her breasts flatten against my chest, our heartbeats syncing. "Wanna see the bedroom?"

Brooke sighs, a lighter smile taking the place of the sad one.

"I thought you'd never ask . . . After all, it's not a proper tour without the bedroom."

"Riiight," I drawl and she gives that small secret smile I'm beginning to love.

Along with everything else.

Brooke

The last two weeks have been the happiest in recent memory. It's almost July and I've been fired from my job and survived a suicide attempt, and yet the grief that was drowning me like the waves I hear crashing from my open window is beginning to subside like a tide gone to sea.

And . . . here I am. In love.

My cell vibrates and I reach underneath my pillow, rolling over on my stomach as I swipe the icon.

Hey dumbass, Lacey says. *Remember me?*

Oh shit. *The time difference,* I think. She's at the airport. I groan, flopping onto my back, forearm tossed over my face.

I have fur on my teeth, I reply. *Ten minutes.*

Make it snappy, I'm dying here in hicksville.

I giggle. *KK,* I type for *okay.* I swipe *reply* and the message spirals out into the ether.

I drag on clean panties that I dyed last weekend at a tie-dye party down on the spit with Evan.

Chance had been fishing.

He wasn't happy with how I spent my day. I remember our conversation perfectly as I brush and spit toothpaste.

"What'd you do today when I was out bringing home the bacon?" Chance asks, stroking my face, our nakedness clinging together.

"Fish, you mean?"

"Oink," he says, sounding remarkably authentic.

"Tie-dye."

His eyebrows lift, then a look of remembrance comes over his face. "Oh yeah, the tie-dye thing at A Better Sweater." A furrow forms between his eyes. "Wait a sec, they sell hippie crap, handmade stuff. I didn't think they did that."

"Actually, it was in their parking lot. Y'know: pallets, pails, hoses, rubber bands. Lots and lots of rubber bands." Chance smirks. I switch subjects, with appropriate guilt. "How's Matt working out?" I knew it should be me working with him instead of flaky Matt.

Chance groans, kissing my nose. I think he's got a nose fetish, he's always kissing it. And a clit fetish . . . and . . .

He interrupts my thoughts. "Don't ask. He shows up when he's not hungover."

"Huh." I lick a path down his bare chest. His eyes go dark with heat, a look I know really well . . . a look I never get tired of seeing.

"What did you tie-dye?" he asks, his breaths coming shorter.

"Panties." I stop and look at him. I sit up on my knees, mine pegged between his legs as he looks up at me from the bed. I survey his muscular body, completely relaxed as he looks up at me, loving his eyes that change color like the sea, his inky

hair, his awesome muscles marked with the symbols of his ancestry. He watches me looking at him and I slowly roll down
the waistband of my yoga pants to reveal the brightly colored
band that used to be white and is now a riot of brilliant jewel
tones.

Chance gives a low whistle then drags me closer as he sits
up, plowing his hands into the back of my pants, grabbing my
butt. "I need a closer look!" he says loudly and I'm suddenly
underneath him, the muscles I'd admired straining against me,
caging me as his hand locks over my wrists and binds them
above my head. He inserts a finger underneath the top of my
pants and inches them down to reveal the beautiful pattern the
tie-dye made.

They clear my ass and his eyes flick to the panties underneath, then to me. "I love them . . ."

"But?" I asked, breathless.

"I like them better off."

He shows me just how much.

Afterward, he takes my wadded-up colorful underwear and
studies the pattern the rubber bands made against the cotton
fabric.

"You went by yourself?" he asks.

"No, Evan came too."

Chance looks at me, his fingers clenching around the vi-
brant fabric. "Evan helped you tie-dye your underwear?" he
asks, incredulous.

I nod.

"Hey, I don't want any guy touching your underwear but
me," Chance says.

"Are you serious?" I ask, slightly uneasy. I can't tell if he's kidding or not.

He leans over me, tucking me underneath him again, trapping me. "No."

Chance kisses me lightly on my lips.

He lifts his head, looking deeply into my eyes, his gaze reaching my toenails. "Yes," he says and moves his mouth over mine, hard.

I open to the bruising pressure of ownership his lips convey—demand.

He lifts his mouth, coming up for breath as I pant beneath him, my panties not there to soak up my arousal. He pushes his finger inside my wetness and I gasp, the intrusion as welcome as it is unexpected.

"Deadly," he says, his finger moving in and out of me as his mouth lowers to own mine again.

Chance proves something to me today. He is lighthearted when he needs to be and can switch gears if he wants to.

Deadly serious.

~

Lacey's at the Homer airport, trying for incognito and missing it by a mile. She has Seattle chic going on: yoga pants, platform flip-flops with a sparkle thong accent, also black, and an aggressive red cami peeking out from underneath her ebony tee. Large movie-star sunglasses cover eyes I know are a clear greenish brown.

"It's gotta be true love for me to brave that wacko journey of a hundred layovers," she says as soon as I come near. Her eyes start at my head and end at my clog-adorned feet. "What's happened?" she asks.

I look down at myself, seeing the metamorphosis of my wardrobe. Certainly Seattle's casual, but Seattleites would look positively uptight compared to the eclectic attire I've seen since coming to Alaska.

"What?" I say, a little self-consciously. Lacey's always been my rock. She's been there for every milestone, big or small. I don't know what I'd do without her. I want her to like what I'm wearing. It's stupid, I know . . . but she's really all the family I have left, and I want her to approve of my new life.

"It's like . . ." She shakes her head, puzzled, her finger tapping her bottom lip. "I don't know: hippie meets girly meets . . . fisherwoman?"

I grin suddenly. "You wait, girlfriend, you haven't seen anything!" I sling an arm around her.

"I can't wait," she replies in a droll voice.

Lacey gets over the shock of seeing the bus in all its psychedelic glory and gingerly slides her butt in. She looks around, her gear already in the cargo hold.

"You're full of surprises," she says noncommittally.

She grills me as I gush about Chance.

"So fisher boy is the new stud?" she asks and I give her a sideways glance, our conversation flowing easily as we wind down East End Road.

"It's Chance, and yes it's L-O-V-E."

Lacey rolls her eyes. "You're not even twenty-one; don't let a case of panty-dropping lust pull a brain fog on you."

I scowl and she shrugs.

We're quiet until we get to Aunt Milli's. "So this is the place Milli was always telling stories about."

I just nod, a choke threatening me. "Yeah," I manage.

Lacey studies me. "I thought you didn't like Milli."

I look at my hands. "I didn't but . . . I didn't want her dead. Then she gives me a house!" I say, sensing the guilt beginning to bubble to the surface again.

Lacey sniffs at the small cabin. Instead of going inside, she noses around the property. When she steps within sight of the outhouse, I can immediately interpret her expression of distaste. She eyes the weathered door, the classic half-moon cutout at the top of the door for ventilation that is now nothing more than decoration.

I don't remember Lacey being this stuck-up. I don't remember feeling so much like an adult either.

I sigh. "It *is* sort of small . . ."

"And . . . awful," Lacey says, sympathy thick in her tone of voice.

I stop. And look critically at the cabin. I've been here almost two months now, Independence Day around the corner, and as I look at the cabin I realize what it represents now.

Home.

I haven't felt right in my own skin for more than half a year . . . and finally, I do.

It's not the six-thousand-square-foot house of my upbringing. But that was filled with my family—our memories. And they're not there anymore so it's not home. Milli's home is fresh and new, at least for me. She was part of my family and a piece of them remains within these four walls, but the house's existense doesn't define them. It's a place of good memories, not the ones I've left behind. So I don't give a shit if it's small . . . it's not awful. Nowhere near.

Lacey sees my expression and regret slides over her features, a shadow of something else chased away before I know what it is.

Maybe better I don't.

"Oh, Brookie . . . I'm so sorry. I . . . *fuck*. I'm an ass."

"Yeah," I say with a nod.

We stand in awkward silence, the buzz of bees lighting on the wildflowers a typical comfort for me. But my heart's full.

To breaking.

Lacey takes my hand. "You know how much I love you?" Her eyes flood with emotion, brimming with sincerity.

I nod, my eyes dry.

"Come on . . . show me the rest."

"Okay," I say, but my heart's not in it. I want Lacey to love Alaska as I've come to love it.

Then I realize: would I love it as much if Chance weren't a part of it?

NINETEEN

~

Chance

The weather is made to order. I've just gotten off a run of three days of balls-to-the-wall fishing, 6 a.m. to almost 9 p.m. of solid sea time, and I'm ready to meet Brooke and Lacey at the Dawg. They've been able to get plenty of girl time in while I've been working. *My turn.*

Maybe Evan can stop worrying about my girlfriend's panties and distract himself with Lacey.

I drive up to the Dawg in the 'Cuda, parking it carefully, tight against an old outdoor streetlamp, my hair still damp from the shower and clinging to the back of my neck like a wet hand. I'm so ready to feel Brooke in my arms I almost forget my guitar. I swing back around, gripping the chrome handle and lifting it as the back door swings open, smooth and heavy. I grab the neck of my guitar and take it out, closing the door. I look at the pool of light cast by the streetlamp and chuckle to myself. As bright as the sun is at 10 p.m., the illumination value is beyond weak. I still like my car packed in tight against something that won't beat the hell out of it with a swinging door.

I stride to the Dawg, the smell of booze, residual smoke, and old wood carry outside, greeting me in a memory trigger of nostalgia. The Salty Dawg will always be the place I first played my music in front of others.

I move inside the gloomy interior, the small, four-pane-divided windows allowing little light to grace the interior. I scan the saloon for Brooke and find her . . . and her friend Lacey.

I note Lacey is good-looking. It takes me about three seconds to lose interest; my eyes are all for Brooke. But Evan's noticed Lacey and is clinging like a fly to shit.

Perfect.

Her blond hair is styled in that overly coiffed way that I think looks like ass, affected. My eyes move to Brooke; her softly waved hair has an untrained and natural look. My gaze doesn't end there but travels to her tight jeans, formfitting cami with a sheer top thrown over it. It's a soft purple color that makes me wish we were outside so I could see her better. Lacey's been a good influence, I notice. I finish my visual sweep at Brooke's high-heeled shoes and smile. Girls don't usually wear heels in Homer. Brooke wore Xtratufs the two times she worked for me and now wears just clogs. Yet here she is in heels and a top so sheer I couldn't tear my stare away from her if I tried.

Brooke smiles, turning her head to whisper something to Lacey, and the two girls' hair mingles together, one black and one like dark gold. Lacey glances my way and giggles. Then Brooke stands and meets me in the middle of the packed bar. My hand has a tight hold on the guitar, but I use my other hand to drag her close. I lean my head down to her neck, closer now from the extra height of the heels.

"You look hot," I say into her ear, the talking all around us loud, way above white noise.

"Thank you," Brooke says, moving sideways until her thigh touches my hard-on. Now bigger thanks to her maneuvering.

I laugh. "Alert: banana in pants."

Brooke's eyes drop. "I like bananas," she says, perfectly deadpan.

I groan—*no shit?*

Suddenly Lacey is there and I move Brooke in front of me, hiding my dick. Her ass moves up against my hardness.

No improvement.

"Nice," I hiss good-naturedly.

"Welcome," she chimes.

Lacey looks puzzled then sticks her hand out. I take it over Brooke's shoulder.

"Brookie's told me so much about you . . ." Her eyes sparkle with humor.

"Brookie?" I ask.

Brooke nods with a short laugh. "We've been best friends since—"

"—kindergarten," Lacey finishes for her as Evan walks up, two drinks in hand.

I raise my brow. "Twenty-one." Lacey answers my unspoken question. She takes the glass from Evan, sipping the cola-colored drink through twin tiny red straws, a cherry centered on top of the ice. "Yum, yum," Lacey says, perfectly pivoting into Evan, her hand on the center of his chest for balance. "Lacey says thank you."

"Simon says come dance with me," Evan says, his mop of

hair pulled back in a ponytail at his nape. A spiral of hair escapes as I watch, as if it refuses the captivity.

"Simon says yes," Lacey purrs. She flutters her fingers at me. "Nice to meet ya . . . Chance."

She saunters off, subtly shaking her ass . . . balanced on heels as fragile as Brooke's.

"Interesting girl," I say. My mind's not made up. But she gets a tally mark on the good side for distracting Evan, though she comes across as brittle somehow. Not fragile, but somehow breakable. Unsteady.

Brooke turns into my arms, and I switch hands with my guitar. "We're totally different, but she's . . ." Brooke bites her lip. "She's the only thing that kept me alive . . . after."

I nod. Tonight isn't about solving the problems of the world, psychoanalyzing Brooke's friends . . . or any of that happy horseshit. It's about being near Brooke, jamming a set, and later . . . being with Brooke.

I smile so wide my cheeks make that creaking sound when you can't grin any harder.

"What's that for, Chance Taylor?" Brooke asks, the smoky coal liner on the tops of her eyelids making that purple gaze look even more arresting. I give a hard swallow, very aware of every part of her body pressing against every part of me.

"Happiness."

Brooke puts the side of her face against my chest. I strain to catch her next words. "Me too."

I tow her behind me, pulling out a chair right in front of where I'll play my guitar. For her.

For us.

I systematically tune my guitar as I do each time I play at the Dawg. When I look up, Brooke's eyes have found my fingers. Her gaze tells me that she's thinking about something other than my playing.

I smile, strumming a chord, and it's her turn to swallow with a dry click I can't hear but see as her delicate throat convulses.

Lacey breaks the sensual tension of the moment, sliding in next to Brooke as Evan sits by her side.

He smirks, giving me a down-low middle finger. I lift my chin. It's okay. I have the faintest glimmer of hope we can move past our butting heads over Brooke.

I play the song that's been on a constant loop in my mind since the moment I knew Brooke had captured me like a fish in my own net: "*Spin.*"

I slowly pick notes on my guitar and the buzz of the saloon grows quiet. I pick up more notes until the chords run into one another and narrow, the melody becoming singular, focused. Brooke's eyes lock with mine and I begin to sing, softly at first, then in a ringing baritone that's meant for her, only her, and I watch her reaction, her cheeks flushing.

"*On the waves of an ocean . . . I can see your inner motive . . .*" I keep my focus on her with steely resolve, every plucked note and strummed chord aimed at her like an arrow, every note I sing wringing out my emotion for the whole place to see. Raw, open.

"*When you wear it on your face . . . indisposed to the world . . .*"

I change the last line, tailoring it for us, my voice going low with the resonating emotion. "*Let yourself be saved . . . by me . . .*"

I hit the last note like a broken heart now healed by love—whole and perfect.

The final note dies and Brooke stands up suddenly, her purse falling to the ground, and I lean my guitar against the log pole that runs floor to ceiling beside where I played.

Brooke runs to me and clasps my face between her hands, and the moment heats—real and alive. Then she wraps her arms around my neck and I lift her off the floor.

I tighten my arms around her as I smile into her shoulder.

The bar erupts in applause and Brooke leans her face away from me, her eyes wet with tears.

And I know we've found it. Both of us.

The joy in the darkness.

Brooke

I'm laying uncomfortably, my head leaning against Chance's shoulder on the drive home as the center console's various parts dig into my side.

I want to touch him so much I don't feel the discomfort, only a thrill of happiness that starts from deep inside and spreads like fire through my body.

He wraps his arm awkwardly around my body, pressing his wrist against my head, pushing me tighter against him, and I feel so lucky for this moment I could die.

I almost did. But for Chance, I would have.

Between Lacey arriving and Chance's guitar nod in front of the crowd, I didn't have a single thought about my family for an entire day. A first.

Chance pulls into his garage and parks the car, turning off

the engine. He slips away from me, charging around the car and ripping the passenger door open. I get up on my knees, eager, wanting. I salivate with anticipation, like before biting into a piece of ripe fruit.

He scoops me up easily and I wrap my legs around his waist, eating at his mouth. If he had words, I took them. My legs squeeze around Chance and he stumbles for the door.

He pushes it open and it swings back behind us, slamming into place. Chance strides with me around his body like a monkey and dumps me on the couch. The ottoman sits beneath me, slid into the center of the sectional like a full-size bed. Perfect.

I gulp air and he strips his shirt off, flinging it to the ground as I count the shadows his abs cast, licking my lips, taking in all of him like the first dessert I've ever seen.

"I love that look," he says, his eyes never leaving mine.

"What look?" I ask, unzipping my jeans. Chance bends down over my feet, his large hand circling my ankle, and he slowly takes my high heel off. His finger strokes my anklebone in a seductive circle that causes warmth to spread and pool just where I want it.

I gasp in a laugh.

"Am I wrong?" he asks.

"No," I shake my head, my hair partly covering my face. Chance moves it out of my eyes and tucks it behind my ear.

We look at each other as I sit up, grabbing the waistband of his jeans while he grips my upper arms. I tear the buttons open on his Levi's and suddenly his penis springs free and my eyes rise to meet his as he wraps his hands in my hair and I can feel myself go wet . . . The pleasure of his hiss of breath when I touch the tip of him makes the heat inside me grow, moisten.

He pushes me back on the widest part of the couch and I watch him crawl toward me, moving until he's suspended above me. "Spread your legs, Brooke."

I do, my legs trembling. But instead of coming inside, he splits my lips with his penis. Spreading me gently, he uses my own wetness as a lubricant, and rocking against my clit, he moves back and forth softly. Chance has his palms planted on either side of my body, driving against me . . . back and forth, faster and faster until the delicious friction swells and I hang on that chasm that comes right before a shattering orgasm.

Chance withdraws and I feel him at the center of me. I pull my legs back, my knees by his ears. "Brooke . . . god," he says, beginning to press wonderfully inside me. Slowly surging forward and drawing back, he puts his palms on the back of my thighs . . . my feet like earrings for him.

Then he's fully inside me with a single thrust and I scream my pleasure into his quiet house, absorbed by all that wood and I come until I can't breathe. The pulses of my orgasm radiate through my tingling body and wash over Chance, grabbing at him as he grows impossibly harder, his own release crashes into him as he pours himself into me. We both gasp, my fingertips digging into his broad shoulders, his arms pulling me closer as he moves inside the deepest part of me, our pulsing orgasms dragging us together tighter.

Chance holds me as the heat subsides, our spent bodies clasped together as he folds his body over mine. My noodle legs dangle over his thighs as he sits up and gently slides out of me. I stay like that, our chests pressed together, slick with sweat, our damp foreheads touching as our breathing slows.

"Brooke."

"Yeah," I choke out. Because my voice won't work. Or my legs. Or anything else. I'm like a pool of languid bones covered by skin that's strung together by a thread of love.

I shut my eyes. My feelings are so overwhelming, I don't even know if I can compartmentalize them all . . . I don't even try.

"I love you," Chance says.

Three words.

The worst words ever. So scary. So necessary.

So everything.

"I love you too," I reply and that broken piece of my heart that began to mend the first night he kissed me, that hole that was there—it's finally closing.

~

Chance has the biggest tub I've ever seen and he tucks me into it, hot and steaming, and I look up at him, my face wet and flushed from the heat of the water and other things.

I hold my hand up, beckoning him. "Come on, fisherman . . . join me."

He shakes his head. "I've never even used a tub . . ."

I pop up out of the water. "Then you have to!"

He sits down on his haunches. Reaching out with his fingertip, he rolls my wet nipple and I feel a tingle in my core and give a slow smile. I could go again. No, I'd be sore. No, I could go again. I laugh and he dips his head to lick the hard pebbled flesh, slowly sucking my nipple. He lifts his head just enough to say, "Naw, I can cook for you . . ."

Well *damn*. I groan but let him off the hook as my stomach does a low growl. Hard to argue with that. I nod my head. He's too good to be true. "Okay," I say.

He laughs at my noisy belly. "Besides, a girl can't live on bananas alone," he says, winking.

"Ha!" I laugh, thinking I'd blow bubbles at him if he had any. Instead I lather up then sit back, relaxing.

Chance looks at me a heartbeat longer, then he walks away, whistling.

I grin like a fool, lying in the water as it gradually cools. The wonderful aroma of whatever Chance is cooking begins to infiltrate my senses when my cell buzzes.

I look across the bathroom and there it sits, half out of my jeans pocket. I get out of the tub, wrapping a towel around me, and make my dripping way to where the cell is. I pluck it out of my jeans and look at the text.

Get lucky? Lacey asks.

Always. I hit *reply*.

She sends a smiley face. *That makes two of us.*

I gasp, covering my mouth. *OMG . . . you did Evan?!*

Yeeeeaaahhhh comes her reply.

Catch ya at the cabin she says.

I send a winking smiley with a heart.

Why not? Love's in the air.

TWENTY

~

Chance

"So, Lacey . . ." I say as a question and meet Brooke's eyes.

She twirls the red wine in the glass and I chuckle. "Contributing to a minor."

Brooke meets my eyes. "Not for long."

"When's your birthday?"

Brooke rolls her eyes. Now I gotta know. "When?" I ask. Then, "Unless you want another tickling session?" I ask, cocking my brows, ready and able.

More than ready.

Her voice drops low, those purple eyes darkening, and I lean across the kitchen table, the better to catch her words. "Will it end like last time?"

"It can," I say.

We stare at each other, then her face breaks out into a big grin. "Independence Day."

I put my palms on the table. "Really?"

"Yeah," she says softly.

"Well that's cool."

There's a cavernous silence and I reach for her hands across the table, knotting them up with mine. I bring one of her hands to my mouth, kissing it softly.

"You need to talk about it, Brooke."

She doesn't lift her eyes, move . . . breathe.

Then, "I was late."

I wait.

Brooke seems to gather herself together, piece by laborious piece, shoring herself up. She takes a deep breath. "It was Christmas break and I was going over the pass, shitty conditions."

I raise my brows.

"Oh." She flicks her eyes away for a moment, remembering. "Interstate 90—Snoqualmie Pass. It crosses the Cascade Mountains in Washington State."

I nod and she goes on. "Anyway, I was on my cell with my mom. She was giving me shit about staying safe and I was missing . . . y'know . . . home—but still kinda irritated about all the 'Brookie be safe' stuff."

Her eyes rise to meet mine. Steady and solemn. I look back levelly. If she can tell it, I can listen. She continues. "And then I heard the doorbell in the background." I watch her take three deep breaths, letting them out slowly, each one seeming more painful than the last, and I squeeze her hands. She looks over my shoulder at some distant spot in the past only she can see.

"I could hear him hurting my family." Her eyes well with tears. "My brother—" She jerks her hand out of mine and covers her mouth. Her horror—mine.

"It's okay, it's not happening now," I tell her.

Brooke nods in quick succession, trying to convince herself.

"Hey," I say, moving around the table to sit beside her on the four-seater bench. I put my arm around her. "I'm here."

"I know," Brooke says, leaning against me. I press my lips to her fragrant hair, still smelling of the soap I use. We sit like that for several moments, then she tells the rest.

"I heard glass crashing and the phone . . . Mom dropped the phone then . . . he . . . killed her."

I wait more. It needs to come from her without urging.

"He picked up the phone. I'll never forget his breathing into that phone." Brooke shudders and I tighten my arms around her.

"And now he might be here . . . somewhere."

"I'll protect you," I say . . . and know that I will. I'd kill anyone who touched a hair on her head. "Besides," I say, stroking her silky hair and tucking her head underneath my chin, "Hardass is watching."

Brooke pulls away, her laughter breaking through the wetness that covers her face like the remnants of a sad storm. "It's Haller, Chance." She shakes her head, a small smile ghosting her lips. "That reminds me of Lacey."

I frown. "How?"

"She can never get Agent Clearwater's name right either."

I smile. Us Alaskans—not much for authority.

"So let's celebrate!" I say, turning her around to face me. I jerk her legs apart and scoot her ass close to my open legs. I straddle the bench and throw her legs over each of mine, putting my hands on the small of her back.

"Celebrate what?" Brooke asks softly, wrapping her arms loosely around my neck.

"Your birthday," I answer, kissing the tip of her nose. It's beautiful and part of her face. Somehow, each little kiss is my way of healing Brooke's many wounds.

Let me heal you, I think, *my mouth speaking for me.*

"It's ten days away."

"Well let's plan then."

She thinks, rolling her bottom lip into her teeth, nibbling on it. I swallow again. Brooke just jacks me up. Any. Little. Thing. "It *is* the big two-one."

"Yeah," I say, my lips going to her throat, then moving up to her jaw.

She tips her head back, giving me better access. Her skin's still moist from the long bath, smelling vaguely of my soap and beneath that, Brooke. I lick and peck along her jawbone and she gives a tight little moan.

"Hungry?" she asks.

"Always," I answer, my hand wrapping the nape of her neck as her lips find mine, the kiss deepening into something more.

"I have to get back to the cabin . . ." she says, even as she strips my shirt off my body. Her words say no but her hands say yes. I dig nonverbal clues.

I move closer, standing with her legs wrapped around me, and Brooke lets my shirt slide to the floor.

"Why?" I ask, already moving to my bedroom.

"Lacey . . ." she says without strength.

"She'll live," I say as I move through my bedroom door

and lay Brooke down as I lower myself on top of her. My body lays cradled between her legs, every bit of me against all of her.

"Yeah," she agrees in a whisper.

"Besides," I say, my fingers trailing down her jaw then moving into her hair, "we finally get to try out *my* bed . . ."

Brooke gives a sardonic laugh. "Novel idea."

"We'll risk it," I say.

We do.

Brooke

I watch Chance's car rumble down my driveway, leaving me at the cabin, and I'm already bereft at his departure.

I've got it bad. So . . . so bad.

I stand out on my front porch and sigh like a lovesick puppy.

Lacey joins me. "God . . . damn. What a shitty hostess you are," she comments.

"Yeah," I agree. I turn to her and notice she seems energized. I feel my brows quirk "I'm sorry . . . I'm crazy about Chance," I answer.

Lacey crosses her arms across her chest. "Or just crazy." Her eyes rest on me with that strange intensity that's riding her.

She's the one that's acting crazy, so I switch topics to avoid a lecture; don't want it. "I'll be better. Promise."

She raises her perfectly plucked eyebrows. "You better." She lifts a finger and I feel my face conform into a tight smile. I'm not escaping without something.

But she surprises me by not talking about Chance. "Have you been practicing?"

I shrug. "Some . . . but not like before."

"Listen, about Juilliard . . ."

My eyes snap to hers. "Yes . . . what about Juilliard?"

"I want what's best for you, Brookie."

I cast my eyes to my feet, my pink flip-flops looking so out of place on the weathered rustic porch. It should be cowboy boots or . . . something.

"I know you do, Lace."

"I'm so sorry about your family," she says.

I breathe deeply. In and out. "Thank you, I know . . . I have no idea how you did it, but I know that you got the Juilliard thing turned around so at least I can have that. I might even be ready to play again." In front of an audience. Without my family.

Lacey doesn't say anything and I look at her.

Finally, she nods. "Your happiness is super important to me and when you took off to this—Lacey sweeps her palm around—"godforsaken place, I got desperate and threw myself at their mercy, playing on the tragic circumstances."

Not too difficult, I think.

"When they said yes and that they'd be sending you the welcome-aboard packet, I booked the first flight."

"And porked the first guy," I say, and Lacey smiles.

"Yeah," she says, and a mild red creeps up her neck and settles into her face. "That was fun."

"Fun?" I ask.

"Well sure . . . I want an Alaskan man too. Y'know, ratio and all."

We smile at each other.

~

Lacey's gone out to be with Evan with promises of being back home at the cabin by midnight.

I realize that I've found a rare moment of solitude. Chance is still fishing and Agent Haller is skulking around somewhere.

I pick up my cell, seeing another message from Agent Clearwater.

I heave a great sigh. I can't hide my head in the sand any longer.

He deserves for me to respond to him. Even if his fellow agent is responsible for me, Clearwater is the one who has come against every wall I've thrown up, still advocating for me.

I need to call him.

First, I cruise through the messages.

Shame hits me like a well-aimed fist when I listen to the first one, over two weeks old by now:

Miss Starr, this is Agent Clearwater. There've been some ongoing developments in the case that I'd like to discuss with you at your earliest convenience. Phone me please.

He recites his number.

I click on the next one.

Hi, Miss Starr, Agent Clearwater again. Did you get my last message?

My guilt sharpens when there's two more of those.

Then: *Miss Starr, because of your continued nonresponsiveness, I have sent a certified return receipt letter. Please phone me the instant it's in your possession.*

I stand, walking over to the table and look for the envelope with all the colorful attachments for delivery confirmation.

I can't find it. All the other mail is where Chance left it, but not the piece I need. I swear he set it on top of the table. I run a finger over the brightly gold-speckled cream Formica, the chrome ribbon border catching on my flesh and drawing a drop of blood. I suck it off my finger, my eyes scanning the interior of the cabin.

I frown as a prickling disquiet surrounds me. It seeps into my body like the sea did on that fateful night Chance saved me.

I listen to Clearwater's final message, my hand losing feeling as I clutch the cell against my ear.

Brooke, I have sent an agent for your protection. We believe that the killer is moving toward you. And . . . we know who it is. We've enlisted the local police to contact you as you won't contact us. Please respond.

That message was left yesterday.

The killer is moving toward you.

I move my thumb over the icon to call Clearwater back as a knock on my door thunders against the wood and I jump.

Shit, I think, moving to the door in slow motion as I slip the phone inside my back pocket.

I press my ear against the wood and say, "Yes?"

"Brooke!" a male voice yells through the wood.

I know that voice. I've never heard it yell, I've never heard it in terror. I recognize it anyway.

I open the door and Agent Haller staggers in, blood pouring out of his mouth like a faucet let go. He slams into me and I stumble under his weight, both of us going down to the floor. He lands on top of me and knocks the wind out of my lungs and I grunt, unable to breathe.

As though from a great distance I see a large knife hilt standing at attention, the blade buried inside his back. The blood runs down his federal-issue threads, pooling beside us like a small lake. From inches away, Agent Haller no longer looks smug.

He looks scared.

Haller's mouth opens and closes like a great gasping fish. He's trying to say a word as my lungs burn for oxygen and his blood slicks our bodies together. I am helpless beneath him. Pinned by his weight, aching to breathe.

"Lay . . . lay . . . lay . . ." he says.

Movement is captured in my peripheral vision. I turn my head, blackness and shock eating at the edges of a brain gone fuzzy, like I'm thinking through Swiss cheese.

Lacey appears over his body as he stammers those syllables over and over.

Thank God, I think as my body recovers, taking a painful first breath. I suck in a lungful, relief sweeping through me. She can get help.

Then in my bewildered state it occurs to me that she's not with Evan.

Suddenly, in one swift movement, she jerks the knife out with both hands, her long nails contrasting against the blood on the blade.

I lie there, the blood roaring in my ears like a great flood, my heartbeats a smothering too-fast rhythm inside the tightness of my chest, my bladder threatening to let go—my terror so great it has its own texture.

Taste.

Suddenly it hits me. *Lay.* Lacey. He'd been trying to warn me.

Her legs are spread and planted on either side of Agent Haller's dying body. Lacey's eyes have a fevered look to them when she slams the blade down into his back, the sound of tenderized meat as it sinks home makes me turn my head and throw up while Haller lies on top of me, bleeding. I retch until my vision triples and nothing else comes out.

The mess I make mixes with the blood from the Fed who lays dying above me.

His eyes meet mine . . . the light inside them fading as his lashes brush his cheek and his head lowers to my chest, his body growing heavy.

With the stillness of death.

I close my eyes; wetness is all around me. The metallic scent of blood thickens the air as I hear the knife find its target and my body takes some of the impact, moving with each stab.

Again and again. Then it stops.

I know when I hear her breathe.

I'd recognize it anywhere.

TWENTY-ONE

~

Chance

I'm whistling to distract myself from how badly I want to be with Brooke.

But fishing can't wait forever. I slice the last one open, hosing off the sea lice, blood, and other disgusting shit, and it runs where I put it, where the pressure of the water directs it. I flop the two fillets, cheeks, and other edibles in my cooler that sits on top of the fish dolly and close the lid. I squint against the low sun, catching the glint of metal as Matt soaps up the hull of the boat with a long-handle brush and nod to myself. At least that chore doesn't await me.

Brooke.

I begin whistling lyrics for a song that's been threading through my mind . . . about love. About her. It looks like something has finally taken the sea away—it no longer calls as strongly.

I hear a clanking of running steps down the plank. They sound strange because the tide's out, making it steep like a ladder.

I look up in time to see a tall man in a suit, a fish out of water, so to speak, jogging down the steel ramp on as dead of a run as a person can manage when it's that vertical.

My gut seizes.

I'd recognize him anywhere. He's the Fed from the phone. From Brooke's cell. The icon tile matches the face, though in the phone there is no fear in his expression: Marshal Clearwater. His black suit jacket flies behind him like a sinister short cape, revealing a gun, snug in its holster.

He reaches the bottom, his head whipping first left then right.

His eyes fall on me with an ominous weight. A buzzing pressure begins in my head. I shake the vertigo that threatens and jog to meet him.

We're an arm's length apart and I notice how black his eyes are, the angles of his face arranged in a way I instantly recognize: Native American.

Not from Alaska.

My scrutiny lasts long enough that it can be counted in seconds, a wound at his neck looking like death has brushed him closely.

My eyes collide with his. "Brooke," I say as both question and statement.

He nods. "Chance Taylor?"

I nod.

"We need you."

I don't wait for an engraved invitation. I leave the fish in its bed of ice.

Frozen and dead.

Agent Clearwater introduces himself as we make our way up East End. One hand wraps the steering wheel so tightly it chases the blood from his knuckles.

"What the fuck is going on?" I begin, forgetting that he's the highest of the law and I'm in his care. He doesn't skip a beat.

Please tell me Brooke's okay. The tension makes my body feel like one solid line of cement, cold and deep—impenetrable.

He doesn't answer right away, instead he gives back story. "In all three homicides there was one pattern that we couldn't make work." His eyes slant my way, his longish hair shifting as he does, then his gaze hits the dirt road again. The shadows make it seem like night when true twilight is still hours away.

"All the families knew the killer. No forced entry, no clue, warning . . . no foresight for the potential for violence."

Interesting at any other time, but now, *who gives a rat's ass?* "Is Brooke okay?" I have to know . . . she's who I breathe for now—live for. The thought of her . . . gone—not possible.

Unacceptable.

His face swivels to mine for a heartbeat, a moment longer. "No."

Jesus—*fuck.* My stomach feels hot and greasy, the food I sucked down for a fast supper threatening to go back up the way it came.

"Then there was the method. The knife work took skill. An accuracy born from practice. When forensics came back with spatter patterns and hand dominance we knew we were no longer looking for a man."

"Serial killers aren't women," I say, trying to convince my-self. Talk instead of puke. Sounds like a plan. My hand slaps the oh-shit handle as we make a corner at forty that should be twenty, the tires lifting. Clearwater's eyes tighten as he checks his speed, the SUV's tires settling, then presses on the gas pedal again.

Insanity.

Brooke.

"No, they're not, usually. But sometimes . . . they are. It's rare, but it does occur. Usually in a male-female pair—"

"Who is it?" I interrupt.

I fight not to punch Clearwater in the chops. Fuck: they're the cops, couldn't they have done something to keep her safe?

Couldn't I?

I've been thinking she's safe while she couldn't be in greater danger.

"Lacey Colbert."

Fuck me, I think, my body breaking out in gooseflesh. Fuck-ing Lacey. Brooke's best friend. I try to wrap my head around that psycho morsel.

It can't be true.

We pull up in front of Milli's cabin, yellow tape like a por-tentous snake winds and twists in front of the porch.

Still, I fight what he's told me. Anybody would. "No, man . . . She's been her best friend since kindergarten. They told me that." I look at him, begging for a different answer, thinking how vulnerable Brooke is with the killer living with her.

"She's more than that, Mr. Taylor," Clearwater says. He

clears his throat, looking over to Milli's cabin as I rip off the belt and my hand goes for the door.

He stays my progress, gripping my forearm.

"Take your fucking hand off me." My voice comes out like a growl, and I hardly recognize it as my own.

Obsidian marbles glitter back at me. "I know you're upset. But Lacey's not here. I need you in the right state of mind so we can find her. Your panic doesn't help us." His eyes search mine and I release the handle. I'm not fucking panicked . . . I'm pissed. Pissed at the circumstances, myself . . . and that nutcase, Lacey.

Brooke.

"She's never been a friend to Brooke. She's . . . obsessed."

My head whips to his. "What?"

He sighs, raking a hand through his hair. He scoops it to his nape and expertly ties it in an elastic band. With his face naked of hair, it looks almost brutal in its angles and planes; the eyes burn with keen intelligence.

"Our field office got permission to search the Colbert home when we had enough evidence to support our suspicions."

"And?" I ask, my hand still gripping the handle of the car.

Clearwater looks at me. "Lacey Colbert is a sick girl. She has every newspaper clipping, photograph, award . . . every scrap of any kind that pertains to Brooke Starr in a hidden shrine in the family attic. And that's just the beginning."

I groan, my head falling back against the headrest on the seat.

I watch the wind move the tape and my eyes burn with tears that I won't shed. Weeping in frustration won't save her.

Brooke's with that psycho bitch.

"What can I do?" I finally ask, the fine trembling of my body begging for action . . . begging to rescue Brooke.

Clearwater looks at me. "Our Anchorage division liaison is dead."

He sees my expression and expounds. "Haller knew who we were looking for . . . I don't know how she got close, anything. He was the expert on this community and we'd been trying to reach Brooke along all the regular channels without success." Clearwater looks around at the rugged landscape, the dense trees, the endless sky, as we hear the crashing ocean below.

"Lacey killed Haller?"

He nods.

How would Lacey kill a trained FBI agent? Women aren't capable of that, are they?

Apparently . . . they are.

My mind moves furiously over the details of meeting her. The sharp gaze, the snarky humor. But always, her restless eyes moving over Brooke.

"Fuck . . . Evan."

"A friend?" Clearwater says.

Kinda. We'd been on the outs because of Brooke, but I'd hoped it was coming around when Lacey entered the scene.

"She hooked up with him last night."

"Yeah," Clearwater says softly.

"No," I say, though I know.

"We haven't identified the male yet, but there's been a stabbing . . . Local police have their hands full in a town that normally doesn't see murder."

They've seen it now.

"Are you sure it's Evan?"

I listen to Clearwater's description. The blond hair and tie-dye apparel give it away.

I hang my head, my chin dipping to my chest. I batten down the hatches on my emotional turmoil, guilt being number one. "Okay . . . What do you need?"

"We need the ten-minute geographical lesson. We're betting that she's familiar with all of this." Clearwater sweeps his hand around the area.

"What makes you so sure?"

"I would be." I look at his serious eyes and think instantly of backup. "I have a couple of people that can help me," I say and he nods.

"We're beyond keeping this under wraps. The longer she has Brooke, the closer it comes to . . ."

Clearwater doesn't finish, but his eyes carry the words easily. Like an unseen wind. You can't see it but you know it's there by the damage.

I text Tucker . . . Then I call Jake. If the three of us can't find Brooke then there's no hope.

I can hear the clock of Brooke's life ticking away.

Brooke

I slowly come to—almost a conscious floating. I become aware of a tuneless humming, grating. Those of us who are lucky enough to possess perfect pitch fight harmonizing with a droning lawn mower or wayward hair dryer.

My eyes pierce the gloom, my head thudding with the beginnings of what promises to be a horrible headache.

The memories crash into me like relentless waves and I'm the shore—battered: *Lacey.*

My eyes softly close, my eyelashes soaked with tears. Tears for everyone, tears for me . . . sadness swallowing my ignorance.

How could I never have a clue about what my best friend is capable of?

"Brookie?"

I open my eyes and there is Lacey, looking fresh as the day she was born.

Her shirt is new, the bloodied one gone.

I swallow, turning my face away, and her fingers grip my chin, forcing me to look into her eyes.

Hazel eyes that have shown compassion, comfort, and, I thought, love. Now that gaze looks empty, like dead marbles in the eye of hurricane, devoid of any shred of humanity. I struggle to grasp that my closest friend, the one person who still feels like family to me, is the monster behind the tragedy that destroyed my life.

"Don't you look away from me, Brooke," Lacey commands in an alien voice, and she drops her hand. I try to move and realize with sickening horror that I'm bound.

"I've sacrificed everything for you, and you'd better be grateful for it."

"I . . ." My unused voice croaks out and I give another dry swallow. "How could I be *grateful* to the person who killed my family?" I stare at her as each word drops from my mouth and Lacey gives me cool eyes back. "Joey . . ." Silent tears huddle at the corners of my eyes. Breaking formation, they run slowly down my face, reaching my collarbone and soaking my shirt. The smell of blood freshens with the dampness. A lump rises in my throat and I try to swallow it down.

Lacey rolls her eyes, swinging a clean blade around, and I flinch as the silver flashes in the low light. She does a deep chortle, the sound such a manic note of evil my breath hitches in a gasping sob. I know I'm hanging by a thread, shock hovering like a vulture seeking carrion.

"I'm not going to kill you, Brooke." Lacey looks off in the distance, the soft rocking underneath me begging to lull me back into the sleep of the truly drugged.

"But I am going to take everything you love."

"Why?" I know I should try to reason with her, but all I want right now is to understand. "Why did you kill my family . . . those other families?" I ignore my wet face, my dry mouth, the throbbing in my head.

Her eyes find mine in the darkness—relentless. "Those other competitors were in your way . . . our way. What better way to incapacitate but by dismantling their emotional framework?" She taps the blade on her jean-clad leg with the movement of long practice, with an ease that speaks of use.

"So you kill their families . . . ?"

Lacey nods smoothly. "Yes, it's almost as easy as surgery. You remove the heart and the spirit is unable to cope. Playing music becomes something that is unbearable in the face of their grief."

I'm trying to understand this . . . her. It's insensible. "Why not just hurt them? Why entire families?"

Lacey laughs, a deep throaty bark. "Too easy," she confesses. "Too small, too targeted." Then, her eyes unnervingly find mine again. "No fun."

My mind stumbles over that phrase: *No fun.*

Evan.

I look at Lacey in horror as a soft smile curls her lips. "Yeah . . . Evan was *fun*. Very fun."

I can't help it, I turn my head, just as I'd done pinned underneath Agent Haller, and dry-retch into the nothingness of where she's holding me.

I finally stop and Lacey rolls her eyes. "Such a weak stomach. Why *do* I love you?"

My eyes widen, my breath coming faster. Suddenly, a horrible idea solidifies. A deep fear like a pincer clamps onto my guts. My stomach hopelessly roils around in a sick, hot lump.

"Chance?" I ask breathlessly. My eyes begin to bulge. Please, God, not Chance.

"Not *yet*," she says in a considering tone. "I need him." Her eyes shift to mine. "And then, when I do not . . ." She slides her index finger down the cool metal of the blade of her knife in a lover's stroke.

I blanch, giving another hoarse retch at thought of Chance walking into a trap because of his association with me.

Then my mind brings images of Chance's hands on me, his mouth kissing away my tears, his loving encouragement against my sadness.

Removing it with his love.

Lacey is suddenly there, grabbing my shoulders, jerking

me to a sitting position, the knife under my nose. "I see you're thinking about lover boy."

I gulp, the blade very silver, very sharp . . . very close.

"You love *only* me. That's why your family isn't here, Brookie. It's about what we are to each other. You don't need them to distract you from me. From us." Her fingers involuntarily squeeze the hilt of the blade as Lacey continues in a reality of her own making, "Just like those other competitors needed to be released from working against you." Her eyes blaze at me with the fire of her belief and I swallow, a hiccup masking an inhale. She smiles at my anxiety. "Once their families were culled from the herd, it'd be just you . . . and me," she says, jamming the hilt into her sternum and making a red mark like an angry comma on the center of her chest.

I search her frantic eyes and see that there's a fire that burns within, a passion that has passed over into zealotry.

I look into her eyes, and they look bloodshot, crazy. She isn't Lacey . . . She isn't sane . . .

It occurs to me then: she's never been sane. My mind flashes on a thousand instances of her trying to control the small details of my life, even from when we were children: what to wear, whom to befriend, whom to date . . . Even recently, with her resistance to my move to Alaska, her insistence on coming here to be with me. Lacey's constant presence . . . but always in the background. An obsessed cheerleader to the hills and valleys of my life.

A clunk distracts her and she lowers her blade as her eyes stay on me. It's not like I can go anywhere: I can feel the plastic zip ties that bind my wrists digging into the soft flesh of my arm.

A knock comes at the door and I pray, so hard I swear God hears me. Until I hear the body drop.

There's no saving me unless it's by my own hand.

Lacey comes back into the dark, soft room she has me in. I don't know where I am, though it seems familiar somehow. I move my cheek against the side of something fuzzy. I can smell the sea but that's normal in a coastal town. There are no windows, but a vague ambient light slithers at the edges, teasing me with its nearness. The lack of light disorients me, making time seem surreal, suspended.

Lacey comes into focus and lifts an object and I flinch, knowing she'll hit me with it.

Instead, she gives a soft chuckle. I look closely and see the ivory of the handle.

Jake's cane.

Oh no, my mind wails, *another casualty of knowing me.* That old man has never hurt anyone.

"Don't cry, Brookie." She brushes my tears away tenderly and I shy from her touch. "What doesn't kill us makes us stronger, right?"

No. *It only makes us wish for death*, I think. But I say nothing.

My eyes follow her progress as she turns the walking stick to put it away and I see a tuft of pewter hair on the cane tip, the blood holding it to the worn surface like glue, very red against the cream.

A rage like a slow-burning fire slides through me and I instantly recognize what it is.

Hatred.

TWENTY-TWO

~

Chance

I take the steps two at a time, banging on the huge sliding metal barn doors of Tucker's shop, the echo of my fist reverberating and shattering the silence of the day. He's a tinker by profession: people need him when their pipes are frozen underground in winter and when their engine block needs an overhaul in summer. He's a modern-day Grizzly Adams . . . of indeterminate age and a true Alaskan man: part MacGyver, part outdoorsman, and all hard living. You'd think someone like him wouldn't do high-tech but that is Tucker's best hidden skill.

He'd known about Brooke for a while, encouraging me to find out for myself, not a gossiper. Tucker had also warned her off me. And to his credit, for what he knew of me, it was warranted.

Not anymore. Her abduction by a deeply deranged killer has necessitated every person on her side. I'm acutely aware that time is against us.

Tucker slides the door open, a quizzical expression on his face. He barely has time to assimilate my frantic presence as I burst through the door.

"What's going on?" he asks, calm as a priest, his dark eyes traveling from my disheveled hair to my dirty boots. Looking for a reason in the madness. He doesn't know the half of it, but he will.

"Brooke's in trouble."

His eyes meet mine. "What kind of trouble?" He sets the socket wrench down.

"The murderer's got her."

Surprise blanks his former expression even as thunder begins to consume it. He stands still for a moment, his contemplative expression darkening.

We look at each other.

"The Feds are here, they've enlisted the help of locals to start a ground search." I don't say that the locals are whoever I think will help—Clearwater has given me that much latitude at least.

Tucker sighs, and I can see the wheels of his brain turning. He'll have to make sense of Brooke being in danger and the unbelievable component of Lacey's deadly involvement. I hope he does it fast; time is our enemy. "Do they know who?" he asks after a lengthy pause.

Thank God, I can't have him floundering on me now. I nod. "Lacey Colbert."

Tucker's features burst like a lightbulb into a slide of surprise. His brows rise then fall in anger. "That blonde Evan wanted to . . ." He lets the sentence go unfinished.

We stare at each other and he sucks in a breath. "No fucking way," he says in disbelief, even as he reads the ready knowledge of Evan's death in my expression. I put that on a faraway mental shelf for analysis later. My friend's death I can grieve over when I have the luxury of time. Brooke has no time.

"Yeah," I answer quietly, regret and sadness thick in my voice.

"Fuck." Tucker hadn't known Evan well, but they'd shared beers; they were Alaskan. And there are few enough of us that, in principle, that's all that matters. We fight for our own. We just do. There's a wildness here that is embraced, which is absent in other place—us against everyone else.

I clench my hands into balls at my sides. "You got any brilliant ideas? Like where?" I ask.

Tucker's eyes flick to mine then away as he palms the short beard on his chin. I wait in torturous silence, the two minutes he deliberates, I die inside. That internal clock ticking. Always ticking.

"You gone by old man Kashirin's?" he asks, his brows popping in question.

"Not yet, you were closer."

He nods, mind made up. "Let's hit his place first. Call the Fed . . ." His brows rise again.

"Clearwater."

He nods. "Tell him where we're going."

I feel my own question on my face and Tucker answers it. "Just in case Goldilocks whacks one of us, they'll still be able to save Brooke."

I lift up my shirt, the gun holster digging into my waistband, the cold butt of the handle warmed by my flesh.

Tucker shakes his head. "I don't think that'll help. This one wants to be up close and personal."

I think about the article describing, in vivid detail, the knife work employed on the victims. I think of Brooke in Lacey's tender care and adrenaline surges through my already beleaguered system.

I don't need to be up close and personal with Lacey. If the opportunity presented itself . . . "I'm taking it. She doesn't have the element of surprise anymore and every Fed in the state is looking for her."

Tucker just stares, then finally he says, "She's smart or she wouldn't have gotten this far. The only advantage we have is we know Alaska like the backs of our hands. She doesn't."

"She's a girl," I say.

Tucker gives a grim laugh. "She's a clever *murdering* girl that's holding your girlfriend hostage," he says as he restates the facts, his level stare locking with mine.

I rake my hand through my hair for the billionth time. "Let's snag Jake. He'll have an idea."

I feel hopeless. Like nothing in the world can save Brooke. Then I think of her guarded trust and we race to Tucker's Bronco, then roar toward the spit . . . toward Jake's junk shack.

I set my feelings aside. One of us has to have hope.

I'll scrape together enough for us both.

Lacey can't take the one thing that's made me live, each breath I take sweeter than the last.

I won't allow it.

I peer through Jake's grimy glass widows, the telltale glow of the laptop absent. I turn to Tucker. "Not here." My hand drops to my side and I want to sound a primal roar in frustration. I dig my cell out: no phone call or text back. *Shit.*

"Damn, man. That's bad news."

I nod in tense agreement. "Could've used his head on this."

I stand still for a second, trying not to let panic overwhelm me. I can hear every second click by like I have a second timer going inside my head.

Tick-tock-tick-tock.

A sudden idea, as horrible as it is sweet, begins to form like a black cloud inside me, a dooming portent.

Tucker sees my face. "What?" he asks, stepping forward, his eyes scanning my face before I utter my suspicion.

"Fuck, I think I know where she is."

Tucker rolls his eyes. "Spit it fucking out, Taylor."

I spin away from him, sprinting to the Bronco. The sun plows into the windshield, breaking away in fragmented splinters of light that pierce my eyes, causing white dots to dance in my vision. My heart climbs into my throat and my body comes to life again, the fight-or-flight instinct kicking in.

It's fight all the fucking way.

"Chance!" Tucker roars, his footsteps stomping behind me like a lumbering giant awakened from slumber.

I whip open his door and jump into the driver's seat and put the still-running rig in gear, slamming the door with a slapped palm on the exterior.

"Don't!" Tucker bellows from a car length away and I toss him my cell out the window.

He catches it smoothly. "Call Clearwater!" I yell over the rumble of the engine and I pull away in a spray of gravel.

I lean out the window screaming over my shoulder, "Marina!" Tucker scowls, punching his fingers through my cell as I travel the short distance to the marina.

I check the rearview mirror and see Tucker speaking heatedly into my cell. Then he disappears from sight and I head for *Life Is Chance.*

Let's hope the name of my boat holds true . . . and that chance is on my side tonight.

I ninja-sprint down the gangplank like a silent ghost for the first time in my life. The steel grating is meant to make noise, but the tide is high so it's not a climb, but almost horizontal—easy for once.

How many times have I shoved dollies full of two hundred pounds of fish up that thing? It's strange to be empty-handed of my catch.

I reach the bottom, my gun naked in my hand. No one with any brains pulls a gun unless they're willing to kill.

And I am willing.

I know that taking a life is a sin. A reduction in the sanctity of humanity's precious tally. But for me, the choice is easy.

Brooke or Lacey.

Prodigy pianist whom I love or obsessed serial murderer?

Everywhere I look I'm greeted with bulging eyes and people who move out of my way, slowly backing up the way I've come.

Everyone wants to avoid a man who looks like I do at that moment: armed, brutal . . . purposeful.

No one wants that kind of attention turned on them.

I move to the last slip where my boat, the same boat that

used to be my folks', gently rocks with the slight disturbance of the quiet harbor.

I know that a storm is coming.

Yet the sky is a cloudless blue, the fabled cool Alaskan weather on hiatus until further notice.

I move toward my boat, which Matt had just been cleaning not two hours ago, Lacey almost certainly using that window of time to stow Brooke. The gun is a familiar comfort in my grip, all those days at the shooting range coming full circle to give me what I need: confidence.

The confidence of a killer, driven by love.

My hand squeezes the handle of my weapon just as I round the corner of the bow and catch sight of Jake. A pool of blood like a halo of death surrounds his body.

And then Lacey steps out of the cabin, an entire half head taller than a stunned Brooke, whose vivid lavender gaze is a window to her terror. I read in her expression a resolute determination. And instinctively guess she might martyr herself for me, sacrificing herself because she feels like she must—some kind of convoluted redemption for her family's death. If she weren't, she'd put herself out of harm's way. But that's not Brooke's design. Death irrevocably changes our life path and Brooke is the proof.

Fuck that.

I can feel the Feds approach like a bitter taste in my throat.

I should wait.

Instead, I put my hand on the starboard side of the ship, pushing up and lifting off, the gun high in the air in my right hand for balance. I sail over the side of the vessel and land on my feet, my toes just inches from Jake's blood.

I stare into Lacey's eyes and see my death reflected back in them.

Brooke

I watch Chance move down the wide-planked dock, his sea legs navigating the moving dock as fluidly as if those boards were rock steady. Chance's bluish-green eyes blaze like cool fire from a face with a perpetual tan, his inky hair standing on end, and I know he's combed it in frustration a hundred times since I've disappeared and I want to cry.

Chance deserves so much more. And Lacey deserves to die. I thought I'd be scared when this moment finally arrived, or maybe try to escape . . . but all I feel is a desperate sort of calm resolution. I know that she'll never stop killing, that somehow I'm the catalyst for her behavior. I can't ignore the deadness behind her eyes.

I thought I loved her.

But maybe I was just so desperate for a connection, loving how much she loved me, that I ignored what I didn't wish to see. And now all I'm left with is hatred. If I have to die to save Chance, and ultimately others, I will.

I watch the muscles of Chance's arm tense as he does a one-handed leap over the right side of the boat, hardly rocking it, and close my eyes against his natural grace, using an athleticism he's not aware of. His left arm's branded by ink, a gun like death in his fist.

"Well hi, lover," Lacey says. As he moves to step forward she presses the knife deeper into my neck and I feel a drop of my blood slide down like a heated trail of fire. It rolls between my breasts and my fear, my determination coalesce into a burning focus.

She can't win. Somehow, I have to end this.

Chance's Adam's apple does a slow bob, those piercing eyes slicing her up like small razor blades. "Let her go, Lacey," he says in a soft voice full of menace, but emboldened by resolve.

He's made up his mind just as I have.

"I think not, Fisherboy. As a point of fact, I like the idea of you taking us somewhere more private. I've always wanted to take a little sea voyage . . ." She gives a tittering giggle and her insanity slips down my spine like an ice cube.

Surprise lights on Chance's face then disappears. I watch him build himself up for what has to happen and I grieve for him.

For me.

"No way." His eyes shoot to mine and whatever he sees there causes him to step forward.

"Don't," Lacey says in a low voice of warning, dragging me back with a strong arm hugging the bottom of my rib cage and pressing the knife harder.

Another drop of blood joins the first. I see Chance track it with his eyes and a low sound of despair rips out of his throat.

"Don't hurt her," he begs, his voice cracking.

"Put the gun up, handsome . . . and see if you can save our Brookie. Like a *man*," she invites in a baiting drawl.

I shake my head at Chance, taking a risk with the knife. I don't care.

I don't care.

Lacey grunts with dissatisfaction. "Brooke, let your sperm donor fight for you. . . . if he's man enough."

Chance slams the gun back into its holster, his eyes burning with frustration, with rage.

There's a sudden groan from the deck and all eyes move to Jake. His pale blue eyes instantly take in the scene, the ragged flap of skin waving off his skull like a flag of flesh.

Jake sees her holding me, the front of my blouse bloody, my eyes bulging in terror while a manic Lacey holds my life with the turn of sharpened metal at my throat.

His gaze silently meets mine. Our eyes lock, then his slide to something on the boat.

I follow it.

The gaff.

Our interchange takes seconds. Jake never sees Chance, who stands behind him. Jake's given me the method.

I take it.

Chance knows what I'll do before I move, watching the interplay and instinctively putting it all together.

"Brooke, no!" he bellows, moving forward. He doesn't lose his footing because of the sea that rocks the boat underneath us but because of the blood that slicks the deck like a fine oil. He slips as I move under and away from the lingering presence of the blade, Lacey's hands momentarily slackened by the surprise of the moment.

"Brooke!" Lacey shrieks as I dive for the gaff. My eyes hit on the brass brackets that hold it in tension pincer grips; the barbed and sharpened end is like an eye that winks at me. I land chest first on the deck, my legs over the top of Jake's, my arms outstretched.

I hear it before I feel it.

A meaty thwack sounds behind me as I crawl forward that last foot. Something tears out of my leg like a burning torch.

When the knife hits my upper thigh again, it feels as though a giant has punched me with his great fist.

I think it should hurt more.

My hand grips the smooth wooden handle of the gaff and I jerk it out of its brass guardians.

The knife exits my thigh in a sucking reverse pop and a flood of blood like a warm bath pours around me.

I ignore the shrieking agony of my body, turning just as Chance avoids a strike. Arching his back, he sucks in his stomach as the knife flashes toward his midsection.

Lacey moves in like a tornado of blades. Both hands now hold knives and she moves with a grace she shouldn't possess.

That I didn't know she possessed.

Her total focus is on Chance, the threat of me forgotten.

I move to my knees in a swivel that brings the momentum of that barbed point in a horizontal arc. I turn it like a baseball bat and hope for that perfect home run as I swing it toward her.

I hear the swish of air as it whistles past my position and sinks into her back. She cries out, looking at me for a shocked moment suspended in time.

The sun sinks behind Lacey, backlighting her in red, and Chance gets close, punching the knife from first one hand, then the other.

They fall with a dull clatter to the deck of a boat now soaked by blood.

Mine.

Jake's . . . *hers*.

A shot thunders and echoes in the stillness of the marina, the sharp retort causing my ears to ring.

A perfect hole appears in her head and blooms like a horrible flower, spraying the bits of what made her Lacey over all of us like a gruesome and final rain.

I crumple to the deck, and as if in a dream, I see Clearwater straighten from his shooter's stance as he yells to a team of suited agents and they swarm like bees around a hive.

But there's no honey here.

Only blood.

And death.

I close my eyes and float into unconsciousness.

⁓

My eyes flutter open and I see a swinging bag, a snakelike IV line running to my taped and abraded arm.

A medic flashes a penlight in my eyes and I groan. Each sense awakens and suddenly I'm ambushed by the noise.

Sirens.

A hand encased in latex checks my pulse then pulls away.

"Hang in there . . . don't you dare die on me, Brooke Starr." Eyes like seawater in sunlight beseech me to stay. I close mine against the sensory overload.

"She's lost a lot of blood . . ." I hear a voice say.

The ambulance rocks and jostles, tossing my limp body with the jogs and ruts in the road.

"Whatever she needs, take it from me," I hear Chance say, as though from a great distance, his voice coming to me through the swamp of my consciousness.

I hear bits and pieces of their conversation: Nicked femoral. Low blood pressure. Shock.

Will to live.

That phrase settles in. I think about it . . . floating on whatever the medics have juiced me with.

Do I want to live?

I feel my hand move and another one, warm and vital, grips mine.

I feel the heat of his lips move over my cool skin and it's the most intimate thing I've ever known. I struggle to live and Chance's lips hold me here to this life, pinned like a butterfly on a board.

His will is imposed this day.

The day I choose to live. For him.

For us.

And finally . . . for me.

TWENTY-THREE

~

Chance

I can't get over the humidity of Seattle. It clings to everything, even in September, when Alaska is cooling, the fireweed having only their tips crowned with purple flowers heralding autumn's approach . . . the Seattle summer is just springing to late life. Whoever says it only rains in Seattle hasn't been here.

It's almost October and three months have passed since Lacey Colbert lay dying on the deck of my boat, true twilight descending as the blood of my cousin Jake and the woman I love mingling with that of the killer's. Three months since Evan's funeral.

One horrible month of Brooke hanging between life and death.

One month of her guilt coming full circle to finally release her from the tragedy of truth: that her best friend had loved her. Not in a healthy way, but in a deadly and obsessive way. To realize that Brooke could never have saved her family. That she's not responsible for any of this.

One month of explaining, cajoling, and finally, under-standing. Juilliard has admitted Brooke. Making the biggest exception of all time to admit someone that eschewed tryouts, regardless of the reason. Of course, there is no precedence. Brooke fought for the other survivors of the two murdered families as well. All three candidates will pull their own weight in a school filled with talent, without their respective families. It was Brooke's catharsis . . . her redemption. Something good had to come out of the tragedy of death.

I slap the steel doors shut and lower the bar across the brackets that hold it, padlocking the doors together. I step away, the orange U-Haul logo covered partly by the lock, and turn to Brooke.

I watch her walk toward me, the storage unit mostly empty, but still holding some of her belongings saved from the sale of her family's home.

She still moves with a slight limp. The physical therapist says she might walk smoothly again one day. Nerve damage can sometimes rectify . . . sometimes not.

Brooke is beautiful to me, scars and all. I have kissed each one as her solemn eyes watch me erase not the pain of the scars, but the pain of the past. I want Brooke to know that her wounds are tangible proof that she survives—lives.

Finally, she is. Living.

Brooke gives me that lopsided smile . . . so perfect it makes my chest constrict. I am just now beginning to stop beating the shit out of myself for not understanding soon enough, guessing, calling Clearwater myself. Finally, it always comes around to the same thing: Brooke's life. I still can't believe how it all happened.

She slides her arms around my waist, gripping me, and I kiss her head. "You okay?" I ask.

She nods. "Have you talked to Jake?"

I smile, thinking about that tough bird. He has a new scar to joke about. He likes to brag that his old ivory-topped cane that was used to bludgeon him with was a spit and polish away from looking good as new. It's so Alaskan of him, I'd laughed— we repurpose everything. Apparently, even weapons used with intent to murder.

I nod at her question. "Yeah, he's happier than a clam at high tide, keeping an eye on the boat."

Brooke sighs, giving a little smile at my pun. "What about your house . . . and . . ." I press my finger to her lips.

"I told you, Tucker is house-sitting until I can move back . . ."

A smile curls her lips. "We," she states, running her tongue on the lower part of her lip and I watch the small movement, an instant distraction.

The ownership in her voice makes every bit of me harden except my heart; it keeps beating, strong and sure—soft. For Brooke.

"Hell yes, *we*," I answer, pressing my mouth to hers. She pushes back, her tongue sliding between my teeth and playing with mine. I forget we're in the middle of the storage parking lot and attack her like it'll be the last time I see her.

It won't. But it's a helluva excuse.

Finally, we break away, both our chests heaving, eyes locked on each other, and I laugh. "I can't get enough," I say, not minding the admission in the slightest.

She grins. "Me either."

Then her grin fades. "We still need to stop by the FBI."

We need to check in with Clearwater before we move to New York for the school term, beginning in September and finishing in May.

"Yeah," I agree, reluctance thick in the one syllable.

I grab her hand and we move to my Ford Bronco, a mirror of Tucker's but a khaki green that Brooke likes to tease me about. I stand by the original color scheme, defending it with its ability to tow nearly anything. Of course, that is after Tucker made a custom hitch, as those early Broncos were averse to towing. But no longer. I hitch the Bronco to the ten-foot U-Haul trailer and chain it.

Ready.

Brooke's already in my Bronco and I can't help but notice how gorgeous her eyes are . . . against the car's baby-shit green. I give a low bark of laughter and she asks, "What?" Her brow furrows in a small frown.

Makes me want to kiss it away.

"I'm just thinking how hot you look in my car with all that green paint."

"Huh . . . Yeah, get in here, clown."

"Don't you 'clown' me or I'll put on a show . . ."

"No," she says, wagging her finger as I rip open the car door and tackle her across the seat.

"Chance!" she squeals as I jerk her underneath me, the wide vintage seats perfect for my nefarious purposes.

I look down at her, my radar having already scoped out our isolation. We are the only ones in a narrow strip of asphalt that bisects the two low-slung rows of garage-style storage units.

"One for the road?" I ask quietly, my heart speeding.

Her lavender eyes darken, sparkling like jewels beneath me, and she nods.

I don't waste time, unbuttoning a blouse so sheer a white Brooke had to wear a tank top underneath. I slip one thin strap off her shoulder and kiss the rounded top of the skin and she sighs. It's such a lonely but contented sound I stop, looking into her eyes again.

"I never thought this was possible," she says in a voice that holds hesitant wonder.

I grin suddenly and answer, "I never did either." And I didn't. How wrong I was.

I work my way down with the lightest kisses I can, really no more than the heat of my breath hovering on top of her skin, and she moves underneath me, opening more of her blouse so I can do more.

And then I do.

My tongue finds her nipple through the sheer material of her bra, her fair skin revealing a tantalizing glimpse of the palest pink leading to the sensitive peak. I move in slow circles, my eyes meeting hers as our gazes lock.

Brooke arches her back, driving her nipple deeper into my mouth, and I mound the flesh with my hand, pushing her breast further inside my mouth and give a long pulling suck and her legs open further as I swim between them.

I let her nipple go with a pop and her breast slides back from my hand, the vague outline of my teeth around the nipple.

It turns me on, seeing any part of myself imprinted on her.

It's a primitive guy thing but it flat-out does it for me.

I take my thumbs and hook her shorts, the elastic giving way to me jerking them off her hips.

I leave Brooke's blouse half on, taking my own shorts off with a pull and dismissive kick behind me as they slide to hide the pedals of my car.

I gaze down at Brooke, her black hair fanning behind her, a portion of it grazing the floorboards of the passenger side, her luminous eyes staring up at me, half-baked with lust, darkened with anticipation, and I don't want it to end.

That look.

Her beneath me.

This moment.

My eyes roam her body, my eyes falling between her legs and my fingers spreading her apart to see the pink within.

"Chance!" Brooke says softly, my thumb driving against her clit while one finger slowly pumps inside her.

"Come for me," I whisper beside her ear, that breast I've had in my mouth shoved hard against my chest as one of her legs flirts with my gearshift and the other is held by my other hand underneath the bend of her knee.

I feel a single wet pulse against my finger and my dick hardens to the point of pain but I hold back. I grit my teeth and feel it as she shatters.

I withdraw my hand and press myself inside her, the crushing rhythm of her orgasm driving me in.

Jesus . . . how she feels . . . slick, swollen . . . soft. "Brooke," I murmur against her skin, my forehead pressing against hers as I get to the end of her and stop to breathe.

I wait, our bodies joined perfectly.

Brooke opens her eyes and I stare into them, my dick throbbing, her pussy caressing me in an almost unbearable rhythmic grip of velvet friction.

"I love you," she says softly.

I withdraw from her, my eyes never leaving hers, and she gasps as I do, her body fighting me, our foreheads locked together. Her face looks like she's in pain but when I look closer I see the glitter of tears.

I rock inside her deeply back and forth as those tears slide out of her eyes. When I can't bear the sweetness of her another second, when she's sucked everything from me, I feel my release and I bury myself inside her so deeply I feel like I'll never be apart from her. Brooke wraps her legs around my pumping hips and groans, pressing her heels into my back.

I catch my breath, the interior smelling like sweat, sex . . . and Brooke. Always Brooke.

I scoot her back against the seat on her side facing me and she smiles, using her free arm to wipe away happy tears. By this time, I know the difference.

We stare at each other for a few moments, our heartbeats slowing together.

"So what do you have to say for yourself, Chance Taylor?" she asks through her tears, ecstasy at the edges like icing on a cake.

It's too easy. "I love you more."

She dips her head against my chest and cries.

I hold her while she does.

Brooke

I sit across from Clearwater's desk, holding hands with Chance. Actually, breaking Chance's hand.

He doesn't even flinch . . . that's the kind of boyfriend he is, though *boyfriend* doesn't do him justice. Avenger, rescuer, lover . . . those seem like better monikers. But to the general public, the press—he's forever part of what brought the killer down.

Lacey.

As I look around my hometown I know I can never go back. There's a wildness inside me now. Alaska's in my blood. A quiet river that flows through my heart and mind, whose path changes yet remains the same.

Wherever Chance is will be my home.

"Miss Starr," Clearwater asks again and I start, Chance squeezing my hand once.

I blush, realizing I've been zoning in my own little world.

"Yes," I reply.

Clearwater smiles, and the scar at his throat lifts slightly with the movement. Somehow, it should ruin the perfection of his face, a blight on the beauty of it.

It doesn't. The raw imperfection showcases how handsome he is and it gives us something to share. My scars don't show like his, but they're there.

Lacey made sure I'd never forget her, dead or alive.

I never will. But what I know now is she can never steal my happiness. Happiness is mine to own or choose—if I want it.

I do. I choose joy.

I turn to Chance and smile at him and he smiles back.

"I hear congratulations are in order," Clearwater remarks.

My face turns to him and I nod as Chance says, "Yes, Brooke's worked really hard to get reinstated."

"That's great . . . and the other victims . . ."

"Survivors," I correct, a hard edge like a steel rod driving down the center of that one word.

Clearwater nods acquiescence, his eyes a quiet study of black, the pupil hiding in all that dark brown. "They are very grateful for your advocacy."

"It wasn't all me," I say, casting my eyes away from his, latching on to my hand laced with Chance's. Still looking down I mutter, "Juilliard was very understanding."

"Bullshit," Clearwater says.

My eyes snap to his and Chance smirks.

"What . . . ?" I begin, confused.

He points a finger in my face. "You. Are. Brave."

I gulp, my eyes burning. The void of my family looms large . . . overwhelming.

"Agreed?" he asks. But his eyes are not really asking. I glance at Chance for help and he stares blankly back.

Dammit. "I guess," I finally say, so softly they both lean toward me.

"Brooke." My eyes rise to meet his. "It's normal to feel bad about . . . killing Lacey, about surviving your family, about her taking a friend."

Evan, I think with a pang of grief. Clearwater's eyes flick to Chance and he gives a subtle nod. Grief doesn't own him.

"It's also normal to be who you were meant to be. Nobody can rob you of that."

I know this. My brain has told me this 101 times. Chance has told me. In that moment I know that reciting something to death doesn't mean it's true.

You have to believe for it to become reality.

I think I do.

I nod.

Satisfied, Clearwater relaxes, leaning back in his chair. "So you guys are off?"

I smile, thinking of making love to Chance in his Bronco in the storage parking lot. I blush and Clearwater's brows rise. "Yes," I answer quickly and Chance gives a soft chuckle.

He *so* knows what I'm thinking about.

"We've got a little slum studio rented," Chance says.

"New York City's damn expensive," Clearwater agrees.

Chance raises our linked hands to his mouth, brushing his lips across my knuckles, and I shiver at the contact, his gaze all for me. "We'll eat Top Ramen," he says.

His eyes say more.

Clearwater lets the undercurrent we have run underneath him as if he's a bridge, watching the water swirl below, guarding our passage.

And like any good guardian, he lets us go.

Marshal Decatur Clearwater stands and we do as well. He lifts his cell, a little different than any I've seen. I guess the FBI might have access to things us civvies don't.

"Thanks for answering my text," he says, his face free of accusation.

I laugh, a little nervously. "Yeah . . . I guess I'm over ignoring FBI messages."

"Good thing," Clearwater says with a wink.

I bob my head, letting go of Chance's hand to shake Clearwater's. Instead, he takes me in his arms, holding me tightly, and after a moment I hug him back.

He releases me and it's only then that I notice his wounded eyes look less hurt. The bruise that's shadowed them is no longer there.

I stand there for a moment with so many emotions I don't know which one to embrace. My eyes move to the scar at his throat and I ask softly, though I know it's the rudest thing ever, "How did that happen?"

He moves his hands to the raw line of twisted red.

"I was protecting a girl . . . a girl like you."

I stand there. I have to know. "Is she . . . did she live?"

Clearwater nods. "She did. Now she's doing what she is meant to."

A fat tear rolls down my face. I don't even know why. Chance wipes it from my cheek with his fingertip.

"That's good," I say quietly.

"Very good," Clearwater agrees. He's speaking about the girl, but the words are for me. All for me.

I turn around and walk away, feeling like I'm more than when I entered his office.

Feeling like myself for the first time in a long time, not stranded, no longer adrift. Not the Brooke Starr from before.

But fully embracing the Brooke I am now.

We drive in peaceful silence, our hands linked as Chance drives the Bronco one-handed, a low whistling seeping through the silence, the old radio in bad need of an overhaul.

I recognize the tune and hum along.

"Will you miss Alaska?" I ask, breaking through the melody like a dull knife through a slab of soft butter.

"Yes," he instantly replies, and I feel bad, noting our random progress through the thick, saunalike heat of an Indian summer in South Dakota, my foot dangling out the window. Cars built in the 1970s aren't big on air-conditioning. Air-conditioning is opening the window. Ours are cranked.

The wind breezes between my toes, my silver toe ring winking in the sunlight as the dusty car travels through endless fields of harvested corn.

Chance slants a glance at me. "But," he says, and I instantly think of halibut, "fishing season conveniently occurs when you're done for the summer . . ."

I look over at him, his left arm tanned to a deep bronze from the driving, his already dusky skin deeper from a summer in Washington. Every muscle stands in stark relief. His legs work the pedals on the floor and I watch the shadows of his strength at the small movements he makes while driving. My eyes move to his arm as his hand grips the wheel, the small muscles of his forearm connected to the huge ones of his bicep and beyond that a thick neck that I've held onto when he's taken me in the middle of nowhere, not a surface in sight, suspended against only him as he drives into me.

The memory gives me goose bumps. "True," I say. Breaking

my contact with his hand, I walk my fingers to his thigh and Chance's eyes darken with my contact.

"Not good for my concentration, Brooke," he warns, and his ominous tone does something to me, pulling everything by invisible strings to loop and knot at my core, the heat bursting from the center of me.

"Oh?" I croon, unbuckling my seat belt and prowling the short distance across the seat, my ass in the air, my boobs hanging down on display.

And Chance is looking. He blinks, his hand turning white on the steering wheel.

"What are you going to do while I play until my fingers fall off?" I ask innocently . . . as those same fingers squeeze the hardness through his shorts and he sucks in a breath.

"Damn . . . Brooke . . ." he says, his breathing a little ragged.

I'm going to cause a wreck and I find . . . I'm not caring much. I have other things on my mind. Lots.

"Answer," I say, giving him a hard squeeze and he moans, jamming his back into the seat, sweat popping on his brow.

"I'm going to play my guitar," he answers through a throat squeezed for air.

His eyes move to mine for a moment, tortured. Then back to the road.

"So you'll play gigs while your girlfriend plays piano . . ." He gasps. I laugh and pull my hand away. We can save that for later.

"I love you," I say, my breath tickling his ear.

"I love you more," he whispers.

TWENTY-FOUR

Nine months later

Chance

I've never wanted to cry as badly as I do now. My eyes are on fire with it . . . but I don't. Instead, I get to my feet like everyone else in a standing ovation.

There are many who do cry. Brook's that great, her talented fingers cause every head to turn, every longing sigh and pause of breath to heave and break.

My Brooke.

She stands and the roses fall, the petals like silky blood, filling the stage with their fragrant praise.

Brooke stands in the middle of the raining petals and gives a small bow, her floor-length velvet skirt a low and shimmering navy, a crisp white blouse that lovingly flows over curves I know so well they're memorized.

Her last recital for the year has come and gone. The final ringing note signals her success as a pianist.

Her success as a human being.

Brooke is becoming who she was meant to be, and I'm so glad I've been there to see it.

The curtains sweep together as a small hand scoops up a rose that made the throw whole. Bringing it to her face she smells the delicate blossoms, and as the sliver of her face is swallowed by the deep red fabric of the curtain, her eyes meet mine.

⌒

The after-party is exactly what I expect it to be: boring. High-class types that I feel about as comfortable with as invading aliens. But Brooke's comfortable with all of them. She moves between the intimate groups, champagne in one hand.

A waiter cruises through with a tray full of hors d'oeuvres and champagne held high. The golden liquid splashes inside with a burst of bubbles and he miraculously spills nothing.

I give him a look and he slides my way, expertly shifting his weight and flattening his body between groups of formal-clad guests, pianists, and one bored Alaskan . . . itching so bad to get back to the sea I can hardly think.

"Sir?" he asks in an affected air, but his eyes flash on me and he immediately knows I'm not part of the beautiful throng that surrounds us.

"How can a guy get a beer in this joint?" I ask and he smiles, despite himself.

"One must only ask, sir," he replies with a poker face and I grin. His lips twitch as he empties his tray on his way back to the kitchen.

I look at everyone, but Brooke is the one where my eyes move back to. She looks so right here—everywhere. She's changed into an outfit I know set her back a grand. She didn't want to buy it; I made her. *A rite of passage,* I'd told her.

The waiter comes back, his tray absent of everything but a single frosted mug with a cold brown bottle beside it—no label.

"Awesome, my man," I say when he appears beside me. I give him a good clap on the back and grab the bottle right off the tray.

"Sir," he sputters as I take a long pull and about die from the chilling pleasure of a cold beer.

"Yeah," I say, ogling Brooke, my eye traveling a slit that nearly reaches her hip.

"Don't you want the mug?" he asks by way of encouragement.

"Nah, but thanks for pulling the strings."

"Yes, sir," he says, following my gaze to Brooke. "Is she your lady?" he asks and I nod.

"She is."

"You are most fortunate," he says. After a moment of our mutual contemplation of Brooke he steps away.

I move toward her.

She gives a great laugh at something and I watch her throw her head back, mouth open, teeth gleaming, throat exposed. And I immediately want to be anywhere but here. Somewhere quiet. Private.

"Hey, Chance," Brooke says, her earlier laughter remaining

in a genuine smile. I'm happy to see it; there's been so many more of those.

"Ready?" I ask.

I'm so ready.

"Yes . . . First, let me introduce you to Marianne and Kenneth."

I look at them, the two who had lost their families, and Kenneth raises a beer bottle and I grin. "Thank God, I thought I was the only one who hated champagne."

"Nope," Kenneth says, rocking back on his heels, one hand stuffed into his pocket and a big smile plastered on his face.

We clink chilled necks and swig.

Brooke laughs. "This is Chance, guys."

"The fisherman," Marianne says.

I nod.

Brooke looks at me with shining eyes. "Yeah . . . he's that and much more."

I take her free hand in mine. "You've got yourself a good woman here, Chance," Kenneth says, tipping his beer toward me.

"Thanks," I say. Then, "A good woman who's getting up early to go north."

Marianne's eyes widen and she slaps her forehead. Her aqua dress in shimmering sequins glitters with the movement. "I forgot, you're running off to no-man's-land to what? Fish?" she ask in disbelief.

Brooke looks down at her feet, the fragile silver heels sparkling with the mix of candles and low amber light of the large room. "Actually, I think I'll play instead . . . and maybe garden."

"Oh that's right! You've got your great-aunt's cabin up there," Kenneth says.

"Yeah," Brooke says softly, and the four of us grow quiet.

"Well, good luck," Marianne says. Her eyes have a sheen and I know she's holding back.

Brooke suddenly looks up. "It's not about luck."

Kenneth looks in my direction, lifting his beer to me in a salute. "Maybe it's Chance."

Brooke gives me a radiant smile, the deep violet of her formal dress making her eyes look like a watercolor in violet, the sweep of her black hair framing them like startled jewels in the ivory of her face.

"That's got a lot to do with it," she admits, her cheeks turning pink as she looks at me.

God, I love her.

I take her into my arms and kiss her.

She kisses me back like no one's watching.

Just the way I like it.

⌒

I speak quietly into the cell. "Are you sure you left it there?" I nod at the next few words. "Right on the keys?" I clarify.

I get an affirmative and heave a sigh of relief.

"Chance!" Brooke yells from the door, the place smelling like a big lemon, better than when we moved in last year with the hot humid summer of New York melting our asses like candles.

"Coming!" I yell back, spying our drop-off keys on the surface of our rented furniture.

Into the phone I tell Jake, "See ya in a two weeks."

"You bet, sonny, and . . . you're a tad sneakier than I gave you credit for," he says in his gruff voice. I can almost see the smoke from his pipe. God I miss Alaska.

I smile. "I've got to have something up my sleeve when I have a clever relative like you running around."

"Humph!" Jake says, hanging up the phone.

He thinks I'm full of shit.

Maybe just a little.

I whistle as I set my matching set of keys on the apartment table, take one last look around, and lock the front door, walking to the Bronco. Still baby-shit green.

Brooke still looks great framed by all that green. One slim ankle and foot hang out the window, spring warming the air, the promise of summer felt like a vibration all around us. The trees' blooms have come and gone and are leafing out in preparation for the heat of June.

But we'll be back in the temperate heart of Alaska in two weeks. I take a deep breath of city air and jog around the front of the car, Brooke's eyes following me like I'm the last solid thing in the world.

She's got it wrong.

Brooke is.

Brooke

My eyes feel like sand has been ground into them I'm so tired, but we're home and this is definitely where my heart is. I turn on my side and watch Chance sleep. The shadow of a beard caresses his chin, black hair a short cap of ink on his head, soft to the touch. Dark lashes lay against the dusky skin of his cheek as he breathes in and out.

Neither one of us will be hurting for money . . . with my inheritance, and Chance's; working is a choice.

However, life is not about money, it's about living. Sometimes it takes tragedy to understand that. I heard a quote once I never forgot: give me the tortured, for they make the best of friends.

Now I have three more years and I am a graduate of the finest music institution in America.

Ask me if that's the thing that makes me most happy, that is the most precious.

If you did, I would answer no.

I look at the man who lies beside me.

No.

It would be a person, not an accomplishment.

Chance is worth the risk.

⁓

"Let me see, Chance!" I say, laughter choking me. His hands are wrapped around my eyes, blinding me.

"No . . . No!" he says, pushing me forward with his front against my back.

"Nice, Chance," I say, but it's a total distraction and I can feel my face heat.

"Did you like that?" he whispers, pressing harder against me and my breath catches.

"You know I do," I hiss at him.

He springs his hands off my eyes and I'm facing Milli's cabin.

Or something that's pretending to be Milli's cabin.

Every single log glows like it's brand-new, every pane of glass glitters in the sunlight like a polished gem. A cedar picket fence and arched arbor crosses the small patch of grass in front of the broad steps leading to the front porch, and the sides run to the backyard where a garden sits. My eyes roam the six-foot-tall chicken-wire fence, anchored in all four corners by six-by-six cedar posts that will weather to a driftwood gray. The raised beds have little green tufts of seedlings sprouting out of the rich black dirt.

Finally my eyes find the outhouse where the small window on the side sports a window box filled to bursting with pansies.

The hollowed-out moon has been painted a deep violet blue.

I turn and look at Chance, speechless.

He grasps both my hands as my tears fall. "How?" I ask through my tears.

"Jake," he answers.

"How . . . could he . . . know?"

Chance gives a soft smile, wrapping me in his arms as we look at the transformed cabin, my eyes taking in more details second by second.

"He remembers what it looked like before . . . when it was new."

I shake my head in wonder. "This must have taken . . ." I don't even know.

"Nine months. In fact, I think he put the seeds in the ground two weeks ago."

I close my eyes and lean back against Chance. A sudden thought occurs to me and I whirl around. "Wait a second!" I say. "You're not going to want to give up your place."

He smiles at me, kissing the tip of my nose, and it shoots tingles everywhere he touches and places he doesn't. "Don't have to."

Chance's eyes are suddenly serious. "It's for posterity, babe."

I cock my eyebrow, dragging him through the new arbor and to the front steps of the cabin. "I can't let that piece of you go. But this!" I say, putting my hand to my chest, and he grabs me around the back and knees, lifting me off my feet, and I squeal.

"It's not all for us."

I look into his face and ask, "Who then?"

"For our children, Brooke. The children we'll have one day."

I stare at him openmouthed, then with a little cry I wrap my hands around his strong neck.

"There's one more surprise," he says, kicking the door open.

This time he doesn't cover my eyes, setting me gently on the top of the stairs that lead to my aunt's quirky basement. I turn, puzzled, and he slaps my butt. "Get going, Brooke."

"Bossy," I say with a giggle and his eyes darken. It almost makes me disobey.

Almost.

I tread softly down the nine or so steps to the bottom and my eyes take in the strange light that floods the low and narrow basement windows. I scan the room, everything as I remember it: the old photos, the small tables with their knickknacks, doilies, and glass paperweights.

My eyes settle on the square grand sitting like a graceful wooden elephant in the center of the room.

Then they stop on a small black box centered perfectly on the ivory keys.

I move toward that tiny velvet cube that sits on the piano keys. I sense Chance's heated presence behind me.

I pick up the box, the press of the velvet caressing my hand, and open it.

A glittering stone lies in the puckered satin, deep, perfect blue riding the fine line of almost-violet. It's obscenely big, and perfect. Tanzanite.

So perfect.

I can see through it like it's a block of ice, cured by violet fire, and suddenly Chance is behind me, pressing his lips to my neck, the hard length of his body behind me like a solid presence of love. His arms slip around my waist, plucking the ring from my hand and slipping it onto my left ring finger.

It shimmers softly in the light that seeps inside this quiet, deep room where my aunt used to play her piano.

Where I got engaged.

I turn in Chance's arms, staring into his eyes.

"Stay with me . . . not for a season, but for life, Brooke."

There's only one response. The only one I've ever had.

"Yes," I say, and he lifts me off my feet, hugging me so tightly I can barely breathe.

Yet I do. I feel like for the first time, I finally can.

ACKNOWLEDGMENTS

I would like to thank:

Levi, who revealed the villain to me.

You, my reader.

My husband, who is my biggest supporter without reading a word.

My parents, who didn't know, but believed anyway.

Erica Spellman-Silverman: smart, savvy, and devoted don't cover it. Thank you for all you do as my advocate. And the team at Trident Media Group for giving me a chance!

Simon and Schuster

Lauren, for believing in me.

Alex, you've improved my work; it's better because of you. Thank you for entreating the tender from the brutal.

Faren, my copy editor.

Angie

Autumn

Crystal

Dianne

Lori

Scott Haller

Shana

Tabitha

Elizabeth and Karie: you kept things straight.

Scott and Josh: for the morale boost this summer.